About the Author

Mary Lavin was born in 1912 in the USA, but moved as a child with her Irish parents to Athenry, Co. Galway, and then to Dublin and her farm in Co. Meath. Lavin wrote two novels, *The House in Clewe Street* and *Mary O'Grady*, but is best known for her many short story collections, including *Tales from Bective Bridge*, *The Becker Wives and Other Stories*, *In the Middle of the Fields*, *Happiness and Other Stories*, and *The Stories of Mary Lavin* (Volumes I, II and III). She enjoyed an eminent reputation in the land of her birth, where she twice served as writer-in-residence at the University of Connecticut and had many stories published in the prestigious *New Yorker* magazine. She won the James Tait Black Memorial Prize, two Guggenheim Fellowships, the Katherine Mansfield Prize and the Allied Irish Banks Literary Award. She was also awarded an honorary doctorate from University College Dublin in 1968. Mary Lavin was also a member of Aosdána, Ireland's state-sponsored affiliation of distinguished creative artists; she was elected Saoi, its highest honour, in 1992 for achieving 'singular and sustained distinction in literature'. In her private life, she was widowed for fifteen years following the death of her first husband, William Walsh, in 1954, with whom she had three daughters. In 1969, she married the distinguished former Australian Jesuit priest Michael McDonald Scott, who predeceased her in 1990. Mary Lavin died in 1996 and is buried with her family in N~~~~~ Co. Meath.

GW00645316

By the same author

The Becker Wives

and Other Stories

The Becker Wives

and Other Stories

Mary Lavin

Foreword by Christine Dwyer Hickey

MODERN IRISH CLASSIC

NEW ISLAND

The Becker Wives and Other Stories
First published in 1946 by Michael Joseph
This edition published in 2018 by
New Island Books
16 Priory Hall Office Park
Stillorgan
County Dublin
Republic of Ireland

www.newisland.ie

Print ISBN: 978-1-84840-694-0
Epub ISBN: 978-1-84840-695-7
Mobi ISBN: 978-1-84840-696-4

Typeset by JVR Creative India
Cover design by Catherine Gaffney
Printed by TJ International Ltd, Padstow, Cornwall

New Island received financial assistance from The Arts Council (*An Chomhairle Ealaíon*), 70 Merrion Square, Dublin 2, Ireland.

Comhairle Chontae na Mí/Meath County Council has given financial support to this republication.

Contents

Foreword

by Christine Dwyer Hickey

Patrick Kavanagh claimed that a would-be writer is best nurtured in an environment of domestic disharmony. If this is the case then Mary Lavin was certainly off to a fine start. She was born in East Walpole, Massachusetts in 1912 to Irish parents who were far from compatible. Her mother, the daughter of a small-town merchant in County Galway, had notions above her station and remained throughout her life a woman disappointed with her lot. Her father, on the other hand, who had come from peasant stock, was self-made and, like many racing men, socialised easily with people from all walks of life.

Like James Joyce before her, also a child of a difficult marriage and a victim of a peripatetic, if – it has to be said – far less comfortable lifestyle, the young Lavin had to adapt to a succession of different surroundings. Each move brought about a new set of people to deal with and a new set of rules to follow. Leaving her father behind, she moved from small-town America to small-town Galway when she was nine years old to live with her mother's people. A year or so later, she moved with her mother to a house in Dublin. Her father, meanwhile, came back to Ireland where he bought a country estate in County Meath on behalf of his wealthy American employers. There he came to live and work as estate manager with Mary spending weekends and holidays in his company. It was divorce Irish style in the twentieth century and Mary soon learned how to divide herself both physically and emotionally between these two very different forces of nature. For a child this lifestyle can cause damage, particularly in the case of an only child, but, from a writer's point of view at least, it would do her no harm. Her observational skills were sharpened, her sense of place developed and most importantly of all, she acquired the ability to switch on her imagination whenever an alternative narrative was required.

Lavin described herself as a great wanderer when she was a child. She often wandered alone. In East Walpole, her solitary rambles brought about a life-long love of nature. In Athenry in County Galway, she roamed the town while other children were at school. She was known there as 'The Yank' and, as something of a novelty, was often invited into people's homes to be quizzed by nosy neighbours about her absent father. Little did these neighbours know that the young Lavin was taking in far more than she was giving away: their rooms and furniture; the food they ate, and the ways in which they betrayed themselves not just through their words but through their silences.

In Dublin she would wander again, a convent schoolgirl, straying from the leafy enclaves of respectable Adelaide Road into the less privileged areas of the city. If Athenry had shown her something of the poverty of the spirit; Dublin's inner city would show her poverty of an entirely different calibre. In any case, it was all going in: landscape, cityscape, the savagery of small-town respectability; the debilitation brought about by the disappointed life. And it would all come out later and flow like an underground river through her work.

My first reading of Lavin was as a child when I came across 'The Widow's Son' in an older cousin's school textbook. I was drawn in by the simplicity of the writing but if I entered that story expecting a country fable, I was in for a shock. The image of the widow beating her son with the dead body of a bloody hen would, for a long time, haunt me. It was the first time I had read a story that stayed with me beyond the page. It also taught me something about life, consequence and chance, and caused me to wonder if those who are in control of our lives are always in the right.

I mark 'The Widow's Son' as my first experience of adult reading and when New Island brought out the *The Long Gaze Back* anthology in 2015 (ed Sinead Gleeson), I was delighted to find myself in the same book as Mary Lavin. In the way that one good thing can lead to another, it was the impending reissue by New Island of Mary Lavin's *In the Middle of the Fields* collection that led to the inclusion of its title story in *The Long Gaze Back* and this followed the reissue in 2011 of *Happiness and Other Stories* also by New Island.

And now we have this collection, *The Becker Wives and Other Stories*, first published in 1946 by Michael Joseph, reissued here by New Island – and so the renaissance of Mary Lavin continues.

There are only four stories in this collection, which is a little unusual. Two of these stories, however, 'The Becker Wives' and 'A Happy Death', could be classified as novellas and in length anyhow they certainly qualify as such. My own feeling is that both stories are so intensely concentrated on the emotional lives of their characters that they read more like long short stories.

It's a balanced selection – the two longer stories are heavily populated; the other two are not. One story concerns the struggles of a well-to-do family; another deals with a family struggling against poverty, or rather against the shame associated with poverty.

'Magenta' and 'The Joy-Ride' are about people who live in the shadow of larger lives: servants and caretakers trapped by circumstances and the whim of the absent landlord.

'The Joy-Ride' and 'The Becker Wives' are both humorous stories although the humour becomes darker as the stories proceed. Even so, they contain more comedy than one has come to expect from Lavin's work, particularly her later work which, despite moments of humour and no shortage of irony, often comes back to grief. But then she was no stranger to grief. In her lifetime she lost two husbands, both of whom she dearly loved and the year before *The Becker Wives* was published, her adored father died leaving her with, some might say, the wrong parent to contend with for another twenty years.

'The Becker Wives' story starts out as a comedy of manners: sleek, sophisticated and fast paced. We are told it is set in Cork although unusually for Lavin, the location of this particular story never really feels specific. In fact, we could just as easily be in small-town America. There is a cinematic texture throughout reminiscent of one of the old Hollywood movie greats such as *Harvey* or *Arsenic and Old Lace* and even the names of some of the characters, Theobald, Honoria, Henrietta – and these may well be old Cork names – sound more like small-town America, to my mind anyhow. It's a story that starts out in a satirical vein, poking fun at the middle classes at work and at play, the desire for social success, the insecurity of those who have married above themselves and the in-house snobbery directed against them. However, what starts out as a comedy of manners gradually darkens into a story about mental illness – a subject that arises to varying degrees in three of the stories in this collection.

'The Joy-Ride' also starts out as a comedy of sorts. Two butlers, caretakers of a house with no master in residence, decide, in the absence of the overseer, to skip off for the day. The butlers, one middle-aged and cautious, the other young and snide, goad each other into taking more and more risks as they embark on their great adventure. In this story, there can be no doubt as to the location: we are back in a Lavin landscape as, with painterly precision, she lays down the countryside of County Meath. The story is a terrific and often hilarious study of male pride. It clips along before delivering us to a dark and twisted ending.

The third story, 'A Happy Death', like many of Lavin's stories is one of love and hatred combined. Love and hatred locked into a cage in a fight to the death. In a way, this is also a story about decay: the slow decay of a marriage; the decay of the spirit within the family too, as the children become, in the all-consuming unhappiness of their parents' marriage, superfluous to requirements.

As in many of her stories, the house in 'A Happy Death' is seen almost as a character. It seems to mirror the experience of the people living within – in this case, decaying and disintegrating alongside Ella and Robert – a couple who were once deeply in love. In a way love remains, although now it is an overpowering and destructive love, the sort that can only turn in on itself.

Finally there is 'Magenta'. There is something joyful about this story for all its unhappy elements.

The young and slightly wild Magenta, daughter of the local herdsman, is full of optimism despite her lowly circumstances. She comes to do the heavier housework in the local big house – again a house without an owner and one that has seen better days. Two elderly maids are the caretakers and have lived there so long that they feel, and often behave, as if they own it. Like Flora in 'The Becker Wives', Magenta breezes in and out of their lives and like Flora, she will pay the price for her *joie de vivre*.

Mary Lavin was thirty-four when *The Becker Wives* was first published. She already had three books to her name and would go on to publish several more collections, two novels, and countless individual stories in anthologies and magazines such as *The New Yorker* where she had a first-read contract for several years. She was often labelled as a writer who dealt with the female aspect of life, an examiner of all things feminine – if not quite a feminist writer. But she is not a writer to be closed into any bracket. As we can see in this collection, she was capable of peeling the skin off any heart, male or female, and subjecting it to forensic inspection. She wrote without gimmickry or regard for passing fads. She worked on instinct and, through her own creative impulse, used her life experience to enrich her stories. She pulled the world into herself, turned it around and then gave it an outer expression that is utterly unique. In other words, she was a true artist.

A photograph taken in a garden, in or around 1914 and reproduced in Leah Levenson's biography *The Four Seasons of Mary Lavin*, shows a child aged eighteen months, seated in the corner of a basket chair. The expression is amused, inquisitive, discerning; it radiates intellectual acuity. Of course, all children are observers at this age – it's how we learn to negotiate the world – but it is hard to believe that the child in this photograph is the average toddler. What is easy to believe, however, is that here is someone recording and more importantly, retaining all that she sees and hears. It's as if there is a camera inside her little head. The fact that the child is alone on the seat, adds to this sense of destiny.

Christine Dwyer Hickey

The Becker Wives

When Ernest, the third of the Beckers to marry, chose a girl with no more to recommend her than the normal attributes of health, respectability and certain superficial good looks, the other two – James and Henrietta – felt they could at last ignore Theobald and his nonsense. Theobald had been a bit young to proffer advice to them, but Ernest had had the full benefit of their youngest brother's counsel and warnings. Yet Ernest had gone his own way too: Julia, the new bride, was no more remarkable than James's wife Charlotte. Both had had to earn their living while in the single state, and neither had brought anything into the family by way of dowry beyond the small amount they had put aside in a savings bank during the period of their engagements, engagements that in both cases had been long enough for the Beckers to ascertain all particulars that could possibly be expected to have a bearing on their suitability for marriage and child-bearing.

'And those, mind you, are the things that count,' James said to Samuel, now the only unmarried Becker – except Theobald. 'Of course every man is entitled to make his own choice,' he added with a touch of patronage, because no matter how Theobald might lump the two wives together, the fact remained that Ernest had taken Julia from behind the counter of the shop where he bought his morning paper, whereas his Charlotte had been a stenographer in the firm of Croker and Croker, a firm that might justifiably consider itself a serious rival to the firm of Becker and Becker. But Theobald ignored such niceties of classification. In his eyes both of his brothers' wives came from the wrong side of the river, as he put it, and neither of them differed much – in anything but their sex – from Robert, the husband of Henrietta. Robert had been just a lading-clerk whom James had met in the course of business, but since it had never been certain that Henrietta would secure a husband of any kind, the rest of the family – except Theobald of course – thought she'd done right to jump at him. Theobald had even expected *her* to make a good marriage. But once Robert had been raised from the status of a clerk to that of husband, it had been a relatively small matter to absorb him into the Becker business.

The Beckers were corn merchants. They carried on their trade in a moderate-sized premise on the quays, and they lived on the premise. But if anyone were foolish enough to entertain doubts about the scale and importance of the business conducted on the ground floor, he had only to be given a glimpse of the comfort and luxury of the upper storeys, to be disabused of his error. The Beckers believed in the solid comforts, and the business paid for them amply.

Old Bartholomew Becker, father of the present members of the firm, had built up a sizeable trade by the good old principles of constant application and prudent transaction. Then, having made room in the firm for each of his three older sons, one after another, and having put his youngest son Theobald into the Law to ensure that the family interests would be fully safeguarded, the old man took to his big brass-bound bed – a bed solemnified by a canopy of red velvet, and made easy of ascent by a tier of mahogany steps clipped to the side rail – and died. He died at exactly the moment most opportune for the business to be brought abreast of the times by a little judicious innovation.

In his last moments, old Bartholomew had gathered his sons around him in the high-ceilinged bedroom in which he had begot them, and ordering them to prop him upright, had given them one final injunction: to marry, and try to see that their sister married too.

The unmarried state had been abhorrent to old Bartholomew. He had held it to be not only dangerous to a man's soul, but destructive to his business as well. In short, to old Bartholomew, marriage represented safety and security. To his own early marriage with Anna, the daughter of his head salesman, he attributed the greater part of his success. He had married Anna when he was twenty-two and she was eighteen. And the dowry she brought with her was Content. By centring her young husband's desires within the four walls of the house on the quayside, Anna had contributed more than she knew to the success of the firm. For, when other young men of that day, associates and rivals, were out till all hours in pursuit of pleasure and the satisfaction of their desires, Bartholomew Becker was to be found in his countinghouse, working at his ledgers, secure in the knowledge that the object of his desires was tucked away upstairs in their great brass bed. And as the years went on, the thought of his big soft Anna more often than not heavy with child, sitting up pretending to read, but in reality yawning and listening for his step on the stairs, had in it just the right blend of desire and promise of fulfilment that enabled him to keep at the ledgers and not go up to her until he'd got through them. In this way he made more and more money for her. Anna might not take credit for every penny Bartholomew made, but she was undoubtedly responsible for those extra pence, earned while other men slept or revelled, that made all the difference between a firm like Beckers and other firms in the same trade. It was inevitable, of course, that the more money Anna inspired her husband to amass, the more her beauty became smothered in the luxury with which he surrounded her. Yet, on his death-bed, his memory being more accurate than his eyesight, it was of Anna's young beauty that he spoke. And reminding her of their own happiness, he laid on her a last injunction to be good to his sons' wives. He made no mention of how she should conduct herself towards a son-in-law, no doubt fearing it unlikely such a person would put in an appearance. Anna gave the dying man an unconditional promise.

Theobald therefore had his mother to contend with as well as his brothers when he objected to each of his sisters-in-law as they came on the scene.

'Have you forgotten your father's last words, Theobald?' Anna pleaded, each time. 'How can you take this absurd attitude? What is to be said against this marriage?'

'What is to be said in its favour?' Theobald snapped back.

And on the occasion of Ernest's engagement, when Theobald had put this infuriating question for the third time, his mother had been goaded into giving him an almost unseemly answer.

'After all,' she said, 'the same could have been said about your father's marriage to me!'

That, of course, was the whole point of Theobald's argument, although he could not very well say so to Anna. Surely he and his brothers ought to do better than their father: to go a step further, as it were, not stay in the same rut. It was one thing for old Bartholomew, at the outset of his career, to give himself the comfort of marrying a girl of his own class, but it was another thing altogether for his sons, whom he had established securely on the road towards success, to turn around and marry wives who were no better than their mother.

'No better than Mother!' Henrietta was outraged. She could hardly credit her ears. She had the highest regard for Charlotte and Julia, but a sister-in-law was a sister-in-law, and the implication that either of them could be put on the same plane as her mother was unthinkable. 'No better than Mother!' she repeated, her voice shrill with vexation. 'As if they could be compared with her for one moment. I'm shocked that you could be so disrespectful, Theobald.'

But Theobald was always twisting people's words.

'So you do agree with me, Henrietta?' he said.

'I do not,' Henrietta shouted, 'but you know very well that both James and Ernest would be the first to admit that no matter how nice Charlotte and Julia are they could never hold a candle to Mother. They've said as much, many many times, and you've heard them.'

It was true.

On his wedding day James had stood up, and putting his arm around his bride's waist and causing her to blush furiously, he had addressed his family and friends.

'If Charlotte is half as good a wife as Mother, I'll be a fortunate man,' he said.

And Ernest, on *his* wedding day, had said exactly the same, giving James a chance to reiterate his sentiments.

'My very words,' James said, and all three wives, Anna, and the two young ones, Charlotte and Julia, had reddened, and all three together in chorus had disclaimed the compliment, although old Anna had chuckled and nodded her head towards the big ormolu sideboard, laden with bottles of wine and spirits and great glittering magnums of champagne, from the excellent cellar laid down by old Bartholomew.

'I never heed compliments paid to me at a wedding,' old Anna said. They all could see though that she was pleased and happy. But just then, happening to catch a glimpse of her youngest son between the red carnations and fronds of maidenhair fern that sprayed out from the silver-bracketed epergne in the centre of the bridal table, Anna leant back in her chair, and lowered her voice for a word with James who was passing behind her with a bottle of Veuve Cliquot that he didn't care to trust to any hands but his own. 'For goodness' sake, fill up Theobald's glass,' she said. 'It makes me nervous just to look at him, sitting there with that face on!'

For Theobald sat sober and glum between Henrietta and Samuel, where he had stubbornly placed himself, thereby entirely altering the arrangement of the table, and causing the bride's elder sister and her maiden aunt to be seated side by side. Theobald had flatly refused to sit between them, and it had been considered unwise to press the matter.

'I would have made him sit where he was told,' Charlotte said to James, when he came back to her side after pouring the champagne and she had ascertained what Anna had whispered to him. 'Theobald is odd, but he'd hardly be impolite to strangers.'

'I don't know about that,' James said morosely. 'Don't forget the way he behaved at our wedding. He wasn't very polite to – ' James stopped short. He'd been about to say 'your people' but he altered the words quickly to 'our guests'.

'Oh, that was different,' Charlotte said. 'That was the first wedding in the family.'

James wasn't listening though. He was trying to read the expression on Theobald's face as, just then, his youngest brother turned and spoke to Henrietta. Henrietta frowned. What was the confounded fellow saying *now*?

It was just as well James could not hear. Theobald was on his hobby-horse. 'The joke of it is, Henrietta,' he said, 'that for all their protestations to the contrary, both James and Ernest would get the shock of their lives if anyone saw the smallest similarity between their wives and our dear mother.'

'Well, there are differences of appearance, of course,' Henrietta said crisply. 'No one denies that.' She always felt that in every criticism of her sister-in-law there was an implied criticism of Robert, and she was annoyed, but on this occasion she was ill at ease as well in case Theobald would be overheard. He hadn't taken the trouble to lower his voice.

'My dear Henrietta,' he exclaimed. 'You would hardly expect our brothers' wives to wear spectacles and elastic stockings on their wedding day and take size forty-eight corsets, would you? Give them a little time. For my own part I'd like to think my wife would have something more to depend upon for attraction than slim ankles and a narrow waist.'

Yet, even Theobald could hardly have foreseen the rapidity with which his sisters-in-law lost their youthful figures. The punctual pregnancy of Julia coinciding with the somewhat delayed pregnancy of Charlotte made both women look prematurely heavy, and there was something about their figures that made it seem they would never again snap back to their original shape.

Indeed, since both of them thought it advisable to conceal their condition under massive fur coats, soon there wasn't a great deal – unless you were at close quarters – to distinguish one from the other of the three Becker wives.

After their confinements, of course, Charlotte and Julia regained some of their differentiating qualities, but even then, due to having followed the advice of Anna and adopted such old-fashioned maxims as 'eating for two' and putting up their feet at every possible chance, neither their ankles nor their waists would ever be slender again. Now, too, Charlotte and Julia felt entitled to accept freely the fur capes, fur tippets, and fleece-lined boots that they had been a bit diffident of demanding when they were dowerless brides. Indeed as the years went on, they came to regard these things more in relation to the effect they made upon each other than to the effect upon their own figures, so that when finally Anna passed to her last reward, and the fallals and fripperies she had won in happy conjugal contest with Bartholomew were dispersed among her three daughters, it seemed at times that instead of passing from the scene Anna had been but divided in three, to dwell with her sons anew. And nowhere was their resemblance to Anna as noticeable as when, in accordance with a custom first started by Bartholomew, and strictly kept up by James, the Beckers went out for an evening meal in a good restaurant. But whereas formerly Anna had sat at the head of the table, comfortable and heavy in furs and jewellery, there were now three replicas of her seated on three sides of the table.

Henrietta, Charlotte, and Julia. There they sat, all three of them, all fat, heavy, and furred, yet like Anna, all emanating, in spite of the money lavished on them, such an air of ordinariness and mediocrity that Theobald, when duty compelled him to be of the party, squirmed in his seat all the time, and rolled bread into pellets from nervousness and embarrassment. Yet he had to attend these family functions. One had to put a face on things, as he explained to Samuel, who came nearest to sharing his views. After all, although it was for the benefit of the family that old Bartholomew had made a lawyer out of his youngest son, Theobald was not without a return of benefit. His practice was mainly dependent on family connections and he just couldn't afford to ignore family ceremonial. But it went against the grain. Indeed, ever since he was a mere youth of sixteen or seventeen Theobald had nurtured strange notions of pride and ambition, and when to these had been added intellectual snobbery and professional stuffiness, it became a positive ordeal for him to have to endure the Becker parties. In Anna's time, a small spark of filial devotion had made them bearable. Without her it was all he could do to force himself to go through with them. But once at the party, however, he could at least make an effort to keep control of the situations that sometimes arose. With a little tact it was possible to gloss over the limitations of the others.

'Not there, Henrietta!' Just in time he'd put his hand under his sister's elbow and shepherd them all to a quiet corner of the restaurant, whereas left to themselves they would have made straight for a table in the centre of the room. 'How about over there?' he'd murmur, and guide them towards a table in a corner behind a pillar, or a pot of ferns.

It was not that he was ashamed of them. There was nothing of which to be ashamed. Indeed, the Beckers were the most respectably dressed people in the restaurant, and they were certainly better mannered than most.

Moreover, one and all they possessed robust palates that almost made up for their hit-and-miss pronunciation of the items on the menu. And James, who as the eldest was always the official host, was more than liberal with tips to the waiters. Nevertheless, Theobald was ill at ease and cordially detested every minute of the meal.

'Are you suffering from nerves, Theobald?' Henrietta asked one evening, frowning at the disgusting pellets of bread all round his plate. She was the one who was most piqued at being led to an out-of-the-way table. 'I don't know why you had us sit here. The table isn't large enough in the first place, and in the second place we can hardly hear ourselves thinking, we're so near the orchestra.'

The table was in a rather dark corner, behind a potted palm, and it was indeed so near the orchestra that James had to point out with his finger the various choices from the menu, in order to come to an understanding with the waiter.

'I wanted to sit over there,' Henrietta said, indicating an undoubtedly larger and better placed table, but just then the orchestra reached a lightly scored passage, and overhearing his sister, James looked up from the menu.

'Would you like to change tables, Henrietta?' he asked. 'It's not too late yet: I haven't given the order.'

Theobald shrank back into his chair at the mere thought of the fuss that would accompany the move. Charlotte and Julia were already gathering up their wraps and their handbags and scraping back their chairs. His left eye had begun to twitch, and the back of his neck had begun to redden uncomfortably.

'Aren't we all right here?' he cried. 'Why should we make ourselves conspicuous?' In spite of herself, Henrietta felt sorry for him.

17

'Oh, we may as well stay here, James,' she said, settling back into her chair again and throwing her fur stole over the arm of it. 'We can't satisfy everyone, although I must say I don't know what Theobald is talking about when he says we'd make ourselves noticeable, because I for one can't see that anyone is taking the least notice of us!'

There was a thin, high note of irritability in his sister's voice that made Theobald more embarrassed than ever. Under the table he crossed and uncrossed his long legs, and took out his handkerchief twice in the course of one minute, as he tried in vain to disassociate himself from them all. The paradox of his sister's words suddenly came home to him. She'd put her finger on what was wrong with them. His discomfort came precisely from the fact that there was no one looking at them. They were the only people in the whole restaurant who were totally inconspicuous. Around them, at every other table, he saw people who were in one way or another distinguished. And those whom he did not recognise looked interesting, too. The women stood out partly because of their appearance, but mostly because of their manner which was in all cases imperious. The men were distinguished by some quality, which although a bit obscure to Theobald, made itself strongly felt by the waiters and where the Beckers often had a wait of ten or even twenty minutes between courses, these men had only to click their fingers to have every waiter in the room at their beck and call. As well as that, most people seemed to know each other. They were constantly calling across to each other, and exchanging gossip from table to table.

Yes, it was true for Henrietta. No one was taking the slightest notice of the Beckers. In that noisy, unself-conscious gathering, the Beckers were conspicuous only by being so very inconspicuous. It was mainly because they liked to stare at other people that the Beckers went out to dinner. Theobald looked around the table at the womenfolk, at his family. There they sat, stolid and silent, their mouths moving as they chewed their food, but their eyes immobile as they stared at someone or other who had caught their fancy at another table. There was little or no conversation among them, such as there was being confined to supply each other's wants in matters of sauces or condiments.

As for the men, Theobald looked at his brothers. They too were unable to keep their eyes upon their own plates, and following the gaze of their wives, their gaze too wandered over the other diners. They had a little more to say to each other than their women, but the flow of their conversation was impeded by having to converse with each other across the intervening bulks of their wives.

Theobald bit his lip in vexation and began to drink his soup with abandon. He felt more critical of them than usual. Was it for this they had dragged him out of his comfortable apartment – to stare at strangers? He was mortified for himself, and still more mortified for them. Such an admission of inferiority! And why should they feel inferior? So far as money was concerned, weren't they in as sound a position as anyone in the city? And as for ability – well, money like theirs wasn't made nowadays by pinheads or duffers. James was probably the most astute business man you'd meet in a day's march. There was no earthly reason why his family should play second fiddle to anyone in the room.

'Look here!' Theobald roused himself. As long as he was of the party, he might as well try to put some spirit into it. He leant across the table. 'I heard an amusing thing today at the Courts,' he said, determined to draw the attention of his family back to some common focus. To help his own concentration he fastened his eyes on a big plated cruet-stand on the table. His story might gather up their scattered attention and make it seem that they were interested in each other, that they had come here to enjoy each other's company, to have a good meal, or even to listen to the music: anything, anything but expose themselves by gaping at other people. 'I said I heard an amusing thing at the Courts this morning,' he repeated, because his remark had passed unheard or unheeded the first time, the gaze of all the Beckers having at that moment gone towards a prominent actor who had just seated himself at an adjoining table. But Theobald's simple ruse seemed doomed to failure. Only James appeared to be listening.

'I didn't think the Courts were sitting yet,' James said. 'I didn't know the Long Vacation was over.' In Theobald's story he displayed no interest at all. He had done no more than, as it were, listlessly lift his fork to pick out a small morsel of familiar food before pushing aside the rest of what was offered.

Theobald did not know for a moment whether to be amused or annoyed. It might perhaps be an idea to try and make a joke of their inattention. If only he could rouse them to one good genuine laugh, he'd be satisfied. If only he could gather them for once into a self-absorbed group! But how? Just then, however, to his surprise he found Charlotte had been attending to what James had said.

'Of course the Courts are sitting,' she said, and the glance she gave her husband had an exasperated glint. Theobald was about to metaphorically link arms with her and enlist her as a supporter, when she leant forward to reprimand her husband. 'How could you be so stupid, James? Didn't you see the Chief Justice and his wife in the foyer when we were coming in here tonight? You know they wouldn't be back in town unless the Supreme Court was sitting.' But after another scathing glance she turned the other way, and this time leaning across Theobald, she caught Henrietta's sleeve and gave it a tug. 'They're sitting at a table to the right of the door, Henrietta, if you'd like to see them. She has a magnificent ring on her finger. I can see it from here. And that's their daughter in the velvet cloak. What do you think of her? She's supposed to be pretty.'

Theobald's story was not mentioned any more that evening by anyone, least of all by himself, and he had the further mortification of knowing that it was due to his abortive attempt to tell it that Henrietta and James, the least curious of the Beckers, and the least given to gossip, were craning their necks all during the meal to see the Chief Justice's wife and daughter. As if they were a different race of beings! Some species of superior animal which they – the Beckers – were kindly permitted to observe.

And those were exactly the words he used, later that night, when he and Samuel were walking home. Being unmarried, they were the only two of the Becker men who were at liberty to walk home from these gatherings. James and Ernest, and Henrietta's husband, had to hire cabs to convey their wives to their abodes.

Samuel and Theobald were in rooms, but not of course in the same locality – Samuel thinking it advisable to reside near the business, and Theobald feeling that for the sake of his practice he had to live further out in a more fashionable area, although he admitted that at times it was inconvenient.

'A good address is essential to a man in my position,' he said. It irritated him that he had to explain this so often to the others. Samuel was the only one who understood. He had even made mention once or twice of doing likewise. For the present, however, Samuel was all right where he was. As bachelor's quarters his rooms were quite comfortable.

The two brothers walked along the streets talking without great interest, but with a certain affection, and looking down as they walked at the pavement vanishing under their feet, except when, intermittently in the patches of pale light from the street lamps they raised their heads and appeared to look at each other, giving the impression that they were attending to what was being said.

Samuel had enjoyed his dinner. He was also enjoying the walk home. The streets late at night had an air of unreality that appealed to him. Like limelight the moon shone greenly down making the lighted windows of the houses appear artificial, as if they were squares of celluloid, illuminated only for the sake of illusion. He hoped Theobald wouldn't insist on dragging him back to reality. But he might have known better.

'Did you see them tonight, Samuel? Did you see them staring at the Chief Justice and his wife? Did you see the way they were turning around in their chairs?'

'I didn't notice particularly,' Samuel said. He still hoped to hold himself aloof. High up in a window on the other side of the street a light went out. What was going on up in that room? What unknown people were intent on what unknown purposes? Vague curiosity stirred in him.

Theobald was relentless. 'What do you mean?' he fumed. 'You were as bad as anyone yourself.'

Samuel reluctantly lowered his eyes and looked at his brother and sighed.

'What harm is it to look at people?' he asked mildly.

Theobald came to a stand. 'You know the answer to that as well as I do, Samuel,' he said. 'You know it marks people off at once as coming from a certain class, to stare at anyone who has raised himself the least bit above the common level. It's tantamount to acknowledging one's own inferiority, and I for one won't do that.' All Theobald's pent-up vexation of the evening threatened to break over the head of the defenceless Samuel. 'How is it no one ever stares at us when we go into these places? Isn't there a single one of us distinguished enough in some way to attract a little attention from others instead of our always being attracted to them?'

Samuel did not reply, not knowing whether it was wiser to reply or to remain silent. Theobald's words might be no more than a protracted exclamation, and a reply might provoke an argument. As they walked on a few more paces in silence it seemed as if he had followed the wisest course. But when they were passing under another lamp-post Theobald stood again.

'I'll never get used to it,' he cried.

This time Samuel was genuinely caught. 'To what?' he asked, taken by surprise.

But it was only the same old pill in another coating.

'To the poor marriages they made,' Theobald said, and of course he was talking about James and Ernest. Samuel sighed. He was into the thick of it. 'It makes me sad every time I think of them,' Theobald went on. 'I don't feel so bad about Henrietta, but I hate to think of the chances our brothers let slip – with their positions and their looks, and above all, with their money. Think of the opportunities they had. They might have made excellent marriages. Instead of that – what did they do?' Unable to find words caustic enough to answer his own question, Theobald made a noise in his throat to indicate the greatest of contempt. Then he put out his hand and patted Samuel on the shoulder. 'The only hope we have rests in you, old man,' he said.

Except for the fact that Theobald was younger than him, which gave an unpleasant sense of patronage to his brother's words and gestures, Samuel felt flattered. He immediately paid more heed than the Beckers normally paid to Theobald. This did not mean he approved of Theobald's nonsense. He was just vaguely titillated by his brother's confidence in him, though there was something about his brother's attitude that he still didn't like.

'When your time comes, Samuel,' Theobald said, 'I hope you'll do a bit better for yourself than the others. I hope you'll have some aspiration towards a better social level.'

That was it. *That* was the undertone Samuel disliked. He had not been able to put his finger on it before. All this talk about lifting themselves up to a higher level implied a criticism of their present level which was decidedly disagreeable to him.

'Look here, Theobald,' he said. They were passing under yet another lamp-post but it was he this time who came to a stand. 'I don't know what you're talking about, and I don't know what levels *you* want to reach, but personally I don't think there is anyone in this city, whatever his position, with whom *I* am unacquainted. Why only this morning I was talking to Sir Joshua Lundon over a cup of coffee and –'

Samuel was trying to speak casually, but as he uttered the baronet's name his voice rose to a higher and thinner note, and his eyes bulged slightly with the strain of trying to appear indifferent. He drew back a pace or two on the pretext of clearing his throat behind a large grey silk handkerchief heavily monogrammed in purple silk to match the silk clocks that ran up the outer sides of his grey lisle socks: he was the most elegant of the Beckers. But he was smart enough to know that the only time their younger brother's views were acceptable to any of them was when the fellow managed to get hold of one of them separately – as now – because while they were all unable to apply his counsels and criticisms to themselves, they came within reasonable distance of agreeing with him when discussing each other.

And, of course, in the present case Samuel felt sure there could not possibly be any personal application intended. Unless Theobald was using the past of the others as a future warning to him, who, though he might have the elegance, had few other attributes of the real dyed-in-the-wool bachelor. Samuel indeed entirely lacked the stamina of the successful bachelor, and at the time of this late night walk with Theobald, he was almost at the end of his tether. So he was at one and the same time drawn towards the dangerous topic of matrimony and anxious to skirt it. He felt, however, that his reference to the baronet had been particularly clever, because it might serve to draw Theobald out in his views without leaving him, Samuel, open to direct examination. Yet when he saw the look that came on Theobald's face, he had an uneasy feeling that he had made a false move, and he was about to be out-flanked.

'Yes,' he said nervously, repeating his words, as if having taken up a poor position he felt it was best to dig himself in – 'Yes, Sir Joshua Lundon. He came over and sat down at my table. We had a most interesting talk.'

But whereas on the first occasion he had looked at Theobald as much as to say 'What do you think of that?' he now looked at him as much as to ask 'What can you say against that?'

Theobald, however, had another most irritating habit, learned no doubt from his profession. He kept people in suspense before replying to their simplest remarks, thereby giving his own words a disturbing preponderance.

'My dear Samuel,' he said at last, 'I have no doubt but that you have often sat down with people as notable – and I hope a lot more interesting – than old Sir Joshua. One meets all kinds of people in public places.'

Under Samuel's heavy chin a blush began to spread. That was a confounded insinuation. No doubt it was another trick of the trade. No Becker had ever been bred to such cute ways. Not that he, Samuel, couldn't summon up certain wiles if needed and beat the damn fellow at his own game. He knew very well what was implied. And he'd give an answer in the same wrapping.

'Curious – that's just what Sir Joshua was saying to me only today,' he said, as casually as possible. 'He was remarking on that very thing – the promiscuity of persons one meets with when one ventures into public places. "As a matter of fact, Becker," he said to me, "I'm always delighted to see you, or someone like you, with whom one can suitably sit down when one is forced to come into this kind of place."'

As he spoke, Samuel's confidence returned, and he felt there was no small skill in the way he parried the laywer's thrust. He even felt for an instant that the Old Man could as readily have sent him, Samuel, for the Bar as the younger brother. Now, of course, after a number of years, training told, but if it came to native wit and natural aptitude he believed he would be prepared to cross swords with Theobald any day. Why Theobald was as good as eating his words. Listen to him!

'I didn't think you knew the baronet so well,' Theobald was saying. And in spite of Samuel's efforts to twitch it away, a look of gratification stole over his face. This was almost an apology. He felt he could afford now to be magnanimous about the whole thing.

'Oh, yes, yes. I've known him a long time,' he said. 'I'd like you to meet him – I must arrange something some day. You might come and have a meal with me in the city?' He looked at his younger brother. The fellow appeared to be thoroughly deflated. Oh, how Samuel wished that James or Ernest could see him. 'Yes,' he said, intent on enjoying his position, 'as a matter of fact I have had it in mind for some time to make you two acquainted. The baronet might be of some assistance to you. And I think he'd be glad of a chance to do me a favour because I don't mind telling you I have obliged him in a number of ways over the years.'

'Thank you, Samuel,' Theobald said, and Samuel could hardly credit the look of humility that he thought he saw on the other's face. But all at once he felt a twinge of uneasiness. Surely there was an excessive quiet in the tone of Theobald's voice? Yes, undoubtedly there was. And what was he saying? However suave it sounded Samuel was on the alert.

But Theobald was only thanking him.

'Thank you, Samuel,' he'd said. 'I'd like that very much indeed.' Then he paused. 'I have often thought that Lady Lundon looked more intelligent than the old man. I'd be most interested in making her acquaintance. For when shall we arrange?'

For one moment Samuel measured eyes with Theobald and thought of taking refuge in dissimulation, saying that he would drop him a line when he had arranged something. But at the thought of the calculating way he had been led into this conversational trap, his temper so got the better of him that dissimulation was impossible. A feeling of positive hatred for Theobald rose within him, and he felt a vein begin to pulse in his forehead, and his jaw to twitch involuntarily. He was only too well aware of these distressing indications of ill temper, and his awareness did nothing to ease them.

The young cur, he apostrophised. He was well suited to the Law. A fox to the snout. He himself could do nothing but bark out the truth.

'If it's Lady Lundon you want to meet you can get someone else to introduce you,' he said sourly. 'I only know the old man.'

This, of course, was what Theobald was waiting to hear. He met the explanation with one simple word.

'Ah!' he said. Just that, no more. 'Ah!' The vein in Samuel's temple throbbed more violently, but Theobald put out his hand and patted him on the shoulder. 'Take it easy, Samuel,' he said. 'I'm sorry for baiting you, but it gets to be a habit with us fellows at the Courts, I'm afraid.'

As he patted his brother approvingly, however, Theobald looked anxiously at him. How the chap shook when he got agitated! But when Samuel relaxed again into his usual complacency, Theobald abruptly withdrew his hand. 'You did rather ask for it though, old fellow,' he said.

They had reached the street in which Samuel resided and had slackened pace to lengthen the time at their disposal, for in spite of a customary invitation to do so, it was not a practice for the brothers to accept hospitality from each other on such occasions. Tonight, however,

Theobald wanted a little more time with Samuel to say something important he thought ought to be said.

'For heaven's sake let's drop the pretence, Samuel,' he cried. 'Don't try to pull the wool over my eyes with your social contacts in public places. Of course, you don't know Lady Lundon, or anyone like her if it comes to that, and if you did you'd keep your mouth shut about it or the rest of the family would be living vicariously on your relationship.' Dropping his normal tone, Theobald affected a thin, high and wholly unnatural tone, instantly recognisable to his brother as the voice of their sister-in-law Julia. 'Oh, Lady Lundon,' he mimicked. 'Oh yes. Oh yes. I haven't met her myself yet, personally, but she's a great friend of Samuel's. I believe she is a charming person – simply charming – and most unassuming. I understand she is a very friendly person, and so simple – just like anyone else in fact.'

Theobald as he imitated her was so like Ernest's wife that Samuel had to smile in spite of himself. And some of his resentment left him.

'Isn't that true?' Theobald asked, although he had not actually formulated a question.

'Well – up to a point I suppose it's true,' Samuel said, knowing what Theobald meant.

'Of course, you understand I have nothing against them,' Theobald said, and in spite of a certain ambiguity in his use of the pronoun, it was possible to tell by the derogatory tone of his voice that Theobald was referring to his sisters-in-law. 'In fact,' he said more explicitly, 'Julia is a very decent sort really. Those socks she knit for me last winter look as if they'll never wear out, although the colour is a bit drastic, but all the same she meant well and poor Charlotte isn't a bad sort either. It's only a pity James and Ernest didn't do a little bit better for themselves.'

Samuel couldn't let this pass.

'They're happy!' he protested weakly.

'Happy! Well, I should hope so!' Theobald said with a flash of contempt. 'That's all they considered at the time, their own comfort and pleasure. If they'd been let down about that I wouldn't know what to say. But happy or not, I still maintain, and will do so till my dying day, that it's a pity their wives hadn't a little more to recommend them.'

'It is certainly regrettable that not one of them – Robert included – had a single penny to bring into the business,' Samuel said with a sudden burst of animation.

'There you are!' Theobald was delighted by Samuel's agreement, although as a matter of fact he himself had not been thinking of his in-laws' lack of money when he'd spoken of their limitations. But it was so encouraging to have someone agree that they did have limitations he let this pass. 'There you are!' he repeated. 'Why, it's ludicrous to think we tolerated it – that no one said 'boo' at the time. In proper levels of society there is some kind of control in these matters: not that I approve altogether of too much interference. In fact interference ought not to be necessary if a family is brought up to an understanding of its obligations, its duties.' He frowned. 'I must, of course, say in defence of James and Ernest that we ourselves were not brought up to have that understanding, but –' He stopped and looked Samuel straight in the eye. '– but how is it, then, that you and I came to have the proper outlook?'

Whatever disparity might still have been between the two brothers was blasted away by this shattering bolt of flattery.

'Oh well,' Samuel said modestly, 'people can't all be alike, I suppose.'

'I suppose not,' Theobald agreed, but more curtly, and he turned aside in case he would laugh out loud at the foolish look on Samuel's face, although it was not indeed a laughing matter, and he felt he was to be congratulated on the evening's conversation. If he had been too late to do anything about the marriages of his older brothers, he believed that at least he had made an impression on Samuel.

There were as a matter of fact two special reasons why Theobald was glad to think he had influenced Samuel. The first was that he had sensed for some time past that the citadel of Samuel's celibacy would not continue to stand much longer, and that he had spoken just in the nick of time. The second reason was that he himself had begun to engage his mind with plans of his own in a certain interesting direction, and he did not want to have any more mediocre connections to have to drag out into the light.

'Well, goodnight, Samuel,' he said abruptly.

They had reached the foot of the steps that led up to the old Georgian house where Samuel still resided in single dignity. Taking a last look at him, Theobald congratulated himself again on having said his say so determinedly. Then having watched his brother admit himself into the house he started to saunter on his way, giving himself up, with more ease of mind than he had done for some time, to the joys of contemplating his own plans – plans which, by the way, he told himself, he would shortly have to divulge to the family.

Before, however, Theobald had time to divulge anything to anyone, Samuel's capitulation had taken place.

' – and I was guided a great deal by you, Theobald, in making my choice,' Samuel said, turning to his younger brother with a special courtesy after he had made the announcement of his forthcoming marriage to the rest of the family. 'I was greatly impressed by that conversation we had the other evening.'

'Did you hear that, Theobald?' Henrietta cried, her face purple with excitement. All the Beckers – bar Theobald – loved weddings. There was nothing they enjoyed more, unless perhaps christenings. 'Did you hear that? Samuel says he was largely guided by you in picking his bride.'

'Is that so?' Theobald said morosely. 'Well, all I can say is that he wasn't guided very far!'

'Theobald! What do you *mean*?' Henrietta cried, but she didn't wait for him to answer. 'Really, there is no understanding you at all,' she said. And indeed it seemed that there was not, because unlike the rest of them Samuel was marrying money. He was in fact marrying a great deal of money. He was uniting himself to Honoria, only daughter of the elder Croker of the firm of Croker and Croker, which was the only other firm of corn merchants in the city which might be said to be in any way comparable in size and importance with the firm of Becker and Becker. Although, as James had quietly expressed himself, there was not much point in making speculations as to the relative importance of the two firms since now undoubtedly there would be an amalgamation between them, Honoria being the sole heiress to Croker and Croker.

'Perhaps you didn't understand that, Theobald?' Henrietta said, willing to give him another chance to alter his extraordinary attitude.

But Theobald understood. He understood every-thing. He shook his head sadly. It was the rest of them that did not understand. To them it seemed that Samuel had scored over him in a way that would pro-tect them for evermore from what they regarded as his notions.

'This will silence Theobald for good and all,' James had said earlier in the day, when as the head of the family he had been given an intimation of what Samuel planned before it was announced to the others.

'Did he get any hint of it at all?' Charlotte had asked eagerly, when it was whispered to her. 'I'd give anything to be there when he's told.'

That was what they all wanted to know – what Theobald would say.

What would Theobald say? What would Theobald do? The question went from lip to lip all that day as one after another the Beckers passed on a hint to each other of the felicitous step Samuel was taking. Julia alone refrained from this eager questioning because Theobald, she maintained, would have nothing to say now. Samuel had cut the ground from under his feet.

And that was exactly what Samuel himself felt he had done.

'He may not come out with it,' Samuel said, 'but I'd dearly like to know what's in his mind.'

And although Samuel got a shock when he was told what Theobald had come out with, he did not let his younger brother's words rankle because he felt that in cases like this one always had to make allowances for a certain amount of jealousy.

Only when he was alone with Honoria did Samuel allow himself to brood over Theobald's reaction.

'Theobald is your youngest brother, isn't he?' Honoria asked. To an only child the Becker family seemed at times bewilderingly large. 'I heard something or other about him, I think,' she said, 'but I can't remember exactly what it was – anyway I'm dying to meet him.'

'You'll shortly be meeting them all, my dear,' Samuel said. 'James is giving a dinner for that purpose I understand.' Then suddenly remembering the last dinner party James had given, and his walk through the empty streets afterwards with Theobald, he frowned. 'I hope James will agree to giving it in his own house,' he said. 'It would be more suitable than in a restaurant, don't you think?'

'Oh, I don't know so much about that,' Honoria said, and she seemed disappointed. 'I love eating out,' she said. 'I love looking at the other people. Father and I go out for dinner occasionally, just for that alone – to look at people. We went out last evening and, Samuel, you'd never guess who was sitting at the next table to us – Father knows him slightly – Sir Joshua Lundon. Father whispered who he was to me. And Lady Lundon was with him. Oh Samuel, she was so nice. Just as simple as could be! She ordered the simplest food too, just like you or me, or anybody else.'

Where had Samuel heard that before? Familiar and unpleasant echoes sounded in his brain. Had he himself not said something like this to Theobald recently and been promptly and severely shown his error?

'It would be more suitable for us to meet in James's house,' he said, and he resolved to insist on it.

When Samuel mentioned the matter to James, James agreed – if reluctantly.

'Very well,' he said. 'I'll tell Charlotte and we'll arrange for some night next week. All right?'

It was more than all right. It was perfect. For once the whole family was in accord in its preference for the betrothal celebrations to be as private as possible. For once their attention was focused fully on themselves. There was not one member of the family but wanted to witness Theobald's reaction to the wealthy bride-to-be. Their interest was centred on their own affairs for another reason too. Was there not a growing rumour that Theobald himself was about to introduce a new member into the family? And might it not be possible that in the intimacy of Samuel's party there could be further disclosures made? The hearts of the Becker women beat faster at the thought. The girl that was good enough for Theobald! How they longed to see her.

Who was she? What would she be like? Above all, would she live up to Theobald's own lofty notions? Not one single member of the family but was sorely tempted to hope she would not. And this, from no more unworthy motive than the common one of self-preservation. It would be such an ease to everyone if Theobald's mouth could be shut once and for ever.

And as the rumour grew this ungenerous feeling grew with it until finally the nearest any of his sisters and brothers could go to letting themselves believe Theobald's principles were inviolable was to disbelieve the rumour entirely.

'It can't be true,' Henrietta declared flatly on the morning of the day James and Charlotte were giving their little dinner for Samuel and Honoria. 'I don't believe it!'

'Well, I do!' Charlotte said. 'And so does Julia.'

'What about you, Robert? What do you think?' Henrietta asked, because Robert had come along with her to James's place to see if they could give a hand in the last-minute preparations.

'I must say I'm inclined to believe the rumours,' Robert said with a grin he couldn't seem to control.

'Why don't you ask Theobald straight out, Henrietta?' Charlotte said slyly.

'That's just what I intend doing,' Henrietta said. 'I'll make a point of asking him the very next opportunity – that is to say the very next time I'm alone with him.'

It was therefore rather unfortunate for Henrietta that a few minutes later, having volunteered to collect a few pot plants in town for Charlotte and having left Robert behind to attend to some hitch in the lighting arrangements, who should she run into – right outside Charlotte's door – right under the windows in fact – but her younger brother. There was nothing to do but take a rush at him.

'Is it true, Theobald?' she demanded, and she actually put out her arm to bar his way as if she feared he might bolt off.

'Is what true?' Theobald asked coldly and looked at her even more coldly. 'Are you feeling all right, Henrietta?'

For the life of her Henrietta could not bring herself to speak any plainer, but feeling forced to say something she took refuge behind further obscurity.

'Well, if it *is* true,' she said, 'all I can say is I hope you'll do as well for yourself as Samuel.'

Then, telling herself she had done what she proclaimed she would do, Henrietta threw a triumphant glance up at the windows of the house behind her, feeling pretty sure that Charlotte would be watching them from behind the curtains. She was so carried away by a sense of her own courage she wished Charlotte could have heard her, as well as seen her.

It was perhaps no harm that her sister-in-law had not heard, because Theobald did not seem to understand what she'd been driving at. Or did he? Really, he was impossible. No one could ever tell what he was thinking. Henrietta stared at him to try and figure out what was in the back of his mind. But the next minute she stepped back in alarm. Theobald's face had begun to work as if he was going to have a fit.

'What's the matter, Theobald?' she cried.

'The matter!' Theobald, although he had calmed down again, still looked very peculiar. 'Pray tell me, Henrietta,' he said then, 'in what way you consider our brother Samuel has done so well for himself?'

Henrietta simply did not know what to make of him. Who were they talking about anyway? Him or Samuel? She'd been under the impression that she was unearthing information about *him*.

'Well,' she said, taken aback, 'Honoria has plenty of money.'

'Money!' Theobald positively sneered at the word. 'What does money matter? To Samuel anyway! What does he want with any more than he has already? Money, my dear Henrietta, is not the only thing in this world.'

Was it not? Henrietta allowed herself to have mental reservations in the matter, but for the moment she was concerned with a less general aspect of what was being revealed. Very quickly she came to a decision. If there was any truth in the rumours about Theobald, well then it looked very much as if *his* intended was penniless. But Theobald was still ranting on about Samuel.

'I never thought he'd be so short-sighted,' he said. 'He's making a worse mistake than any of you.'

Henrietta had swallowed too many of these jibes to object to one more, and anyway she was just beginning to think she might draw him out a bit after all.

'How is that?' she asked faintly.

'Oh, can't you see!' Theobald cried impatiently. 'What difference does it make to Samuel whether he has thirty thousand or fifty thousand. It isn't more money Samuel needs: it's less. And that applies to all of us.'

'Less?' The daughter of the Beckers felt faint at the suggestion.

'Exactly,' Theobald said. 'I thought Samuel would have had the wit to forget about money for once and try and acquire some of the things of which this family stands in such sore need.'

'And what are they?' Henrietta gaped.

Theobald fixed her with a cold eye.

'Social position for one thing, and distinction for another; preferably the latter. But instead of that Samuel turns up with this mediocre Croker person. As I said before, he's made a worse mistake than any of you. What did the rest of you do? – Well, to put it bluntly you did no worse than keep within, whereas Samuel has widened, the circle of our mediocrity.'

In his vexation Theobald made several extravagant gestures, that to Henrietta appeared most unseemly in the street, but when his arms fell suddenly to his sides she felt still more uneasy about him.

'Tell me,' he said in a low despairing voice, 'I expect this girl has a horde of relatives? How many of them do you think there will be at James's tonight?'

'Only her father, I think,' Henrietta said quickly, 'and maybe an old aunt, but the aunt is deaf.' The question had made her very anxious. 'Why?'

'Because,' Theobald said, 'I was thinking that if there weren't too many Crokers there, tonight might be as good a time as any for the family to meet my Flora.'

'Flora?' Henrietta said stupidly, and then with a rush of blood to the head, she realised that this Flora, whoever she was, must be the living embodiment of the very rumours she had been trying to run to earth. 'Why, Theobald,' she cried, 'is her name Flora? I mean is it true? What I mean to say is we heard a rumour but –'

'That's all right, Henrietta,' Theobald said, cutting her short, and he allowed her to find and briefly hold the hand she was vaguely feeling for, as her words stumbled and tumbled over each other. Her muttered incoherence was painful to him, and it was painful too for him to have to watch what he took to be her embarrassment, knowing that Flora would call it gaucherie.

But Theobald was wrong, for although Henrietta was confused, her confusion came, not from embarrassment, but from trying to do two things at the one time: to talk, and to think. She was thinking furiously. Apparently whatever attributes this Flora of his might possess, she, Henrietta, must be right in assuming that untold wealth was not one of them. Flora certainly couldn't claim to be the heiress that Honoria was. How far therefore was it wise – she was thinking in terms of worldly wisdom, of course – to make use of the party given in honour of Honoria to introduce into the family another prospective bride who could, money apart, if Theobald's prognostications were true, put poor Honoria's nose out of joint? Was it even fair? And above all, was she, Henrietta, to be the only one to know of the bombshell that her young brother was planning to throw into their midst that night? If so, the responsibility was just too much for one pair of shoulders. Should she tell him so? Decidedly she would have to tell him.

These were the thoughts that were running through her head while actually she was shaking his hand in felicitation.

'Of course I'm longing to meet her, Theobald,' she said, when she regained her hand. 'I'm just wondering if tonight is the proper occasion for introducing her to us?'

'Why not?' Theobald said. 'She has to meet you sometime.'

Memories of certain scathing remarks Theobald had made about Robert still rankled with Henrietta, and they bred a sudden vicious hope in her mind. Was he ashamed of this Flora?

But she was quickly and in fact rudely shown how wrong she was. It was not of Flora Theobald was ashamed.

'I'll have to get it over some time or another,' he said. 'It's something that will have to be faced sooner or later, and anyhow I'm sure Flora will make allowances. It is always people like her who are most understanding when it comes to the shortcomings of others.'

Henrietta swallowed quickly, and took a deep breath. Was it possible Theobald had accomplished the feat he expected of himself? She swallowed again. All the more reason, then, to protect poor Honoria from the hazards of a comparison.

'All the same, Theobald,' she said firmly, 'I think it wouldn't be nice – for your Flora, I mean – to introduce her to us casually like that. I think we ought to wait and talk to James and get him to name a definite evening for the purpose. It's nice to be formal about these things don't you think?'

She spoke so primly Theobald threw back his head and gave a loud guffaw.

'Formal? Is it Flora? Easily seen you don't know her. My dear Henrietta – don't you think for a moment that she's the kind of person who'd sit down to one of our vulgar spreads. Why, I don't believe Flora knows such orgies exist. After all, they *are* purely middle-class functions. As a matter of fact when I was telling her about this evening's party I must confess that I more or less conveyed that we ourselves didn't ordinarily go in for this kind of gathering. I'm afraid I told a white lie – I rather gave the impression that we were going through with it mainly to please the Crokers, who were a bit old-fashioned. I sort of suggested that for us it was going to be quite an ordeal. So I'd be glad, Henrietta' – this time it was he who reached for her hand – 'if you'd help me out a bit and play up that suggestion?'

'Well –' Henrietta said slowly, 'if you insist on bringing her, I suppose I can't show you up for a liar. But it will be very hard to do it convincingly.'

'I know that,' said Theobald dryly.

Henrietta wasn't sure what he meant, and she didn't at all like his tone, but she felt she more or less had him at a disadvantage.

'We must warn the others, Theobald,' she said.

'On no account must that be done, Henrietta,' Theobald cried. His voice rose urgently and he glanced over Henrietta's head towards the windows of the house in case the wind might have carried their words in that direction. 'I don't want anyone to know about it, only you and me and Flora. I want to take everyone by surprise. Indeed those were the only conditions under which I could make Flora consent to come. She wouldn't come under any other.'

'But, Theobald!' Henrietta protested once more. She felt her responsibility in the matter come down on her with an insuperable weight. 'I'll have to tell James. And I'll have to tell Charlotte. We might get away with keeping it from the others, but we'll have to tell them. You can't possibly expect to land an extra person down on them without notice – and for that matter – you can't let Flora arrive and find no place set for her! There mightn't even be enough chairs!' Henrietta was as embarrassed as if she were the hostess and Theobald's bombshell was about to fall on *her* dinner table.

Theobald only laughed. 'Don't worry about that, Henrietta,' he said. 'We're only going to look in on you for a minute or two towards the end of the meal. We're not going to stay. We're not to be counted as far as place setting and that are concerned.' He looked sternly at her. 'I thought I made it plain to you that Flora wouldn't understand sitting down to the big gorges that James and Charlotte provide.' He gave another laugh, a different sort: a pleased laugh. 'Flora doesn't eat as much as a bird.'

A bird? All the time they'd been talking, Henrietta had been trying unsuccessfully to visualise the appearance of this person, Flora. Now, all at once, with Theobald's mention of her birdly appetite, Henrietta's imagination rose with a beat of wings, and before her mind's eye flew gaudy images of brightly plumed creatures of the air. They made her quite dizzy, those images, until they merged at last into one final image of a little creature, volatile as a lark, a summer warbler, a creature so light and airy that it hardly rested on the ground at all. Perhaps not a lark – a chaffinch, maybe? A minute little creature with yellowy golden hair.

'Oh, is it wise, Theobald?' she cried again. 'Is it wise under the circumstances?'

'What circumstances?' Theobald asked obtusely, but then as he saw Henrietta redden he understood. 'Oh, you needn't worry on that score either. Flora's life is too rich, too filled with variety, to notice that at all. I assure you she isn't the kind of person to take in little details.'

'Little details!' Henrietta reddened, this time with annoyance. There was only one detail and she wouldn't call it little. You wouldn't have to stare very hard to be aware of it. One of the circumstances to which she had alluded was the fact that she was pregnant again, and beginning to be more than a little remarkable. The other circumstances were the pregnancies of her two sisters-in-law, both of whom were in the same condition, only more advanced. A nice time, she thought, to bring to the house a giddy little bird like this Flora. Because now Henrietta's conception of Flora's appearance had hardened like cement.

'You don't understand, Theobald,' she said stiffly. 'It could be embarrassing for an unmarried young woman.'

'Nonsense!' Theobald said. 'But if so, what about embarrassing Honoria?'

'Oh, it's different for Honoria,' Henrietta replied, although immediately after she'd spoken, it occurred to her that she hadn't been very kind to Samuel's intended. Honoria's plump, well-fed figure was furred and beribboned as much as any matron in token of her independent means, and there wouldn't be anything like the same embarrassment for her that there could be for a birdy bride-like creature with a name like Flora. Why Honoria might as well have been a matron already.

'Oh, it's altogether different for Honoria,' she said, trying to make emphasis do for explanation. It was not a matter one could explain to a man: least of all a man like Theobald who was so lacking in understanding.

Lacking in understanding Theobald certainly appeared to be that day.

'I think you're absurd, Henrietta,' he said. 'I can only attribute it to your condition. I'm sorry I mentioned the matter. Please forget it.' Raising his hat, her brother was about to move away.

Henrietta was speechless. This made things worse. She did not know whether he was going to carry out his intention or not? It was impossible to remain in such uncertainty.

'Theobald!' she called.

Theobald, upon being called, turned with forced politeness.

'Does that mean you are not going to bring her?' Henrietta asked.

'It does not!' Theobald stopped. 'I'm not going to miss an opportunity like this for killing two stones with the one – I mean two *birds* with the one *stone*. Good morning, Henrietta.' This time he quite definitely walked away.

Henrietta stared after him, more upset than ever. Her brother usually affected such a slow and deliberate manner of speech there was seldom danger of a verbal mishap such as he had just suffered. Henrietta shook her head. He must be out of his mind about this Flora, she thought, and she shivered. To think of having to meet and entertain a person capable of turning the head of a man like Theobald!

All during that morning as Henrietta tried to do Charlotte's messages for her, she continued to experience unpleasant shivers of apprehension, and several times when Theobald's slip of the tongue came to her mind, she had a sensation of the ground going from under her. But at bottom Henrietta was a sound and sensible woman. By the time she'd done the messages and got back to James's house she had made up her mind – Theobald's injunctions apart. She'd say nothing at all about the impending surprise. For, unlikely as it seemed that

Theobald would play a joke, the thought had occurred to her that he might be having her on. And if that were the case, what a fool she'd make of herself in the eyes of the others. Henrietta deposited with Charlotte the flowers, the frills for the cutlets, and an extra carton of fresh cream, and departed with Robert, taking with her the secret about Flora.

It was really only later that evening when she took her place at Charlotte's beautifully appointed table where she'd been seated between Honoria's father and Ernest that the burden of her guilty knowledge began to tell.

'Are you feeling all right, Henrietta?' Charlotte asked on at least two occasions, once during the soup, and once during the fish, when Henrietta, thinking she'd heard a footfall on the stairs, began to perspire across her forehead.

Oh, why hadn't she told someone – if only Robert? She looked across the table at him in desperation. Could she, even now, convey her fears to him? But Robert was not attending to Julia on his left, much less to Henrietta across the board, because Robert was nervous of swallowing small fish bones. He made it a rule never to talk when eating fish.

The fish, however, had gone the way of the soup and there was no sign of Theobald, and soon the dinner was mid-way through its courses at least with regard to the number of dishes consumed, although considering the rich nature of these first dishes it might perhaps be said to be nearing an end. The guests having, as it were, successfully crossed the biggest of the fences, were coming into the straight, and would no doubt gather speed now for the gallop home. In other words, having consumed the turtle soup, the curled whiting, the crown of roast young pork (accompanied by mounds of mashed potatoes, little heaps of brussels sprouts and a ladle or two of apple sauce), might be expected to make quicker progress through the green salad, the peach melba, the anchovy on toast, the coffee, and the crème de menthe. Still no sign of Theobald! He must arrive soon if he expected them to be still at the table as Henrietta understood him to have intended.

In spite of her irritation with him, Henrietta found herself trying to go slow with her peach melba, until feeling Charlotte's eye upon her, and fearing her sister-in-law might think there was something wrong with the dessert, she had to act like everybody else and gobble it up.

In a trice the anchovies were being passed. In a trice their remains were being removed, and the cheese and crackers were being carried on stage.

It was then, just as the crunch of crackers made hearing difficult that Henrietta once more fancied she heard sounds indicative of Theobald's arrival. A cab had stopped in the street below, right outside James's door. It must be Theobald. Henrietta told herself that she might have known that a person like Flora would have insisted on arriving by cab. She put down her cracker and listened. Yes, there were voices in the hall. There was laughing. She looked around the table. Did no one else hear? Apparently not. Henrietta's heart stood still. Then, all at once, with a belated access of loyalty she came to a decision: she'd have to let the others know what was about to befall them: she must prepare them for the shock.

'Excuse me. Forgive me for interrupting,' she cried, breaking in upon what, unfortunately, was the first time the whole evening that Honoria had essayed to display the confidence to which her position entitled her by telling a story. Realising how unfortunate her interruption was, Henrietta felt she had no option but to continue. 'I must tell you all something,' she went on desperately. 'I knew it since morning, but he wanted it to be a surprise.'

Normally, having a rather squeaky voice, Henrietta might not have made herself heard if she tried to address the whole table, but as everyone was giving punctilious attention to the story Honoria was trying to tell, ever single word of what Henrietta had to say fell on upright ears.

'What's that?' several of the Beckers cried, speaking all together, and looking first at Henrietta and then at each other.

James alone kept his head.

'Who wanted what to be a surprise?' he asked, almost shouting at Henrietta.

'Theobald, of course,' Henrietta said impatiently, because surely the others had ears as well as herself and ought to be able to recognise Theobald's laugh, rare as it was, and he had just given a hearty laugh on the stairs. 'Theobald, of course, who else?' she said, permitting herself this tick-off, before she fastened her own eyes on the dining-room door.

'Theobald?' James seemed to affect some diminution of interest at the sound of his brother's name. Indeed a curious frigidity had fallen on the company in general, because if Theobald had not come this would have been the first occasion that a member of the Becker family had voluntarily absented himself from a family celebration. And although on this occasion Theobald had been formally excused, there was an underground feeling of dissatisfaction with him.

'Theobald?' Honoria's deaf aunt asked loudly, addressing herself to no one in particular.

'Oh, he's another brother,' Honoria replied impatiently.

'Is it the one you dislike so much?' Honoria's father asked, and as the Beckers all seemed to be at hounds and hares, he didn't feel it necessary to lower his voice all that much. Charlotte, in fact, was the only one to hear and as hostess felt obliged to cover up for her brother, Theobald.

'It's nice that he's been able to join us after all,' she said. Truth will out, however, and she added an unfortunate rider. 'I can't believe that whatever appointment he said he had would have kept him busy all day *and* all evening. I'm glad he has decided to look in on us even for a few minutes!'

'But that –' Henrietta cried, addressing herself to Charlotte first and foremost, and then the whole family – 'that is just what I wanted to tell you. He is coming! It was to be a surprise!' In her excitement she rose in her chair. 'And now he's here with her!'

'With *her*? With *whom*?' they all cried.

'Flora!' Henrietta almost screamed the name. 'Flora was to be the surprise.'

'Flora?' James gave a startled look at Henrietta. 'Are you out of your mind, Henrietta?' he cried, because at the sound of the name a vague memory stirred in him and gaudy and tinsel images pirouetted before his mind's eye. Hadn't there been an operetta in his youth called *The Flora Doras*? What on earth was coming over Henrietta, he wondered? Flora? Flora? 'What are you talking about?' he demanded.

It was all Henrietta could do to refrain from saying that Flora was a bird. But suddenly she recalled Theobald's slip of the tongue about killing two stones with the one bird, and whatever about his fiancée, it seemed to her that when, at that moment the dining-room door was flung open by Theobald, all the seated Beckers, and all their seated guests, seemed to have been turned into stone.

And the bird?

Henrietta stared. Perched on Theobald's arm, or rather hanging from it by one small hand, was the little chaffinch-type of thing she had expected to see.

Flora was small. She was exceedingly small. She was fine-boned as well, so that, as with a bird, you felt if you pressed her too hard she would be crushed. But in spite of her smallness, like a bird she was exquisitely proportioned, and her clothes, that were an assortment of light colours, seemed to cling to her like feathers, a part of her being, a part moreover of which she herself was entirely unconscious. She accepted her clothes as the birds their feathers: an inevitable raiment.

Indeed Flora appeared to be entirely unconscious of her person. She was hardly into the room before her bright eyes darted from one face to another, her own small pointed face eager with interest in them. It was a birdlike face, thin and sharp, and since her chin was slightly undershot, she gave the impression that like a bird her head was tilted at right angles to her little body. She was evidently very curious about them all, but unlike the curiosity of the Beckers that strove to conceal itself, her curiosity had taken open possession of her. It almost seemed that the excited beating of her heart was causing her frail frame to vibrate and tremble, and that she would simply have to find some outlet: beat her wings, flutter her feathers, or clutch at her perch and burst into song, song so rapturous the perch too would sway up and down.

Theobald, however, was not that kind of perch, and no tremor of Flora's excitement shook the arm to which she clung. Theobald was intent on making his entry.

'Well, everybody?' he said, and with his free hand he possessively clamped to his arm Flora's little hand with its long varnished fingernails. 'Hello, Samuel. Hello, Honoria. I want you all to meet another future Becker bride.'

Had the Beckers been totally unprepared for this shock there is no knowing how the seated table would have reacted, but Henrietta had, as it were, broken the fall for them. And so when Theobald looked around for evidence of surprise, all he saw was stupefaction. The faces that stared at Flora and himself seemed to stare at them out of a coma.

'Well?' he repeated, a little half-heartedly. 'Aren't you going to welcome us?'

At this, James, who had been the most stunned of all, upon being given a dig in the ribs by Julia, got awkwardly to his feet.

'We are unfortunately nearly finished dinner,' he said, looking around the table, 'but we are just going to have coffee.' He ventured his first real look at Flora – 'Perhaps you'd care for a cup?'

Ah! That was better. Good old James! The Beckers relaxed and began to breathe again.

'Where will they sit?' Julia asked, and she went to move her chair to one side. Not that there was much room for movement round the massive mahogany table because it was already so crowded. It was doubtful if a single extra chair, much less two, could be squeezed in at any point. And since, to add to the difficulty, everyone at the table was following Julia's example and trying to make room for the newcomers, there was soon complete confusion. As Julia moved her chair to the right, Henrietta at the same moment was trying to move hers to the left, and on Henrietta's other side Ernest, moving right, was clashing with Charlotte, moving left.

'They look as if they are playing some game,' Flora said to Theobald in a whisper, but a whisper which Charlotte to her intense mortification overheard while she was leaning forward to try and catch the attention of that stupid, stupid James, as she crossly apostrophised him in her mind. Giving up discretion, Charlotte shouted at him.

'Why don't we have coffee in the other room?'

'Just a minute!'

To everyone's surprise the voice that sang out was as sweet and melodious as a bar of music. It was Flora's.

'Please don't move, any of you!' she cried. 'Please, please stay as you are. We've had dinner. Just ignore us.'

There was such poised authority in Flora's voice that one or two of the Beckers who had stood up, sat down again immediately. In fact only James remained standing, and he did so from uncertainty about his duties as host. But Charlotte gratefully seized on Flora's words.

'Don't tease them, James,' she said, and she turned to Theobald. 'If you're sure you've had your dinner, why don't you both go into the drawing-room while we finish our coffee. You can show Flora the albums while you're waiting.'

But as she made the suggestion, Charlotte knew it was not a very good one. Yet what was the alternative? They couldn't be let stand there. Really this was an outrageous thing for Theobald to have done. To bring a strange girl in on top of them like this, and take them at such a disadvantage, particularly when – as Charlotte couldn't fail to see – there was something so distinctive about the girl, something unusual, something indeed downright remarkable.

All at once, irrelevant though it might seem, Charlotte was shot through with bitter regret that she had not had the dining-room redecorated last month as she had intended. But enough of that! What was to be done with the pair now – they didn't seem to be moving off into the drawing-room?

During her brief reverie, however, Charlotte had missed something. Flora had smiled, and Flora's smile was not something to be missed. It was what the Beckers were always to remember about her – her sudden, luminous smile. And on that first occasion that it shone out, it transformed their awkwardness into gaiety. Flora had saved the situation.

'You simply mustn't move!' she cried. 'Such a charming group as you make.' Then, from the purely exclamatory, her voice changed to the intimately conversational as she turned to Theobald. 'Isn't it a wonder photographers never seem to think of posing people around a table this way?' With a charming gesture she indicated the group before her, and smiled again. This time Charlotte didn't miss the smile, and she too, like the rest of the Beckers, felt warmed by it, as by yellow sunlight. 'Oh,' Flora cried, 'oh how I wish *I* was a photographer.' Then suddenly she did the funniest thing. 'Let's pretend that I *am* one,' she cried, and bending down her head in the drollest way, just as if she had a tripod in front of her, and letting her yellow hair fall down over her face like a shutter curtain, she made a circle with her fingers and held them up to her eyes to act as a lens for her make-believe camera. 'I think I can get you all in,' she said, turning her head from side to side to get them in better focus. 'Keep still, everyone. Look at the dickie-bird. And smile! Smile!' Then, when she had them all smiling, she reached down her hand and squeezed the imaginary rubber bulb that controlled the shutter.

It was the most unexpected thing that could possibly have happened. It was exactly as if she was a real photographer. The Beckers had unconsciously stiffened into the unnatural and rigid postures of people being taken by the camera. Then, when the girl straightened up and pushed back her hair, the group came to life again. Realising how ridiculous they must have looked, Julia laughed. Then they all laughed, even the parlour-maid, even Honoria, who looked as if she didn't often do so. Above all, Theobald laughed. He was delighted with himself. He looked proudly at his fiancée. She'd be able for any situation.

'Isn't she wonderful?' he said to Charlotte.

But they must be introduced to her.

'Come, Flora,' he said, starting to lead her round the table, beginning, of course, with the head of the house. 'This is James,' he said, and in no way constrained now, he laid his hand on his older brother's shoulder.

In the hilarious mood that had developed, no one really expected Flora to put out her hand and utter conventional commonplaces. They watched her eagerly.

'James?' Flora said, and there was a pert little note in her voice that made some of the family titter. Then, to the accompaniment of general laughter, she circled her eyes with her fingers again and bent once more over her make-believe camera and took a head-and-shoulders portrait of James.

It was quite a few minutes before anyone could speak, they were laughing so much, and James himself, although he was startled for a second, soon saw what the funny girl was up to, and he too gave way to the merriment.

'I hope I didn't break the camera, my dear?' he said.

Theobald's pride in Flora was infectious. It even infected stuffy old James. He was charmed by her.

Flora herself didn't smile. She was doing something to her camera.

And her serious expression convulsed the group. She straightened again.

'I must take one of each of you,' she said, and she turned to her next subject. 'Who are you? You're Julia, aren't you?' she asked, while she was adjusting the lens. 'Just a minute please. Try not to move.' From the intent way she was looking at her it seemed Julia was a difficult subject, which fortunately Julia found flattering. 'Smile!' Flora ordered suddenly. But when Julia laughed as the bulb was being squeezed, the photographer was quite annoyed. 'You moved,' she said severely. 'Your picture will be blurred.' She turned around. 'Who's next?'

It was Samuel, and she had to speak sternly to him too. 'I can't take you, you know, while you're grinning like that! Please try to keep still. Look at the dickie-bird!' When she'd taken him she didn't seem altogether satisfied, and she took another shot. 'You're Samuel, aren't you?' she said. 'You're a bad subject I'm afraid, but with a bit of luck it may come out quite well.' She moved her apparatus further along. Her sobriety was the best part of the fun.

'Who have I now?' she asked. It was Henrietta. 'You're very photogenic,' she said to the delighted Henrietta. 'Your face is so angular. Turn your head a little to one side, if you please. Yes – I think a profile would be best in your case.'

It was side-splitting. Never in their lives had the Beckers met anyone remotely like this.

'Well, what do you think of her?' Theobald asked James in an undertone. 'This performance is nothing! She's a sort of genius really. You've no idea how people stare at her everywhere we go. Of course, she's well-known anyway; she comes from a very old family, but that doesn't account for all the attention she attracts. It's because she's so amazing. There is nothing she cannot do.' He laughed. 'And nothing she won't attempt too, if she takes it into her head. She's very accomplished.

You should hear her play the piano. And she paints. You should see her water colours. She's going to hold an exhibition one of these days. And I believe she has tried her hand at poetry too, if you don't mind! Some publisher has approached her with a view to bringing out a little volume. Oh, there's no end to her gifts. But I always tell her that her real talent is for acting. You've just seen for yourself! And she's a wonderful mimic. You should see her impersonations!'

'Well, if that was any indication!' Samuel said admiringly, coming up to the other two just then, because the party had loosened up and one or two people were going around with Flora pretending to be her assistants, helping to move her equipment and pose those yet to be taken.

They were just about to photograph Honoria's father, and at the expression on the father's face even Honoria burst out laughing, although up to now her laughter had only been following suit.

'Look at my father's face. Please, please,' she begged, and she was laughing so much she had to hold her sides to keep from shaking the whole table.

'That girl is a born actress,' Samuel said, happy to be able to give free rein to his admiration because up to then he'd had some misgivings about offending Honoria, having noticed that her merriment had been somewhat more subdued than that of his family. Now he could let himself go and enjoy this extraordinarily exciting young woman who unbelievably – thanks to that dry stick Theobald – was about to become one of them.

Samuel ventured a good look at Flora. This he had avoided doing previously, as it didn't seem generous to do so with Honoria present. And he was surprised at a boyish quality about her, because unconsciously, and perhaps because of her name, his first impression had been of quite extravagant girlishness. In fact before he'd met her at all, from the first instant he'd heard the name Flora, it had brought a vision to his mind of a nymph in a misty white dress, with bare feet and cloudy yellow hair, who in a flowering meadow skipped about, gathering flower heads and entwining them in a garland. It was a bit of a shock to see she was wearing a trim black suit and that her small black shoes had buckles, not bows. There was just one thing about her that was flowery though: her perfume. Honoria never wore perfume. Samuel wished she would. It was captivating.

Captivating was the word; all the Beckers were captivated. Flora was not in their midst more than a few minutes before they had all succumbed to her charm. As Ernest expressed it afterwards when he and Julia were going home, there was only one thing that bothered him and that was to think that such a fascinating person should be tying herself up to a bore like Theobald.

'He is a bore, Julia, you know, with all his theories and principles.'

'He has put them into practice, though,' Julia said, 'you must admit that. I'll confess something now, Ernest: it was always my belief he'd make a fool of himself in the long run. People who are too particular always do. I felt certain he'd make a disastrous marriage. I really did.'

Ernest would have liked to confess that he too had often thought the same, but at that moment he felt so well disposed towards his young brother that he hedged.

'Theobald hasn't made many mistakes in his day,' he said.

'That's what I mean!' Julia cried. 'It's that kind of person who makes the worst mistake of all in the end.'

But Ernest wasn't listening. He was thinking about his brother. So there had been something behind his nonsense. He wasn't such a blower after all. Ernest felt subdued. He wondered if Flora had money? The jewellery she was wearing must have cost something. He tried to recall it in greater detail, but as he did he got confused. Had she jewellery on at all? He was puzzled. It didn't seem possible that someone as observant as he prided himself on being could be uncertain about such a significant detail. Ernest was so perplexed his wife had to repeat herself twice before she got his attention.

'What is the matter with you, Ernest? Are you deaf? I said her fake photography was the cleverest thing I've seen in years.'

'Oh yes, yes. She certainly is a bit of an actress.'

'More than a bit I'd say!' Julia replied, but there was something in the tone of her voice that made Ernest look at her out of the corner of his eye.

'What do you mean by that?'

'Oh nothing,' Julia said lightly. 'Only I thought once or twice that she carried it just a bit too far. I'd say she doesn't believe in hiding her light under a bushel. And quite honestly, I thought she went into the realms of absurdity altogether when we were saying good-bye on the steps.'

'Why? I didn't notice.'

'Oh, you must have heard what she said to James? He was shaking hands with her, when with a deadly straight face, she said she'd let him have the proofs of the photographs as soon as ever she had them developed.'

But in spite of the small trace of censoriousness with which she had started to relate the incident, Julia couldn't help laughing herself at the recollection. 'James's face was a scream,' she said, 'and that wasn't all! When James got her meaning at last and started to laugh, she really carried the thing to extremes. She put on an injured air, as if her dignity had been offended, and took Theobald's arm and went off down the steps without another word. Oh, it was really funny. I don't believe one person in ten thousand would have been able to go away like that without dropping the pretence at *some* point.'

'There is no doubt about it,' Ernest said, 'Theobald is right. There is a touch of genius about her. Now that you mention it, I think I did notice that she was carrying the thing a bit far at the end of the evening. I saw her pretending to pack up her photographic equipment, and when Theobald gave her his arm, she made as if she was changing it to her other hand. As a matter of fact Theobald didn't twig it at all: he's a bit slow sometimes in spite of his high opinion of himself. I saw the joke immediately. And I let her see I did. 'Why don't you let Theobald carry it for you?' I said, and went as if to assist her myself. 'That's all right,' she said. 'I can manage.' And she smiled. Good lord, that smile!'

'Oh, she's something new in our lives and no mistake,' Julia said, but seeing that they had reached their own street and were approaching their own door, she waited until Ernest had turned the key and admitted them before she gave him a little jab.

'I still can't help thinking it's a pity Theobald has had the satisfaction of knowing he's done so much better for himself than the rest of you.'

This just about expressed the reaction of all the Beckers. Not one of them but could see the distinction and talents possessed by his intended, yet not one but felt that in the long run these would only add to his conceit.

Never mind though. Their wedding would be the next thing. They had that to look forward to anyway. When would it be?

The wedding would take place quite soon. Flora didn't believe in long engagements, it seemed, a fact which might have elicited some cynical remarks were it not that the family all agreed. Theobald wasn't half good enough for her, and the quicker he made sure of her the better.

James kept his head, though, and pointed out that family protocol demanded that Samuel's wedding be first. He glanced at Flora's hand; Theobald had not got the engagement ring yet.

But, it appeared, that was another thing Flora didn't believe in – engagement rings. And this the Becker women found completely baffling.

'She says the feel of a ring on her finger makes her fidgety,' Charlotte reported.

'She'll have to wear a wedding ring, won't she?' Julia said.

'I wouldn't be too sure of that either,' Charlotte said. 'I heard her saying they look dowdy.'

Charlotte and Julia looked down at their own thick bands of gold, guarded by big solitaires set in massive claws. They used to be so proud of them, but now at every minute they found their notions of things suffering a jolt. And soon the jolting was as good as continuous.

First of all Theobald broke it to them that he was not going to buy a house. He and Flora were going to live in apartments. It now appeared Flora could not saddle herself with a house. She was at that particular time engaged in bringing out her book of poems, and she had a responsibility to her publisher. Afterwards they might consider the possibility of a house; but not until afterwards.

'That may be all very well now,' James said, 'but it could be awkward later on.'

The others nodded. They knew what he meant.

'Although, mind you, I wouldn't be surprised –' Henrietta said, beginning to say something, but stopping. She had recollected the presence among them of Honoria, who although only one month married might take offence. Afterwards she had a private word with Charlotte.

'Of course,' she said to Charlotte, 'it would not matter so much in Flora's case, she is so gifted in other directions. And I don't believe Theobald would mind as much as another man – he'd have such a lot of compensations.'

Flora's gifts were indeed many. A few weeks before the wedding her book of poems came out, and although frankly the Beckers were unable to understand two words of it, their pride in her was even greater than Theobald's. Samuel was particularly pleased. He made it his business to go down to the club every day to see if there were any reviews of the book.

'She should have had it illustrated,' he maintained every time the book was mentioned. 'She should bring out an illustrated edition.'

Samuel in fact went one further than them all at times in his admiration for her, and actually took a censorious attitude towards poor Theobald.

'That fellow doesn't realise a man has responsibilities towards a woman like Flora,' he muttered. 'He should take her around more. There was an exhibition of modern paintings last week in Charleville House. I read about it in the paper. But I bet Theobald knew nothing about it. I hope she didn't have to go without an escort, because I'm sure it's the kind of thing she wouldn't want to miss.'

And there and then he promised himself that when she was his sister-in-law, he'd make a point of remedying Theobald's deficiencies in such matters. He was beginning to suspect that Theobald, for all his talk, did not really have a very deep feeling for the Arts. He, Samuel, might not understand a great deal about art, and with one thing and another he hadn't had much time for it, but he intended to do something about it. And now, with the added security of Honoria's dowry he might even venture to buy a few pictures; start a small private collection perhaps. If bought wisely, pictures could be a profitable investment he'd heard. And in this sphere Flora's advice would probably be invaluable. He'd make a start at once; go to a few galleries, make a few enquiries. If Flora were with him he'd feel safe. Yes, they'd make a few tentative expeditions.

The prospect of entering the realm of art in the company of Flora was a particularly pleasant one for Samuel just then, because he would soon be temporarily deprived of Honoria's company. A few weeks after Henrietta's tactful regard for her feelings on a certain subject, Honoria had given evidence that such tact was superfluous. But he must not let his enthusiasm run away with him. The proprieties had to be considered. Oh well! The wedding was just around the corner.

Meanwhile there was the question of the wedding presents.

Presents were a main concern with the Beckers. Every occasion for making an exchange of gifts was eagerly seized on by them, weddings of course being the best occasions of all. The giving and receiving of presents had always been a way of expressing emotions which nervous reticence made it impossible to express in any other way. Presents were a silent symbol of their family solidarity. They spoke loud to the Beckers, and in a language they understood. Thus, when the James Beckers went to visit the Ernest Beckers it always gave them a feeling of family unity to drink coffee after dinner from the Crown Derby service they themselves had given the couple on their wedding day. The Ernest Beckers in turn felt something identical when having spent an evening with James and Charlotte, they were obliged to acquaint themselves with the time by consulting the big ormolu clock of which they were the donors on a recent anniversary of the marriage of their host and hostess. And both the James Beckers and the Ernest Beckers found it pleasurable, when visiting Henrietta and Robert, to be given tea from an old Georgian silver service, the tray of which had been the gift of one and the service itself of the other, both bought separately, as it happened, but matching exactly due to the tact and intelligence of the very reliable antique dealer from whom the Beckers had bought all their furniture, porcelain and silver since time began.

The Becker men, and Henrietta, of course, had grown up in an aura of good sound taste, and it hadn't taken the Becker wives long to learn from them. It hadn't taken them long to profit by good example and to realise the stigma that attached itself to the brand-new furniture that in their single state they used to admire in the shop windows of Grafton Street. Just exactly what the stigma was they were not certain, but nevertheless they weren't long in resolving at all costs to avoid having it attach itself to anything belonging to them. They rapidly reduced their disturbing new knowledge to the working formula that nothing was worth buying that was less than a hundred years old.

It was therefore the biggest jolt of all for the Becker wives to learn that Flora had other ideas about furniture and decoration. Flora, or so she declared, would not tolerate anything in her home that wasn't as fresh as paint. They were not only startled; they were dumbfounded. This was clearly not another case of their own former ignorance, when they had been unable to distinguish between the merely old and the antique and had contemptuously classed both as second-hand. Not that they often dwelt on those days. Sometimes, however, they had to entertain friends from those early days, friends who had made less fortunate marriages – and who were inclined to voice surprise that they, the Becker wives, having married money, did not have newer furniture, and then, smugly, Julia and Charlotte would put these people right. And if they failed to convince their friends they contented themselves by thinking to what zenith their own taste had soared.

Yet here was Flora making positively heretical statements, not only about tables and chairs, but about glass and table-ware and even jewellery. And with her it was clear they were up against something different from their own early lack of knowledge. There was more behind her prejudice than there had been behind their former ignorance, no matter what the surface similarities. It was most bewildering, and a disturbing thought entered their minds – was there perhaps another world more esoteric even than the world of antiques? A world of which they yet knew nothing? Oh, but how willing and eager they were to learn!

Flora had a phrase and they grasped at it. *The antiques of tomorrow*. That was what the new bride intended to have in her apartment, and for weeks prior to the wedding her conversation abounded in the names of joiners and cabinet-makers, designers, brass-workers and handlers of gold leaf, craftsmen of whom neither James nor Ernest had ever heard, living in streets not even Robert knew existed, peculiar lanes, dead ends, and back alleys. It was odd. It was distinctly odd. And although the James Beckers and Henrietta and Robert too made valiant efforts to catch and memorise the names of some of these obscure craftsmen, and track them down to their haunts, they found it exceedingly hard to believe that any value could be set upon the shapeless and colourless articles they were seriously offering for sale.

Samuel was the only one with an ounce of real courage, and one day he instructed Honoria not to hesitate any longer, but go out and buy, as their present for Flora, a large canvas on which there was inscribed a name he had definitely heard Flora mention, although, apart from the signature, there was nothing else intelligible to him on the canvas.

After Samuel had purchased the painting and Flora had been quite pleased with it, some of the others took courage. Ernest and Julia bought an etching, and Henrietta a most uncomfortable modern chair. But they never got the same feeling of pride in these presents that they formerly used to get buying things for each other. They could not feel either that they would get the same pleasure when dining with the Theobalds that they got when dining with each other, that is to say the feeling of pride in their own selective judgment. There would be little or nothing of themselves in their gifts, and they had had no fun in buying them. Of course they had to allow that they might not see very much of these presents after they left their hands, because they might not be very prominently displayed by the Theobalds, or even displayed at all. Not that they would resent this, recognising that the fault could be in themselves: they might not have really mastered all the nuances of the new brand of good taste.

In consequence Flora became vested with still greater charm. Only Samuel claimed to come anywhere near understanding her. He had in fact confided to Henrietta that in some ways he had a greater affinity with her than Theobald. And when he was requested to be the best man at their wedding, he felt it was a tribute to this affinity and that Flora was behind the request.

'My height is about right, I dare say,' he said deprecatingly when talking to James. 'I expect they have to look into that kind of thing at a large fashionable wedding where there will be newsmen galore and photographers.'

'Will there be a lot of photographers?' James asked. He really was stupid at times, Samuel thought, in spite of his business capabilities.

'Don't you know there will!' Samuel said curtly, 'with a bride like that!'

'I suppose you're right,' James said, and he began to feel nervous at the prospect of such publicity. But his nervousness was quickly superseded by a feeling of family pride. Theobald's acquisition of Flora was the best thing that had happened to the Beckers for a long time.

Everywhere she went Flora attracted attention. Shades of the days when Theobald had sighed over the nonentity of his family! Now, wherever they went – that is to say if Flora was with them – they were followed at every step by glances of admiration or curiosity. And if they happened to take a meal out in a public restaurant, which they did not do so often nowadays, far from worrying Theobald by staring around the room, it was almost absurd the way the Beckers fastened their eyes on Flora and kept them on her. They certainly had a common focus now, as indeed did everyone in the room. The funny part of it was that it began to look as if in this regard Theobald could have had too much of a good thing. To the amusement of his brothers and sister it seemed at times that he rather wished he could hide Flora's light under a bushel.

'I think he's jealous,' Flora herself said jokingly in his hearing to Samuel the day she and Theobald came home from their honeymoon, when he and some of the others called at the apartment to pay their respects to the happy pair.

'That is absurd,' Theobald replied, disclaiming such unworthy motives. He'd only been trying to put some small curb on a wife who didn't really seem to know when to stop. It wasn't everyone who could appreciate her high-flying acts and antics. At the hotel where they'd been staying when they were away she had been unique. To the other guests her energy, her fire, her undiminishable vitality had made her seem like someone from another planet. Her wit, her sallies, her vivid word-pictures had left them breathless. As for her impersonations, these had left everyone, including himself, exhausted.

'You have no idea, Flora, the effect you had upon those people,' he said, trying to speak a little crossly to her because it really had been embarrassing. He turned to the others. 'She was like a flame playing over them incessantly, withering the life out of them.'

'A flame?' Flora had heard him. 'Oh, how lovely!' she cried. She ran over and gave him a kiss. 'That's the nicest thing you've ever said to me, Theobald.' She closed her eyes and a frail smile played over her face, a reflection perhaps of some inward thought that caused her also to sway slightly from side to side and then, after a minute, to tremble.

Watching her Samuel saw that she had begun to glow, to grow more vivid and more vital. Under the influence of the compliment she seemed to vibrate as if a strange new force ran through her. The flesh and blood Flora had vanished, and where her feet had rested a flame struggled in the air.

But that was absurd, he thought. He was getting over-imaginative and he would have been a bit worried about himself only Theobald just then got very cross with her.

'I know what you're up to, Flora. Stop it,' Theobald said. 'See! She's at it again,' he said, turning to Samuel. 'Trying to imagine what it's like to be a flame!'

Samuel sighed with relief. It had not been his imagination then. He was greatly reassured and pleased, too. It just showed how alive he was to Flora's moods. No longer alarmed, he looked at her appraisingly. It was hard to see why Theobald was so put out. What a dull dog he was!

'It was this way all the time at the hotel,' Theobald said. 'You'd only to mention something and Flora would start to personify it.' He took her arm and shook it, rather violently. 'Stop it, Flora.'

As if drenched with cold water, the flame that was Flora died down. Theobald looked ridiculously relieved. He laughed uncomfortably.

'I wish you wouldn't encourage her, Samuel,' he said, because Samuel was complimenting her.

'You have a great gift, my dear,' his brother was saying as he pressed her hand.

'Now, Theobald! Do you hear that?' Flora cried. She turned confidingly to Samuel. 'I wish Theobald had your appreciation of things. Why, he was even annoyed with my little green dragon!'

In spite of himself Theobald had to laugh at her this time. He didn't approve greatly, but there was something irresistible about the casual, intimate way Flora spoke of these imaginative creations of hers.

'What green dragon? Is this something new?' Samuel asked.

'A green dragon?' At the other end of the room Henrietta had overheard and given a little fictitious scream as she hurried over to them. 'What are you talking about?' she cried, and in a minute everyone was clamouring for an explanation.

The green dragon was evidently one of Flora's most successful performances, and the one she had put on most frequently at the hotel. The affair of the photography on the first day they met her had been impromptu, but the green dragon was apparently part of a steady repertoire.

'Oh, do it for us. Do it! Please, Flora,' several of her new relatives cried, speaking all together.

'I don't *do* it,' Flora said. 'I *see* it.'

They did not understand.

'It's really very clever.' Theobald was softening. 'I have to admit that. It's absurd of her to say I was annoyed about it. It was only that I thought she put on the act too often. And that strangers wouldn't understand anyway. They were a dull lot on the whole in that hotel!'

Samuel appealed to his new sister-in-law.

'I beg you, Flora, please remove the imputed stigma that we are no better than that dull lot. May we please see the green dragon?'

Theobald nodded his consent. He even tried to make it easier for his family to enter into the spirit of the thing.

'It's quite a simple trick, basically,' he explained. 'Flora just stands up and looks in front of her and claims she sees it – sitting on the table or on a chair – anywhere in fact. That's all there is to it, but the way she stares at it you'd swear it was there. Her way of looking at it is so convincing. And she puts on such a comical expression.'

'Oh, it sounds most amusing,' Henrietta said. 'Please, Flora, please.'

'Please what?' Flora asked, and truly her expression was masterly at that moment. No one could have been more serious. That was the core of her genius: that she could keep her face straight when everyone else was doubled up with laughter. They were all sure that she was going to oblige with the entertainment. There was a look of expectancy on every face.

But Theobald, who was able to read Flora's face a little better now than before they were married, saw an obstinacy in it that the others didn't see. For a moment he had the feeling that he used to have years earlier, when Henrietta was a girl – a big awkward girl – who when asked to perform on the piano used to wear away the whole evening with wearisome refusals that were part vanity, part hysteria. There wasn't going to be that kind of stupid scene now, was there? He looked uneasily at his wife. But he'd misjudged her. Turning suddenly she looked around at one of the small gilt chairs that were so fragile the Beckers were afraid to sit on them, and then at the curious marble table that they found so hard to consider suitable for a meal, and when finally she looked at Henrietta it was with the faintest trace of contempt.

'I'm sorry I can't show it to you,' she said. 'I don't see it anywhere. It must have gone into the garden.'

Such roguishness, but at the same time such a graceful way to refuse. It was almost as good as putting on the act. Everyone was looking around the room, and Samuel stepped over to the window and looked out. The green dragon's absence was almost as positive as his presence would have been. Theobald saw that his family could almost visualise the little creature. All his own pride in Flora came back. He didn't mind how she showed off in the bosom of the family. And this wasn't just showing off. She had handled the situation very neatly. She hadn't felt like performing and she'd got out of it with tact. That of course was the reason her little charades were always so successful: she did not attempt them unless she felt the compulsion, or the inspiration, or whatever you fancied calling it.

Then, as if to corroborate her husband and just as the others were taking their leave and were about to go, the wives secure in their warm wraps and James and Ernest with their mufflers already round their necks, Flora, who had come to the door with Theobald to see them off, peered suddenly out of the open doorway into the dark street.

'Ah, there he is!' she cried. 'I'm glad he came back before you left. See him?'

'See who?' some of the slower ones asked, staring out.

'The green dragon, of course – who else?' Flora said, affecting impatience as she bent down and held out her arms. 'Come here, my pet,' she said, and she made a feint of catching something that had, as it were, leapt through the air at her bidding and was now cuddled against her.

'Well, isn't that the most amazing thing you could see in a month of Sundays,' James said. 'You'd swear she had something in her arms.'

'Isn't he a darling?' Flora said. 'Look! He likes me to tickle him behind his ear.'

'Oh please, please, Flora.' The Becker ladies begged for mercy. They had already laughed so much they couldn't bear to watch any more. But Flora went on. It was exactly – oh but exactly – as if she had a little animal in her arms, cuddling it and talking to it and tickling it, in much the same way that they themselves – some of them anyway – Robert perhaps? – might play with a kitten or puppy; except – and this was important – except that Flora's fingers moved delicately, guardedly, as if her pet had some prohibitive quality, such as a scaly skin.

'Genius. Sheer genius,' Samuel said.

Even James rose to the occasion with another rare flash of wit.

'Take him inside, my dear,' he said. 'Good night, good night. We'll find our way ourselves. Don't stand out here in the night air. *The little fellow might catch cold.*'

The little fellow! He meant the little dragon. James had never been known to make such a good joke. It showed how he responded to his new sister-in-law.

There was a further peal of laughter, and shaking with merriment the women had difficulty finding their feet on the steps. Theobald stared after them. Had the Beckers ever before laughed out loud like that in the street? A change had certainly come over them. And this was only the beginning. With Flora around, new and surprising things would be happening every hour.

Some days, with no more than a few hours' warning, the Theobald Beckers would invite the whole family to join them at the theatre, and all because Flora, when she went out to buy fish, had booked a whole row of seats for the theatre, and it would take every available Becker to fill them if Theobald's money was not to be thrown upon the waters.

Another time it would be a picnic in the country. Theobald would have to make a hurried round of calls to gather the James Beckers or the Ernests or the Samuels or Henrietta and Robert to fill the seats on a side-car that Flora had seen outside the Shelbourne Hotel and couldn't resist hiring. And if any of them felt it made them too remarkable to be seen sitting up on an old-fashioned vehicle, no matter, the next week it could be a char-à-banc. Forward in time or back in time, it made no difference to Flora as long as she could escape from the tedium and boredom of the present, just as it didn't matter to her whether it was Henrietta or Honoria she was impersonating as long as she stepped out of her own personality and became another being. When this desire for change came over her nothing was allowed to come between her and making the change. Often in the middle of a conversation, a sentence, a word, she had been known to spring to her feet and turn a picture face to the wall.

'I couldn't stand it a single minute longer,' she'd explain. In her own apartment this didn't matter so much, of course, but Julia felt it was going a bit far when she did it in Charlotte's to a water colour which, as a matter of fact, Julia herself had given to James and Charlotte. Another day it was a vase to which she took exception and put out of sight.

'It may be only a little affectation,' Charlotte said, when she and Julia were discussing the matter later.

'That's no excuse,' Julia said. She was still the only one of the Beckers who had not completely capitulated to Flora's charm.

'Julia is jealous if you ask me,' Honoria said to Charlotte when Charlotte told her about Julia's attitude. 'She's just plain jealous because Flora has got such good taste. I think Flora was quite right about the vase. It was hideous,' she added, feeling no disrespect in speaking her mind about the vase because it was she who had given it to Charlotte. 'As a matter of fact,' she went on, looking around her own lavishly furnished drawing-room, 'I'm always nervous when her eye falls on those china dogs my aunt gave me.' She stood up, moved heavily over to the mantelpiece and took down the dogs. Holding them out from her, as if they had the mange, she rang the bell for the servant.

'Throw these out, please,' she said to the astonished maid, 'and this too,' she added as an afterthought, reaching up and taking down a water colour that was over the mantelpiece. 'And if I were you, Charlotte,' she said, 'I'd take your condition into consideration and get rid of that Buddha James gave you last year. It can't be good for you at present to have to stare it in the face – well, to have to stare at it anyway – every time you sit down in your own drawing-room.'

'But what could I do with it?' Charlotte asked, although after seeing Honoria's treatment of the china dogs she could guess what her sister-in-law would say. Honoria did not go in for short measures.

Honoria's vandalism was of course a lot easier to take than Julia's and Charlotte's, neither of whom had brought a penny of dowry into the family, and when they too began to throw things out their husbands were more critical. The only good that could be said for taking such drastic steps was that they were influenced by Flora. That and the fact that their rooms looked unquestionably better without the old junk. Into all their homes, as into their lives, more air had come, more colour, more light. Even Henrietta made changes, and Charlotte finally did throw out the Buddha, or rather she gave it to the washerwoman.

Charlotte's washerwoman was what was called a 'character'. She was one of the people that Flora could imitate to the life. If there was a dull moment in a conversation, or even a lull, Flora was liable to say something in a voice utterly unlike her own.

'Charlotte's washerwoman!' four or five people would shout out at once, as if it was a guessing game. There was

never any need to tell them who was being imperson-
ated, yet Flora's appearance hadn't altered in any way.
Of course there were times when she took more trouble,
pulled her hair over her face and dragged her clothes half
off to make herself look disorderly. When she did that
you'd swear it *was* the washerwoman: she even looked
like her.

Flora really enjoyed impersonating people but she
liked them to recognise at once who it was she was
representing. And it was surprising how irritable she
could become if anyone guessed wrongly.

'No! How could you be so stupid!' she said crossly to
poor James one evening when he took her to be doing
Henrietta. 'I'm Charlotte,' she said. 'Are you blind? Didn't
you see me bending when I came in the door?' For Charlotte
being unusually tall had a nervous tendency to dip her
head when she came through the doorway although there
was no danger of hitting her head in her own home where
the rooms were spacious and high-ceilinged.

'But you weren't Charlotte when you were coming
into the room!' James said a bit argumentatively, Samuel
thought, because looking at Flora now anyone could see
she was holding herself exactly like Charlotte.

Flora herself gave James a deadly look.

'Charlotte I was born,' she said, 'and Charlotte I will
remain!'

There was a peal of laughter at this which James did
not quite understand, not having been of the company
on the previous evening when, in answer to a suggestion
from Flora that she should call herself Lottie, Charlotte
had taken umbrage, and uttered almost the same words
in identically that tone.

'Charlotte I was born and Charlotte I will remain
until I die!' Flora was Charlotte to the life.

There were, however, times when Flora's impersonations were a bit too subtle for anyone to guess. These were times when avoiding the obvious landmarks of voice and gesture, she ventured into the interpretation of some inner characteristic, some quality normally hidden in the other person. There were even times when regardless of an audience, almost it seemed indifferent to one, undesirous of one, for some purely creative satisfaction she could be observed trying to project herself into another person. That, Samuel thought, was the mark of the real artist. He had caught her at this on a number of occasions. He'd see her stare at someone, and then after a minute her lovely agate eyes would alter and fill with curiosity, a curiosity which would grow stronger, would make her eyes deeper and their light more inward. It was really awe-inspiring then to see how her whole face would change, and her eyes would lose their lustre, their vivacity, their depth, but above all, their luminous glow and take on instead an actual physical resemblance to the eyes of the person at whom Flora had been staring. He had seen her lovely eyes grow narrow, and the lids come down obliquely as into them crept the chilly, supercilious expression that was habitual to Julia. He had seen them empty of all depth and stare outward with the naive and childish expression of Honoria. He had seen them become so cold and shallow they seemed to have changed colour like the sea over sand, and he knew Flora was being Theobald.

It was becoming Samuel's biggest pleasure to watch his new sister-in-law in the act of departing from her own body and entering that of someone else. But he was careful to guard her secret for her, and even when he saw the transformation coming, he'd bend one part of himself to the task of diverting the attention of the family, while the other part of him he'd give over to furtively watching her and sharing in her adventure. Only when he was in doubt as to who she was taking off, would he venture to intrude his curiosity upon her. He'd go up to her then, quietly, and bending down understandingly, he'd whisper a name in her ear.

'Charlotte?'

If he was right Flora would look up and smile. If he was wrong – but this rarely happened – although she was not able to conceal her annoyance, she never failed to make a witty answer, correcting his error in some original or comical way.

'What's the matter with you?' she would ask. 'Are you blind? That's Charlotte over there!'

Samuel, however, was seldom wrong. Even when one evening in the very act of raising a glass of claret to her lips at a small party given in a restaurant by the Ernest Beckers, he saw Flora pause and look into her glass for a second before she drank, in that instant, although there had been neither word nor gesture to fasten upon, he knew Flora had become Theobald – Theobald arresting the flow of his consciousness, becoming aware of himself, trying to catch himself as it were, in the act of living. That evening Samuel could not forbear leaning across the table to her.

'Theobald?' he whispered.

For a moment Flora seemed startled. Then she nodded, but curtly, and at once for some reason – possibly to cover embarrassment – she answered out loud, and her voice was impatient. 'What do you want?' she said.

Samuel was always very understanding. He made allowances. She was probably afraid the others would discover her secret game. He resolved not to intrude on her in that way again. And when a few days later he did, it was only under the compulsion of unbearable curiosity, because not for the world would he want to forfeit her friendship. He was becoming more and more dependent on it, particularly of late, because Honoria, although in no way noticeable yet, had already taken to staying home in the evenings and having Charlotte or Henrietta come over to sit with her. Very considerately she refused to keep Samuel tied to the house. One or two nights a week at least she insisted he go out, and if it weren't for having Theobald and Flora, where would he spend those evenings? Certainly not with James or Ernest. And to put oneself voluntarily into Robert's company would, of course, have been ludicrous. So to Flora's he went, every evening Honoria could spare him.

Then came one particular evening. Samuel had had dinner at home, but after dinner he walked over to the Theobald Beckers to spend a short while with them before retiring. It was a summer evening and the lamps were not lit when the servant admitted him. The master, she said, was dining at the club that evening, but the mistress was in the drawing-room. Would she announce him, or would he go in to her?

Samuel went across the hall and opened the dining-room door. For a moment he thought there was no one at all in the room. It was only faintly lit by the paling daylight and the furniture had begun to confound itself with its own long shadows on the wall. Beyond the window the trees in the garden were still visible. Samuel was staring at the black branches when he saw Flora.

She was standing by the side of the window, leaning back against the white woodwork to which her back was closely pressed, her shoulder blades drawn downward, and her face tilted upward more than usual. She seemed to be staring through the upper panes of the glass, and when he moved nearer, Samuel saw the thin spikes of the first stars. She was like the bowsprit of an ancient ship, he thought, and as sightless – at any rate sightless so far as he was concerned. She was unaware of him until he came close – or so it seemed, although he did not think it possible she had not heard him when he first entered. But then, when he'd come close and seen the rigidity of her body and the intensity of her expression, he was paralysed with embarrassment. He did not dare to break in upon her, but stood silent too, afraid to breathe. He felt as if he was in the presence of someone he had never known, and he began to tremble and his face to twitch in a way it had not done for a long time.

This was not Theobald's wife. This was someone else. But who? It was someone Samuel had never seen before. He pulled himself together. It was, of course, quite possible that it was some former acquaintance of hers. Or it could even be some person who did not exist at all except in her imagination, someone who borrowed life from her as characters in a book borrow life from their creator. If novelists and dramatists could invent people, well then, why not Flora? She must write, he thought. A play perhaps? She must! She must! She must! Breathing more than speaking it, he whispered the question that tormented him.

'Who is it?' he whispered. 'Who are you now?'

First Theobald's wife shuddered. Then she turned, and her eyes were sad and wearied. Samuel felt a catch at his heart. Was there something wrong? But her voice was normal enough when she spoke.

'Why Samuel! What a strange thing to ask! I'm Flora, of course, who else?'

Who else indeed? Who else would have made such an answer?

Yes, it was Flora: but if ever a person was caught in the act of self-impersonation, that person was Theobald's wife, for in that tense, motionless figure which a moment before had been unaware of his presence, he realised that Flora had concentrated her whole personality. And the essence of that personality was so salt-bitter that a salt-sadness came into his heart too.

'I understand,' he said quickly. 'I won't intrude.' Turning away swiftly he went out of the house.

Yet, the next evening Flora was as gay as ever. If possible she was more hilarious, in higher spirits, and more irrepressible than they'd ever seen her. Except for Julia, the Beckers were all enthralled.

'Irresponsible is what I'd call her, not just irrepressible,' Julia said when during the course of the evening Flora had twice mimicked Theobald when he was out of the room. 'If he ever finds out he'll never forgive her.'

'Oh, he won't find out,' Charlotte said. She'd hate to have missed that particular take-off: it was the one she enjoyed the best of the lot. 'It was so amusing,' she said, laughing again at the thought of it. 'She only stood with her back to us but there was something about her that would make you swear she was Theobald.'

'All the same,' Julia carped, 'I think it is disloyal of her, and what is more, I think some of her other impersonations are coarse.'

'Coarse? Julia!' Charlotte was astonished at the viciousness of the accusation.

'Well,' Julia said, determined to be even more explicit, 'I suppose I oughtn't to mind as long as Honoria herself doesn't seem to care.'

'Oh that!' Charlotte was relieved and she laughed again. It was, perhaps, a bit coarse, but at the same time it was comical to watch a little scrap of a thing like

Flora imitating – and with such success – a big lump like Honoria, particularly in view of Honoria's increased size. 'Anyway, Honoria enjoys it as much as any of us,' she said, defending Flora further. Charlotte, being the most insipid of the Beckers except for her height, had up to then been relatively safe from Flora's mimicry, and so, next after Samuel, she had the keenest appreciation of it. But it was true that Honoria took the imitations in surprisingly good part, considering how often she was the victim.

In fact, where, at the beginning of her relationship with the Beckers, Flora had been continually calling upon them to witness that she was now Henrietta, now Charlotte, now James, now Julia, now Ernest, and now perhaps one of the servants, or a tradesman with whom they were all familiar, of late she had confined herself to making Honoria the butt of her humour. She had merely to smile in a certain way, or go up to Samuel and pick a bit of fluff off his sleeve, or do no more than take out her handkerchief and blow her nose, and everybody screamed.

'Look at Honoria!' they'd cry.

Once or twice Flora carried things so far as to answer for the real Honoria when Samuel came into the room and called his wife.

'I'm here, Samuel,' she said. 'What do you want?' And once when Honoria answered at the same time, Flora was so funny, so amusing. She turned on the real Honoria and gave her a chilling look, calling *her* Flora.

'Please, Flora,' she said. 'Please give up these childish impersonations.' As if it was Honoria who had been pretending!

It was side-splitting.

And in spite of Julia's misgivings, when summer came and at Flora's instigation the Beckers made a big family party and rented a villa on the coast, it was enlivening for them all in the monotony of their rural surroundings, to have her with them, up to her pranks and antics.

'I realise all that,' Julia said, when this was pointed out to her, 'but I still say she shouldn't pick on Honoria. If I were you, Samuel, I'd put an end to it quick, now that Honoria is so near to her time.'

'Oh but surely,' Charlotte interrupted, and she was about to say that Flora would have too great a delicacy to continue making fun of Honoria much longer, until at that very moment she saw Theobald's wife going over to Samuel, and she was walking with a most peculiar gait. Julia saw her too.

'Look at her now!' Julia cried. 'What did I tell you! It's disgusting. It's shameless. Poor Honoria: it's so unfair! Her first baby, too!'

It being the third time that her own figure had become somewhat grotesque – and the fourth time for Charlotte – she felt they could be supposed less sensitive than Honoria who was pregnant for the first time. 'I'm going to put a stop to it at once,' she said, and she went straight over to Flora. 'Look here, Flora, what do you think you're doing?' she asked in a harsh tone.

But Flora answered so sweetly Julia was momentarily disarmed.

'Please don't call me by the wrong name, Julia,' Flora said sweetly. 'Can't you see I'm not Flora: I'm Honoria. How can you mix us up, particularly now?'

In spite of himself Samuel chuckled. Julia turned on him. 'What is wrong with you?' she cried. 'Why do you think it so funny?' Then she shrugged her shoulders. 'If that's the attitude you intend to take, I may as well mind my own business.'

It was on the tip of Samuel's tongue to say 'Please do,' but instead he smiled falsely and turned to the rest of the company.

'How about some music, ladies?' he asked, and only after he'd spoken did he realise how rarely it was they played the piano since Flora had come among them with her diverting ways. 'Well, how about some music?' he repeated, although he was surprised at his duplicity because Julia was the musician of the family, and his suggestion might appease her. But before Julia had time to lift the piano-lid, Flora had snatched at the suggestion and converted it to her own use.

'I'll play,' she said, still speaking with the voice of Honoria. 'I'll play the tune Samuel likes best!' she cried, and the next minute she was seated on the piano stool playing the only tune that Honoria's memory had managed to retain from all the long and expensive music lessons that had formed the largest part of her education.

Flora played Honoria's tune. She played it and replayed it. And she might as well have been Honoria, so faithfully did she reproduce all the little twists of the wrist, turns of the waist and nods of the head by which Honoria had learned to make up for the deficiencies of her musical talent.

'Well?' Charlotte whispered to Henrietta. 'That seems harmless enough.'

'Do you think so?' Julia hissed, cutting in on them. 'Well, if you think that, please look at the way she is sitting on the piano stool.'

True enough, Flora was sitting peculiarly. Charlotte and Henrietta both had to admit there was something awkward about it. She was sitting at least a foot further away from the keyboard than was either necessary or normal.

'It's disgusting! I've said so before,' Julia said, 'I'll say it again.' She glanced around her to make sure the women were alone. 'I hope the men don't notice,' she said. 'It's making a mockery of motherhood.' And having glanced pertinently at the waist-line of the other two, she indicated her own loosely slung garments. 'It's all due to jealousy, I hope you realise that. Flora is jealous of all of us, but particularly of Honoria because they were married so nearly the same time.'

Whatever malice underlay these words however miscarried of its effect because both Charlotte and Henrietta suffered a sudden suffusion of pity for Theobald's poor little bride.

'Oh, poor, poor Flora,' they cried, and then both together they looked in her direction. 'Perhaps –?' they began eagerly, but Flora's waist was as slim as ever, and her figure gave a complete denial to their kindly hopes for her. Julia hadn't bothered to look at Flora at all.

'Quite the contrary,' she said, then she lowered her voice. 'And if I'm any judge of these things, that will be the fly in Theobald's ointment.'

'Oh!' Charlotte exclaimed. 'You don't think so, really, do you? It would be such a pity.' Her thoughts raced to the nursery upstairs where her big pale baby lay sucking its thumb. 'Why, I've heard of dozens of cases where there was no sign of anything for much, much longer than this, and yet there was success before the end!'

But two days later, it was Charlotte herself who had to bring up the subject again.

'Are you sure, Julia?' she asked. 'Are you sure there couldn't be some possibility of mistake in what you said yesterday?'

'Why?' Julia said coldly.

'Because,' Charlotte said, 'I couldn't help noticing how she acted at supper last night.' No need now to name names. 'She used to love pickled onions, you know that? Well, last night she didn't have any. Wouldn't touch them in fact! And it was the same with the apple sauce. She used to love that too. I couldn't help thinking it odd after what you were saying because I myself couldn't bear anything with the slightest flavour of onion in it when I was expecting, and I couldn't touch apple sauce. It used to give me the most appalling heartburn. But that wasn't all. During supper – the whole time in fact – she sat – well she sat a foot out from the table just like when she was playing the piano. It may be that the thing has got on my nerves, but as well as everything else, I thought she was *walking* queerly after supper when she and I went for a short stroll in the garden. The stroll was at *her* suggestion, mind you, which I thought odd – and here's another thing! – I hope you won't think me coarse to mention it, but I couldn't help noticing that she never buttons her coat, not properly anyway: she lets it hang out loosely from her. Now why on earth is that, do you think?'

'Why do you think?' Julia asked. But she was only leading Charlotte on for a fall.

'Well,' Charlotte said, 'I was wondering if there was any possibility that you could be wrong, and that she might be going to have a baby after all?'

This was what Julia had anticipated, and she was ready for it.

'In that case,' she said acidly, 'isn't it odd that it's thinner Flora is getting, not stouter?'

For a moment Charlotte was defeated. Then she came to the fore again. 'Some women do get thin in the early stages.'

'Is that so?' Julia was more than doubtful. 'Then tell me, in a case like that does the woman have to sit a full foot out from the table? Does she have to wear her coat unbuttoned? And above all, does she have to walk like Flora walks?' For Flora had certainly taken to a most peculiar gait. 'No,' said Julia, answering her own questions so emphatically that Charlotte was silenced. 'I tell you, I'm tired of your talk of impersonations. It's not impersonation. It's mockery. Flora is making a mockery out of poor defenceless Honoria.'

'Oh for goodness' sake, Julia,' Charlotte cried. 'Are you losing your sense of humour? Anyway, if what you say is true, why would Flora be doing it when she's alone?'

'What on earth do you mean, Charlotte?'

Julia's startled look made Charlotte falter.

'Well, I wasn't going to mention it,' she said, 'but the evening before we came down here, I called in to Theobald's with a message from James, and I was shown into the drawing-room, and for an instant I thought I was alone there until suddenly I saw there was someone else there after all. Oh, Julia, I know it sounds a bit daft – the lamps weren't lit – but for a minute I was positive it was Honoria. I nearly said the name. But it was Flora. She was walking up and down her own drawing-room floor, and if you only saw the way her hips were swaying. Why, even Samuel would have been forgiven if he mistook her for his wife. And when the maid had carried in the lamps and after I knew it was Flora, I still couldn't take my eyes off her, because I could still have sworn she was twice the size she'd appeared when I first came in the door. I've often heard of optical illusions, but I never thought I'd experience one!'

Julia said nothing for a minute.

'It seems to me,' she said then slowly, 'that we are all experiencing them these days. Ernest was saying only this morning that James had commented on the resemblance between Flora and Honoria. Resemblance! Did you ever hear anything more absurd?'

'It does seem a bit absurd, doesn't it?' Charlotte said. 'On the other hand, I must say I did think once or twice that Flora was beginning to have a look of Honoria. I'm interested to hear James noticed it. I wonder if any of the others did?'

When discreet enquiries were made in the course of that same afternoon, Henrietta too thought she had noticed a slight resemblance.

'I thought it was only my imagination,' she declared, 'and I didn't like to mention it to anyone in case it might be put down to my condition. I'd hate anyone to think I was getting nervy or hysterical, or beginning to get fancies.'

That, however, was just exactly what was happening to all the Beckers, and especially to the Becker wives.

'It's all Flora's fault,' Julia said.

'Isn't it strange, though, that Honoria doesn't appear to notice?' Charlotte said.

'Oh, that's part of her nature,' Henrietta said, 'but all the same it's my belief she's more upset than we think. I came across her by surprise the other day and I could have sworn she had been crying.'

'Crying?' The other two women started up in matronly concern.

'A fit of crying would be the worst thing in the world for her at the present time. It could be the cause of anything!' With this far from lucid statement Julia stood up. 'I'm going to speak to Samuel again,' she said.

Charlotte felt her knees tremble. Samuel was Flora's stoutest champion. She'd have thought it would be more difficult to approach him than Theobald, and to approach Theobald of course was unthinkable.

Samuel, however, was no match for Julia. When he tried to pooh-pooh her complaints, she went for him with fire in her eyes.

'Samuel Becker,' she cried. 'Are you going to put Flora before Honoria? I'm telling you that for some reason or other, Theobald's wife is deliberately trying to make your wife look ridiculous, and what is more, Honoria is beginning to notice.'

Samuel's face was white and drawn. He made one last effort to evade the issue.

'It's not deliberate,' he said speaking lowly. 'If Flora is giving offence I am certain she is unconscious of it.'

So he was willing to admit offence was given. Julia relaxed somewhat.

'Consciously or unconsciously,' she said, 'it has got to stop, and stop immediately. Today! Did you know that Honoria has been having fits of crying lately? And what do you think is the cause of that? Above all, may I ask what effect you suppose this state of mind will have on your unborn child?'

Samuel's face went whiter.

'Where is Flora now?' he asked. 'I'll speak to her.'

Flora was not far away. She was in the breakfast room sitting by the window, sewing. As a matter of fact Charlotte and Julia thought Samuel could hardly have gone farther than the end of the passage when he was back again, but they knew at once by his face that something had happened.

'What's the matter?' Charlotte cried. Then a sudden inexplicable fear came over her and she shouted for James.

'James, James!' she called, relieved to remember that he was sitting on a garden seat just under the open window, reading in the sunshine.

'What in heaven's name do you want, Charlotte?' James said, starting up and leaning in across the window-sill, but instantly he too felt there was something wrong. 'Ernest! Robert!' he cried, seeing the two men walking along a gravel path to one side of the villa. Then, without waiting to go around to the door, stiff as he was, he put his leg over the window ledge and joined the women at once. 'Oh, you're here too, Samuel,' he said with relief.

But whatever had upset Samuel he was now fuming at the fuss that was being made. 'What is the matter with you people?' He turned to Julia. 'I only wanted to speak to you, Julia,' he said. 'I don't understand   what is the meaning of this commotion?' Yet when Ernest and Robert hurried in he couldn't help deriving some comfort from the proximity of so many Beckers. 'There's nothing wrong,' he said. 'I only wanted to have a word with Julia – or Charlotte – or Henrietta.' He hesitated. 'I wanted one of them to step to the door of the other room with me.' He hesitated again. 'It's Flora.'

Charlotte put her hand to her heart. 'Is there something the matter with her?' she cried.

'Oh no – at least I don't think so,' Samuel said, 'but I was a bit worried because she didn't answer when I spoke to her. She was sewing, and when I called her she just went on drawing the needle in and out and didn't even turn her head.'

'She didn't hear you: that's all,' James said, with an elderly frown. He'd given his knee a knock on the window ledge. It was vexatious. 'Was it to tell us she was deaf you brought us in from the sunshine? I thought the place was on fire.' He was turning to go out again when Samuel put out his hand and laid it on his older brother's arm.

'Wait a minute, James. The odd thing is that I know she heard me.' He turned back to the women: they were more understanding. 'I know she did. I called her by name, not once, but twice or three times, and yet she went on sewing. And the last time I called she was putting the thread between her teeth to break it, and I could see by the way she paused that she was listening. Then, ignoring me, she bit the thread and broke it and bent her head again.'

It wasn't much – but it was decidedly odd.

'What is she sewing anyway?' James asked suddenly. 'She's at it all the time.'

'Oh, for goodness' sake, James,' Charlotte said, 'what does it matter what she's sewing!' It was so like James to fasten on something trivial. She turned back to Samuel. 'Why didn't you go over to her?'

It was only after Samuel answered that they all began to feel anxious.

'I thought one of you women should do that,' he said. 'That's why I came back for one of you,' He looked at Julia. 'I thought you might be best, Julia.'

'Me?' In spite of being the most aggressive earlier on in her assertions that something ought to be done, Julia was most reluctant to put herself forward now. 'Will you come with me, Charlotte?'

'I will of course,' Charlotte said readily enough, but she made a sign to the men. 'Please stay near at hand,' she said. Then she addressed herself to Samuel in particular, and her voice was very kind. 'We'll leave the door open,' she said, 'and you can stand outside and listen.'

'But be quiet,' Julia warned, because James was still inclined to protest that they were making a fuss about nothing. 'Where is Theobald?' they could hear him ask. 'Why isn't he here? Why didn't someone fetch him along? If there's anything wrong it's his business more than it's ours.'

Afterwards everyone remembered what James had said, but they all felt it was fortunate that Theobald was not there. For Flora gave Julia and Charlotte a very different reception from the one she had given Samuel. Being prepared for similar treatment, they were paralysed with fright when she sprang to her feet the instant they called her name. They'd only called once, and as casually as possible.

'Flora?' they'd said timidly. 'Flora?'

But the name had hardly left their lips when Flora sprang up. Lithe as a cat, she swung herself around, and gripped the back of the chair in which she had been sitting. Her sewing had fallen to the floor. Her eyes were blazing.

'What is the matter with you all?' she demanded. 'Have you gone mad? Why are you coming in here and calling me names?' And then, as it she saw – or in some way divined – that the rest of the family was there too, huddled together outside the door, she shook her fist in their direction. Julia and Charlotte drew together, and didn't advance any further. 'Tell me this, Julia Becker, or you, Charlotte Becker!' Flora cried. 'Is it a joke? Because, if it is, you'd better stop it at once. You must know by now that one thing I detest is being called names.'

'But I never called you names, Flora,' Julia cried.

'None of us did, Flora,' Charlotte said.

They seemed to have only made things worse, however. Flora's face became convulsed.

'There you go again,' she cried, and she nodded towards the hallway where the others were rooted to the ground. With her long thin finger she pointed out through the window that looked on the garden. 'As for that one,' she said, 'that wretched creature out there: if someone doesn't stop her from driving me mad, I won't answer for what will become of her.'

They looked.

Out in the sun, on a stone bench, not too far from the house but just beyond earshot of what had gone on within it, Julia saw that Honoria was taking her mid-day rest with her eyes shut and a newspaper over her face to keep her skin from getting too red.

Sensing that behind her the others had come close, Julia called out to them.

'You'd better come in altogether,' she said.

Flora swung around. 'Yes, come in. All of you,' she cried. 'Let's have this out. And make her come in too,' she added, nodding back over her shoulder to indicate the figure at the end of the garden.

James was the first to enter the room.

'Now, now,' he said placatingly, 'there's no need to disturb Honoria. If we have had some little disturbance among ourselves, there is no need to drag poor Honoria into it. It's best for her to be kept as quiet as possible under the circumstances.'

Something in James's words seemed to sting Flora into another ungovernable fury. There was moisture gathering on her forehead and more alarmingly at the corners of her mouth –

'Honoria?' she echoed. 'Under the circumstances? So you are all playing the same game.' She caught at the neck of her dress and tore it open. "Very well. I warned you. I won't stand it. It was bad enough when it was only her that was tormenting me' – she pointed again at the unsuspecting Honoria. 'I pretended not to take any notice. But if you're all at it, I can't stand it. I can't and I won't!' She clapped her hands over her ears, and tears sprang into her eyes.

'But what are we doing?' Charlotte cried. 'We don't know what you're talking about, Flora!'

'Flora! Flora! Flora!' The girl was almost beside herself. 'You *do* want to drive me mad. You do! You do!' Her eyes ran over the faces one by one, and then she scanned them all as a group in a wild sweeping glance. 'It's a shame for you!' she said. 'You ought at least to consider my condition.'

From where he stood at the back of the group, looking down at the carpet, Samuel started violently and looked up.

'Yes – a shame,' Flora repeated. 'If people only knew how I'm treated,' She wrung her hands. 'Oh, how terrible – I have no one to help me.' Suddenly she placed her hands on her small flat abdomen. 'It's not myself I'm thinking about – it's the child!'

At that the Beckers, all except Charlotte, went rigid. Charlotte laughed hysterically.

'Oh, it's only an impersonation,' she shrilled, but even as she spoke her blood ran cold. Flora's tears had dried as quickly as they'd rushed forth.

'If it's only an impersonation,' she cried, 'then it's time an end was put to it!' She ran over to the window. 'Look at her now. Look at the brazen creature. At this very moment she's out there making a mockery of me. Oh, how can she do it? How can she be so coarse? How can you all see her at it day after day and not be revolted? Don't you notice the way she sits at the table? Don't you notice the way she wears her clothes, not fastening the buttons?' Suddenly she stooped and picked up the piece of material she had been sewing. 'She even went to my work-basket and took out this and pretended it was hers.'

The frightened gaze of the Becker women fell on a small white flannel chemise that was only half-finished. But as she held it up the sight of it made Flora wail. 'I wouldn't mind if she were a normal woman,' she cried, 'a woman that might have a child of her own some day, but look at her, with her hips like a scissors, and her chest like a cardboard doll! *She'll* never have a child. It's just that she's jealous; jealous of me. That's what it is!'

For one moment Flora's face became radiant, glorified, and then the light died out and it was once more haggard and harassed and aged – looking. 'Oh, I can't stand it,' she said in a voice that was now small and whimpering. She put her hand up to her head as if it ached. 'She's got me so confused.' Then, as if she was taking them into her confidence, she tried to steady her voice. 'I'm fighting against it,' she told them. 'See!' Fumbling among the laces on the front of her dress she pulled out a crumpled piece of paper. 'When she says something to put me astray I look at this paper. It has my name written on it. Oh, I won't let her get the better of me. She won't drive *me* mad!'

Urgently, frantically, she pushed the paper into James's hand, then before he had time to uncrumple it, she pulled it back and shoved it into another hand and then into another and another. But all any of them could see was a blur of wretchedly bad handwriting. Snatching it back she stuffed it back into her bodice. And now the look on her face was crafty.

'You see, I'm able for her,' she said. 'I'm able for all of you.' She spread out her fingers and again placed them over her boyish body.

'I have to think of my child,' she said. And it was the change in her voice that was hardest to bear: it had become wondrously gentle again.

'Oh my God!' Charlotte said, muffling her cry with her handkerchief. Next minute she was sobbing convulsively and James had to call on Samuel and Ernest.

'Get her out of here quick,' he ordered.

Flora, however, had not understood it was Charlotte he meant.

'Get who out of here?' she screamed, starting up like a hare. 'No one is going to lay a hand on me.'

'Hush, hush, he wasn't talking about you, my dear,' Samuel said, and he endeavoured to take her hand.

'Are you sure?' Flora's eyes filled first with suspicion and then with fear, and finally with something else, indefinable to the Beckers. They stared at their brother Samuel, who had pushed James aside and seemed to have taken over command of the situation. Flora too recognised that Samuel had put himself in authority. She caught at his lapels. 'That's what she wants, you know – to have me sent away.' She let go the front of his jacket and seizing his hands she clutched them so that the skin went thin on her knuckles and the bone showed through. 'You'll help me, won't you?' she pleaded. 'You're the only one I trust. You won't let her drive me mad, will you, like she's been driven mad herself. That's it, you see. No one knows but me and I didn't tell anyone before now. But I knew it all the time. She's mad. Mad! She was really always mad. Her family was mad – all of them. Her father died in a madhouse. She didn't tell that to Theobald, I bet? She didn't tell it to any of you. But I found out and that's why she had this set against me. She wants to make me mad too. But she won't. None of you will. You can keep on calling me Flora all you like. Flora! Go on! Call it to me, Flora! Flora! Flora! I won't listen. I'll stick my fingers in my ears so I won't hear.' With a wild distracted gesture Theobald's wife pulled her hands away from Samuel's again and went to stick her fingers in her ears, but halfway through the gesture her hands dropped to her sides. 'Where is my piece of paper?' she cried and again she fumbled and found it once more. 'As long as I have my name written down on this bit of paper no one will succeed in getting me mixed up,' she said. Then, having stared at the piece of paper and soundlessly moved her lips two or three times as if memorising something, she stowed it away again, and rammed her fingers into her ears as far as they'd go.

'She'll pierce her ear-drums,' James said. And as if Flora had gone out of the room the Beckers' tongues were loosened.

'What happened to her?' that was what they all wanted to know.

But Samuel raised his hand and it looked as if he'd scourge them. 'Oh, you fools!' he yelled. 'Get out of here, all of you. Leave this to me.' There was such a look on his face that Robert was already backing out of the room.

'Are you sure it's all right for you to stay alone with her?' James asked from the doorway.

'Oh, James, what do you mean?' Charlotte cried. 'You don't mean –?' But she didn't dare finish the sentence.

James's meaning was made clear, however, before the door shut. They saw Samuel put his arm around Flora's thin shoulders, and his words sent a chill through their hearts.

'Hush, Honoria. Hush, hush,' Samuel was saying. To Flora!

'Please, Honoria – please hush!'

Then the door shut them out.

'Oh God in heaven,' Charlotte said, and burst into tears again.

'What on earth will we do with her?' Julia asked.

'How was it we didn't find this out before now?' That was what puzzled Henrietta.

'I kept telling you all that something was wrong,' Julia said, 'but none of you wanted to believe me.'

'What good would it have done if we had listened to you?' Henrietta said tartly. 'Sooner or later – what difference does it make – the disgrace is the same.'

'Disgrace? Oh, how can you speak about it like that?' Charlotte stopped crying out loud but tears ran silently down her face. 'How can you use such a word! It's all so terribly sad.'

'And there's Theobald to think about!' James said suddenly. 'What about him? Where is he? When will he be back? And who is going to break this to him?' But knowing it would probably be up to him to do it, he sank down on a chair in the hall and began to mop his forehead with the handkerchief out of his breast pocket that was normally only for show. 'This is only the beginning,' he said.

But inside in the room with Flora this was not what Samuel was thinking as he held her hands tightly in his, and tried to keep her calm by lending himself to her delusion, calling her Honoria over and over again. It was all over. That's what Samuel was thinking.

'Hush, Honoria. Hush, hush,' he said. They would have to send for Theobald. They would have to get a doctor and make arrangements to have her taken away somewhere – for a time at least – to try and restore the balance of her poor jangled mind. It might not be for ever, or even for very long, but all the same Samuel knew that the terrible, terrible sadness that had settled on his heart would lie upon it for ever.

It was all over; the fun and the gaiety. Their brief journey into another world had been rudely cut short. They had merely glimpsed from afar a strange and exciting vista, but they had established no foothold in that far place. And the bright enchanting creature that had opened that vista to them had been but a flitting spirit never meant to mix with the likes of them.

Across Flora's shoulder he looked out the window into the garden. The children of Charlotte and Julia and Henrietta had come back from a walk with their nanny and were playing under a tree: a heavy-set little girl, and two stodgy boys. And on the grass Charlotte's fat baby sat sucking its thumb. Beckers to the bone, all of them And the child that his wife Honoria was carrying would be like them, as like as peas in a pea-pod.

His eyes came back to rest on Flora. The tempest of her passion had died down.

'You'll be all right in a little while, my dear. Try to rest. Try to forget everything. Rest on me –' he paused. rest on me, Honoria.'

But when Flora's sobbing finally ceased and, exhausted, she rested against him, her weight was so slight he started. It was as if she had begun to dissolve once more into the wraith-like creature of light that had first flashed on them all in its airy brilliance on the night of his own betrothal party; a spirit which they in their presumption had come to regard – so erroneously – as one of themselves, just another of the Becker wives, like Julia or Charlotte, or the real Honoria.

The Joy-Ride

The two butlers stood outside the door and watched the overseer's car go down the driveway. Crickem, a lank, pimply fellow, the younger of the two, turned around and looked up at the solid mass of the manor house behind him, all of hewn granite, three storeys high, and showing a frontage of fourteen windows and a colonnaded porch.

'I suppose he thinks the old house would run away,' he said, and he spat contemptuously into the dewy grass beyond the granite steps.

The overseer had just gone away for three days. The likelihood was that he had gone to the Galway Races, but the butlers had been given to understand that he was going to Dublin on business.

It was seven o'clock in the morning. The dew was still on the ground. And the two lackeys stared disconsolately at the wheel-tracks of the departed car that were printed fast on the dewy moisture of the gravel. The younger man was even more disconsolate than his companion. He had counted on their being given at least one day out during the overseer's absence. Purdy, the older fellow, did not really care one way or the other, but for Crickem's sake he was ready to abuse the overseer.

'If you were working for him as long as me you wouldn't have expected anything better,' he said, and he too spat into the dewy grass.

The estate on which the manor house stood occupied some 400 acres of the best land in Meath and was owned by a young man not yet of age, who was heir to at least two other estates as well, in both of which he appeared to have more interest than in this one. The countryside, however, was consoled for his never visiting this estate, and for the likelihood of his never bothering much about it, by the fact that the overseer was himself a man of such gentlemanly habits, who ran the house on a scale that approximated to their idea of ownership, and treated them with what they regarded as a proper rudeness and contempt.

It was generally believed in the district that Malcolm would eventually purchase the property for himself, and in this assurance the countryside relied upon no knowledge of the overseer's financial position but rather upon the fact that he had an aquiline nose, called them all by their surnames, and wore a yellow tie printed over with a pattern of foxes' heads.

The house was certainly kept in good order. The owner might walk into it at any hour and find it not only habitable but exceedingly comfortable and pleasant. Malcolm believed that the best preservative for anything was constant use, and so the rooms were unshuttered every day, the fires lighted, the furniture dusted, and the windows kept clean. The curtains were always hanging. There was no dismal shrouding of pictures and chandeliers. There was no rolling up of carpets; the house was kept in running order.

And for this order, Crickem and Purdy were solely responsible. They comprised the entire indoor staff. Crickem, the young man, was responsible for the care of the front part of the house, for the airing of the rooms and the preservation of the furniture. Purdy helped, but although he too was a butler by training, he was, on account of his age, and the lesser likelihood of his being able to pick and choose his jobs, forced to undertake a few other chores, such as the preparation of the food, the making up of the overseer's bed, the polishing of his boots, and, of late, although it was understood to be a temporary arrangement, the laundering of the overseer's shirts, and the pressing of his trousers. Recently, these multifarious duties had induced Purdy to abandon the wearing of his black suit, and although the two men worked together amicably enough, it occasionally galled the older man to see Crickem going about resplendent in his black suit with the silk lapels, his white shirt and his black tie. To counteract any extra authority which Crickem's black suit might give him in the eyes of the outdoor workers, Purdy took care to keep his own black suit always in sight, hanging on a coat-hanger from a nail on the kitchen dresser.

Purdy was a small man of about forty, with a bald head and a round belly. His glossy face wore at all times a timid look, which was absurd on one of his age and bulk, but a natural timidity had, in his case been increased by the feeling of vulnerability that comes to people who have been a great many years in the same employment and who have come to feel that their security is dependent on a single thread. In spite of this timidity and sense of dependence, however, two days after getting his salary Purdy seldom had a penny in his pocket, for as regularly as pay-day came around, Purdy put on his black suit and his bowler hat and went down to the village to empty the contents of his pay-envelope on the counter of the local public-house.

Lest, however, such improvident behaviour with money should seem to be inconsistent with the expression of timidity and dependence that sat upon Purdy's features, it is necessary to revert to an incident in Purdy's past to which Purdy himself never willingly referred at all, and which, in all but one particular he had effaced from memory. It was this: Purdy was a married man. Or perhaps it would be more correct to say that twenty years ago he had been married for a period of six weeks, to one, Amelia Purdy, a housekeeper, whose idea of marriage having proved somewhat different from that of the young Purdy, a separation had been mutually sought and mutually granted. To this Amelia Purdy however, Purdy paid every week one third of his salary in alimony, the alimony being by the provision of the Court, sent direct to Mrs. Amelia Purdy by Purdy's employer. The sum, therefore, which Purdy got in his envelope each week represented the legal residue over which he had full liberty. Now, in spite of a poor opinion of women in general, and of Amelia in particular, Purdy was able all the same to discriminate between virtues and faults, and the fact that Amelia proved difficult to live with did not blind Purdy to the fact that she was an exceptionally thrifty woman, with the double capacity of making money and of keeping it. And Purdy knew that not one penny of that alimony would be squandered by Amelia; that not one penny of it would, as it were, be let go down a crack in the floor. It would, on the contrary, be saved up carefully, and as likely as not more would have been added to it, until it must by now represent a tidy sum in the vaults of Amelia's bank. Yes; that alimony must, by now, have accumulated into a tidy heap. And in Purdy's mind, that alimony was still his money. He had never lost this feeling of ownership over it, as for that matter, he had never lost his feeling of ownership over the tall and forbidding Amelia. And it was always at the back of Purdy's mind that if all went to all, if the worst came to the worst; if, that is to say, he was really up against it, he could patch things up with Amelia. Two could live easily on the interest from that accumulated alimony. Without adding another penny to it, two could live on it in comfort. So, every Friday night Purdy went down to the village and confidently emptied his pockets.

Yet, in spite of having Amelia and her alimony to fall back upon, Purdy had no wish to jeopardise his job at The Manse. And so Crickem, who in a short and rapid career had occupied some thirty to forty jobs, was able to enliven himself any time he wished by taking a rise out of the older man. When restrictions and duties weighed heavy on him he used to glance slyly at Purdy.

'After all,' he would say, 'there's no obligation on us to stay here. Nobody can force us to stay. We can walk out any minute we like!'

And after this, or some such remark, he had nothing to do but sit down and watch the absolute terror that would come into Purdy's eyes.

On this particular day, the day of the overseer's departure, Purdy was more placid than ever under the restrictions that irked his callow companion. A day out coming in the middle of the week would not be much use to him with his salary all spent. But he hadn't forgotten what it was to be young, and so when the overseer's car had gone out of sight, he put his hand on the young man's shoulder and patted him understandingly.

'I know how you feel,' he said, 'but there's no reason why we should both stay in all the time. If you like you can take a day out and I'll be able to manage.'

'Oh, what fun can a fellow have alone?' said Crickem, irritably shaking off the patting hand. 'I don't see why we can't both get out. As I said before, the house isn't going to run away, is it?'

'No,' said Purdy seriously, 'but I wouldn't like to go out and leave no one here.'

'If it's bolted and barred what can happen to it?' demanded Crickem.

'But it won't be bolted and barred,' said Purdy. 'I got particular orders that the shutters were to be taken down as usual.'

Crickem snorted. 'That was to tie us down,' he said, savagely spitting out once more.

Purdy moved over to the door.

'There's no use standing out here in the cold,' he said. 'Are you coming inside?' and when Crickem had stepped in after him Purdy automatically bolted and barred the hall door, and put up his hands to close over the heavy shutters inside the door. But suddenly he stopped. 'What's the use of locking up?' he said. 'We'll be opening the house again in an hour or so?' He let his hands drop. 'As long as we're here,' he said then eagerly, 'why don't we take down all the shutters?' For Purdy was not at ease about Crickem, and he felt that the sooner the house was laid bare and open, the windows thrown up and the doors unbarred, the sooner Crickem would see the necessity for someone to remain in charge of it.

But Crickem pushed him aside impatiently and clattered the shutters into place over the door.

'Wait till we decide what we're going to do,' he said ominously, and in case the old fellow would burst with apprehension, he turned around more tractably. 'We'll have our breakfast first in any case,' he said. 'It's too early to open the house anyway. The dew is still in the air. It would do more harm than good to open up the place at this hour! Come on!'

Tightly shuttered now, the hall was as dark as a vault, except for the pale streaks of yellow sunlight that came through the joinings of the boards. These gave no light, beyond their own long narrow reflections on the floor, and were little better than strokes of paint to guide the two butlers back to the kitchen regions.

In the back regions the windows were without shutters, protected only by black bars and railings. Here the cold north light was permitted to make its bleak entry through high sashed narrow windows overhung with ivy. The two men turned into the kitchen.

In the kitchen the two butlers took their breakfast without any further reference to the day in front of them, but Purdy was uneasy, and from time to time he glanced nervously at Crickem, and wondered what was in his mind. The young man, he thought, had a peculiar look in his eye, and his eye was, moreover, directed on him, Purdy.

Crickem, as a matter of fact, who had never spent more than a year in any job, had for some time past been feeling that his term in this one was running short. He was familiar with this unsettled feeling although he could never decide whether it was a premonition of dismissal, or a contributory factor to it. At any rate it made him reckless. And although a few hours of stolen liberty would not make much of a meal for a reckless young man, a piquant sauce would be added to it if he could induce the cautious Purdy to eat the same fare. The young man had already got a good deal of satisfaction out of shaking Purdy up with the suggestion that they both take a day out and he knew that now the old fellow was suffering the discomfort of suspense. But the suspense must not be drawn out too long. The next thing to do was to give him a false impression of security. Crickem stood up suddenly and with an elaborate air of resignation he walked over to the door.

'Well,' he said, 'If we were ordered to open those shutters,' he said, 'we'd better open them. Are you coming?'

As he expected, Purdy nearly strained a blood vessel in his anxiety to get to this feet and comply with this suggestion, which he no doubt took to mean that there would be no more talk about illicit outings. Crickem had to hurry out the door ahead of him to hide the smirk on his face.

The usual procedure in this matter of opening up the shutters was for Purdy to take the left of the house and Crickem the right. They began with the windows to each side of the hall door, and then Purdy went into the drawing-room and Crickem into the library. From then on they saw no more of each other until they emerged into the hall again after a complete round of the house, although as Purdy carefully folded back each shutter under his care, he could hear, in the distance, the clatter made by Crickem who was less particular about the noise he made. On this morning, however, while Purdy made his way around the rooms on the left, there was nothing distant or faint about the clatter that came from the other side of the house. Clatter after clatter sounded through the house, and in the brief moments between the clatters, there were ear-shattering sounds as of someone recklessly plunging about in a dark room. Purdy tried to feel amused. After all there was no one to hear, no one to be disturbed, no one to worry in case any damage might be done. If this was the only advantage Crickem took of the overseer's absence things would not be too bad. Nevertheless, Purdy felt himself quake every time there was a fresh clatter on the other side of the house, and after a few minutes he found himself counting the clatters. The fellow ought to be at the last one soon. Only about one more to be done, Purdy estimated, and he carefully let down the hasp on the last window on his side of the house, and silently folded back the shutters. But the deafening clatter that came at the same time from the other side of the house was not the last. It was immediately succeeded by another. And that was succeeded by another. And then, as Purdy made his way back to the hall the clatters continued one after another, and if possible, one louder than another.

That was strange! Purdy hurried along towards the hall. Had he miscalculated the number of windows on the other side? He had always taken for granted that there were about the same number on each side. How then was he finished today so much sooner than Crickem? Even as he hurried along there was another and then still another violent clatter in the distance. But this time, strange to say, it seemed to Purdy that the clattering came from one of the rooms that he himself had shortly vacated.

Purdy opened the door of the passage leading in to the hall. Here in the bright light from all the opened rooms that radiated from it, he and Crickem would join company to engage upon the next task of the day: But as Purdy rushed into the hall this morning, to the accompaniment of another deafening clatter somewhere behind him, to his astonishment the hall was just as it had been at seven o'clock that morning; as dark as a vault, the only possible difference being that in the yellow streaks of sunlight from the cracks and joinings of the shutters, particles of dust danced deliriously like midges and there was a smell of dust in the air.

Purdy stood like one bewitched. Hadn't he himself opened one of the shutters in this hall? And the other rooms, opening off the hall, why was there no light coming from them? He groped his way over to the drawing-room and fumbled in the dark for the handle of the door. It was a minute or two before he grasped that the door was wide open, and beyond it the drawing-room yawned as black as a pit.

Like a sleep-walker Purdy put one foot inside the threshold of the drawing-room. There was no mistake. It was a black pit, slashed only with the familiar yellow streaks where the reshuttered windows let in cracks of light. Purdy stood with his mouth opened and gaped into the blackness. Far away, this time unmistakably to the left of him, there was a last and violent clatter, and after a few moments there was a sound of footsteps and whistling coming along the passage. The next minute Crickem opened the door leading into the hall.

'Are you there, Purdy?' he called out, and in the thin light from the regions behind him, Purdy saw with a sinking heart the unmistakable grin of mischief on the young fellow's face. 'Come on!' cried Crickem. 'Now we can do what we like. Malcolm may be smart, but he's not smarter than me. He gave orders to open up the house, did he? Well. His orders were obeyed. We opened up the house. But there was nothing said about closing it again. That's where we have him! Come on now, let's get out of this dungeon. What are you doing standing there in the dark?'

Crickem held open the passage-door, and beckoned Purdy towards it. He wanted to hurry the old fellow back to the lighted regions where he could see the expression on his face. He wanted to get a laugh at the old chap's fright.

But, when Purdy emerged into the lighted hall Crickem got a surprise. Purdy's face had changed. There was no doubt about that. But to Crickem's astonishment instead of a look of fright, Purdy's face wore an entirely unexpected expression. It was not fright. It was not nervousness. It was not even disapproval.

Crickem stared.

Purdy, yes, Purdy, had undergone some extraordinary change. He was transformed. And on his face there was what could only be called a grin.

Yes; Purdy was grinning.

And the outer was only a reflection of the inner change. Something had happened to Purdy in the few minutes when he realised the way Crickem had compromised between obedience and revolt. Something had stirred inside in him. And what had stirred was a memory of youth. This was the kind of compromise that had characterised every boyish prank that Purdy had ever dared upon. A feeling of boyish irresponsibility had come over Purdy, and all of a sudden looking at Crickem, Purdy forgot that he was fat as a barrel, bald, and middle-aged, and timid, and that he was moreover married to a six-foot shrew to whom he paid one-third of his salary in alimony. It seemed to him, that he and the raw youth in front of him, who was thin as a pea-rod and pimpled with the bad-living of youth, were partners cut to the one pattern. He chuckled and rubbed his hands together. Then as Crickem stared at him in astonishment, Purdy's eye fell on Crickem's trouser leg, and it appeared to him all of a sudden that if there was any difference at all between them it was in the manner of their attire.

'Just a minute,' he said, as Crickem opened the kitchen door, and dashing in ahead of the young man Purdy grabbed his black suit off the nail of the dresser, and disappeared up the servants' staircase. A minute later he too was resplendent in black and white, a proper butler; a proper dandy.

In his black suit, it would not be correct to say that Purdy still felt like a boy; rather he felt like a young man; just exactly, indeed, as he used to feel twenty years ago when he was apprenticed to the head waiter in the Centreside Hotel in North Great Georges Street, Dublin, where pranks and larks and sprees were the order of the day. Purdy looked himself up and down, and yet he hesitated to go downstairs. In the old days he had a name for thinking up pranks, and now he felt it was up to him to keep pace with Crickem. It was up to him to take some daring step on his own two feet. Crickem had gone a good bit. He, Purdy, must go one better. He sat down on the side of his bed and thought furiously for a moment or two and then a look of great daring came over his face, and standing up he made his way up to the overseer's dressing-room. A few minutes later he was going down the passage to join Crickem, trying not to run in his excitement, and what he had of straight black hair was plastered as close to his head as paint, with liberal handfuls of the overseer's hair lotion that came in specially prepared proportions all the way from Dublin, and of which the overseer was himself so careful he used only as much as moistened the palms of his hand, while on the elderly butler's feet, instead of his usual square-toed boots of black leather, there were a high-polished pair of Malcolm's bright yellow shoes, with pointed toes.

The monkey was up in Purdy. He was ready to spend the day in pranks, pranks one more daring than another, but all of them somehow of the same nature as using the boss's hair oil and wearing his yellow boots. For these were the pranks that had been popular in the Centreside

Hotel, twenty years back. These were the larks they had when Purdy was a boy.

Crickem however was not a boy. And when Purdy came into the kitchen the young butler looked at his foolishly-plastered pate, and at the pointed boots that made him walk like a spinster on the tops of his toes, and he felt that he was in danger of being put into a ludicrous position. He didn't want any tom-boy pranks.

'Well, what are we going to do?' he said brusquely. 'The house is bolted and barred. The doors are all locked, the windows are shut. There's no need for us to sit around the place all day.'

A twinge of returning apprehension shot through the joy that filled Purdy's soul. He looked at Crickem.

'What could we do?' he said half-heartedly, but no sooner had he said it than he took confidence. There was nothing to do. Crickem might be filled with daring, but what was there to do at ten-thirty in the morning, in the heart of the country, four miles from the nearest town, and two miles from the railway station from which the only outgoing train had already departed some two hours! Purdy took heart again. He felt he might even show off a bit.

'It's a pity there isn't another motor car!' he said. 'We could go for a jaunt somewhere.'

In spite of himself, Crickem was impressed.

'Can you drive?' he asked.

Purdy couldn't drive, but he didn't let himself down.

'What's the use of being able to drive,' he said, 'when there's no car!'

Crickem stared at him. Had he underestimated Purdy? But Purdy was a new man. This wasn't the old Purdy.

'The petrol might be missed,' said Crickem, determined to put him to the test.

'Pouf!' said Purdy. 'There are plenty of petrol stations between here and where I'd go!'

Curiosity overcame Crickem.

'Where would you go?' he asked, and he was humble as a pupil at the foot of the Master.

Purdy waved away the question deprecatingly.

'What's the use of talking about it!' he said. 'There's no car, and that's the end of it!'

Inside the tight yellow boots that pinched his toes, Purdy seemed to be rising up taller and more lofty. Peaks of daring loomed up ahead of him, and rising on the pointed toes of the overseer's boots, Purdy got ready to scale those peaks. But rising, he fell.

'God be with the times,' he said, 'when you didn't have to bother with cars and petrol, and when, if you wanted to go for a joy-ride you had nothing more to do than to walk down to the yard and hitch up a pony and trap!'

'A pony and trap!' Crickem sat up. 'Purdy!' he cried, running over to Purdy and slapping him on the back. 'Purdy! You're a genius!'

This was when Purdy first felt his feet slip. He saw disaster ahead. What did Crickem mean? Why was he so excited? Purdy trembled in his boots. His jaw shook. His eye wobbled. And he stared open-mouthed at Crickem. Crickem saw his advantage.

'Oh well,' he said patronisingly, 'If you didn't think of the idea, you put it into my head.'

'What idea?' asked Purdy in a small weak voice.

'The pony and trap!' cried Crickem, and then the whole significance of the affair became clear to him. He saw through Purdy's pretence of daring. 'Do you mean to say you didn't know there was an old pony cart down in the yard?' he cried, and he rubbed his hands together with delight in Purdy's discomfort. 'I don't know what I was doing down there, but I remember one day when I was poking about in the stables I saw an old trap pushed into a corner of one of them.'

Purdy's vague prognostication of coming disaster resolved itself into a certainty. Instantly he recalled what he had not thought of for years, that away at the back of one of the stables, stowed in away behind a few rusty and out-dated farm implements, which like itself had long ago been supplanted in use by mechanical implements, there was, indeed, as Crickem said, an old pony cart. Instantly it rose in a vision before Purdy's eyes; a delapidated but undeniably entire, pony trap of the kind used for the nursery governesses in the days of horse transport; the body painted to resemble basketry, the shafts, wheels and the sockets of the gig-lamps painted black with yellow stripes, and the whole vehicle, shafts and chassis, dulled with dust, and draped with cobwebs as a cheese is shrouded in muslin. Desperately Purdy clutched at the one possibility that remained.

'It's all covered with dust and cobwebs,' he said. 'It's probably falling to pieces.'

'Not at all,' said Crickem. 'Those old traps were made to last for ever. Come on! Let's go down and have a look at it!'

Purdy could do no less than follow and although he did so reluctantly he gave the impression of being in a greater hurry than Crickem because, with his short, fat little legs, he took two or three steps to every one of the long lanky butler.

'See! It's covered with cobwebs,' the little fellow panted again, when he followed Crickem into the inner depths of the stable a few minutes later.

But the cobwebs, alas, only proved that the old trap had been left undisturbed and intact and that it had escaped the usual fate of such outmoded vehicles. None of its various portions had been detached for other uses. And when Crickem pushed an old swing-plough out of his way and caught the shafts of the pony-cart and pulled it out of the dark stable on to the sunlit cobblestones, there it was, as good as the day some distracted governess had driven it into the yard for the last time. There were the yellow-buttoned leather cushions, piled one on top of the other. There was the fringed rug, folded neatly on the seat, although no doubt riddled inside with moths. And there, above all, like a mast on a schooner, the small yellow whip stuck up from the whip socket, with two white sails of cobweb hoisted to either side of it.

Without waiting to brush aside the shrouding webs and spider strings along which the startled spiders were scurrying on short black legs, Crickem caught up the shafts and setting himself between them, began to run up and down the cobbles, dragging the trap behind him.

It was the sight of Crickem between the shafts that gave Purdy another moment of hope.

'A pony!' he exclaimed. 'We've no pony!' and he could not keep the elation out of his voice.

But Crickem turned around in the shafts and with a jerk of his head he indicated the loose boxes at the other end of the yard.

'What's wrong with those nags?' he asked, and he let the shafts drop on the ground with a clatter. Purdy was speechless.

There were only two horses kept, but they were the apples of the overseer's eye.

'The hunters!' he gasped.

'Sure!' said Crickem. 'If they're as good as Malcolm says they are they'll go like lambs under the trap.' He looked critically in the direction of the loose boxes, over the half-doors of which the two horses looked out at them with mild equine curiosity. 'We'll take the bay,' he said.

Now, if there was anything to choose between the two horses, the excess of excellence in its owner's eyes, rested with the bay.

'The bay!' said Purdy weakly, like a man in a dream, and he followed Crickem over to the largest of the stalls, where a handsome bay horse, with a white star on its face, drew back its head with a nervous tremor.

To lead out this magnificent animal and throw the harness over her, was only a matter of moments, and as Crickem expected, right from the moment she was led up to the trap, she showed herself willing and ready to draw it. Freely of her own accord she backed into the shafts and stood waiting to be hitched.

But at this point there was a small delay as Crickem wrestled with the intricacies of the harness.

He had started confidently enough and thrown the neck collar over the animal's head, the breeching across its back. He had fastened the traces to the wagon. But when he had done all this between the shafts and the bay mare there still hung down a bewildering number of leather straps that had not been pulled through the brass buckles, also of considerable numbers, on the upper parts of the harness.

Crickem scratched his head and stood back from the job.

'Just a minute! Just a minute!' he said, as if poor Purdy was complaining of the delay. He surveyed the hanging leathers. 'The main thing,' he said, catching up the belly-band and mistakenly plaiting it in with the trace, 'The main thing is to get the horse secured to the wagon. It doesn't matter much how you do it.'

Purdy, in the pointed boots, wobbled on the cobblestones in his indecision as to whether or not he should let this erroneous idea be put into practice. On the one hand they wouldn't get far but on the other hand, he shuddered to think of what might happen to the waggon on that short journey—to say nothing of what might happen to the handsome bay mare whose legs, to Purdy's troubled eye, looked as fragile as glass.

Meanwhile, as Purdy hesitated, Crickem had again tackled the job. Twice he succeeded in buckling all the buckles, but twice it was necessary to unbuckle them again. And in the course of the latter effort he had once inadvertently loosened the traces and let the shafts fall to the ground with a splintering crash, and three times he had run in and out under the bay mare's belly. But still the mare and trap were as independent of each other as they were when the mare was in her stall and the trap was in the stable.

And under the stress of coping with these unlooked-for obstacles, Crickem, who, for purposes of his own usually treated Purdy as an equal, was reaching that point at which his patience was worn so thin that truth was likely at any minute to make a sudden fissure. Several times he knocked into him as he ran from one side of the trap to the other. And although Purdy stood at a good distance from the scene of this activity, Crickem began to mutter at him under his breath.

'Can he find nowhere else to stand?' he muttered at one moment.

'How is it some people haven't the wit to get out of a person's way?'

In the course of this muttering, however, during which he had once again let the shafts fall, and twice again run in and out under the horse's belly, Crickem chanced to glance at his companion. Before Purdy had time to efface it, on his glossy countenance was a supercilious smile.

'Well?' demanded Crickem. 'What are you smiling at? Eh?' He had reached the point at which he would readily have kicked the mare, but for an instinctive feeling that a horse was not perhaps the best animal in the world with whom to engage upon a kicking match. By the gleam in his eye when it fell on Purdy it looked as if he might satisfy his impulse by kicking his fellow man. But suddenly the gleam faded.

'Look here!' he said, partly sneering, and partly in earnest, 'you're not by any chance an expert at this job?'

Purdy said nothing for a moment. Then he stooped down and caught up the belly-band. In an instant it was slipped into position, and Purdy darting around the mare had secured it in its buckles on the far side. Then the trace was slipped into its hook. Every strap was tightened and buckled, and in a few minutes nothing remained to do but jump into the trap and they would be on their way, fully equipped and as smart as paint.

Positions were once more reversed. Purdy was top-dog again. He sprang into the trap, and caught up the whip. And then on another impulse he sprang out again and threw the reins to Crickem.

'Wait a minute!' he said. 'We must bring something to eat with us.'

For he was once again back in the old days when the staff of the Centreside took their annual outing, and in those days there was always a fat hamper of food strapped under the axle of the wagonette.

'Can't we stop on the way and get something to eat in a public house?' asked Crickem, who was impatient to go spanking down the road.

Purdy looked at him with pity for his inexperience.

'You can't leave a horse on the side of the road, you know!' he said, and his little legs twinkled as he sped across the yard towards the house.

He was hardly inside the larder however when he heard a step in the yard, and there was Crickem.

'I tied the reins to the yard door,' said Crickem quickly, anticipating the look of disapproval on Purdy's face.

Only slightly relieved, Purdy again turned his attention to the food he had collected, and laid on the table. It was a mixed lot; a loaf of bread and a slab of yellow cake, a tin of sardines, a hunk of dry cheese, and in a small stone crock to keep it from melting there was a pound of strong butter. But chief among all these was a large ham-bone on which there was a certain amount of ragged pink meat.

Crickem looked critically at this collection.

Then he went into the larder, and after poking on an upper shelf he came out a few minutes later with another loaf and a bottle of green pickles. Purdy eyed the pickles. He regretted not having seen them. They seemed to give Crickem back some of his advantage over him. He looked around to see if he could go one better than the green pickles. After a minute he clicked his fingers.

'Where are the keys of the wine cellar?' he asked.

Crickem nearly let the bottle of pickles fall on the floor. So great a temerity overpowered him completely.

'Don't you know every bottle in the cellar is counted and listed,' he said. 'There's no chance of taking a bottle without it being missed.' But as he saw that Purdy was continuing to look around for the key of the cellar he looked at him with admiration. 'Are you going to take a bottle?' he asked.

'We'll see!' said Purdy. 'We'll see!' in the tone of one speaking to a child. 'Let's find the key first.'

The truth was that Purdy had suddenly remembered that several years before, Malcolm had ordered a case of liqueurs among which there had been one or two bottles of curacao for which he could not acquire a taste and which he intended to return. They had never been returned however, and if his, Purdy's, memory was correct, they were stowed away in a dark corner of the wine cellar. It was almost a certainty that these bottles of curacao would not be missed or that if they were missed it would be possible to persuade the overseer that they had been sent back to the wine merchant. On the other hand, the whole affair of the liqueurs had taken place before the arrival of Crickem, and he would not be aware that there was anything to mitigate the enormity of Purdy's daring.

When however the key of the wine cellar was located and the wine cellar was opened, a little difficulty arose as Crickem ran in ahead of Purdy, smacking his lips and uttering exclamations.

'What will we take?' he cried, and he rubbed his hands and smacked his lips. 'How about a bottle of sherry!' He snatched up a bottle of sherry and ran out of the dark cellar to hold it up to the light, but almost at once he ran back again, exclaiming and rummaging in the shelves. 'How about port? How about claret?' In all his transports he was careful, however, to cede the choice to Purdy, for with the choice went the guilt. 'What are you going to take?' he cried.

'Just a minute; just a minute!' said Purdy, and he began to take out bottle after bottle and search around in the dark recesses at the back of the vaults.

'Clever lad!' said Crickem. 'You're taking from the back where it won't be missed.'

But Purdy spurned such a suggestion.

'I'm looking for something in particular,' he cried. 'Confound the dark. Here! Light a match for me.'

But ten, twenty, matches were lit and burnt out to the tip, and still Purdy's bottles had not come into view.

'Oh let's take anything,' said Crickem, getting tired of lighting match after match. 'There's only one match left anyway,' he said as he hastily dropped the second last match and sucked his singed fingers.

Purdy faltered. Could it be that he had been mistaken? Could the curacao have been returned after all? And if this were so, what then? He had got himself into this fix. He would have to take something. He couldn't let himself down. Crickem was about to strike the last match.

'Wait! Give me that match,' cried Purdy, and taking it into his own hand he struck it carefully and guarding the flame with his hands he crawled into the last, the sole remaining vault of the wine cellar. In the shelter of the vault the flame burned brightly, and quickly ran along the thin stick of the match. Already Purdy felt the heat; he would soon have to blow it out or drop it. In despair he ran his eye around the vault.

'Ah!' Just as the flame had reached his finger-tips, just as he felt the first nip of pain, there, in the far corner of the vault, shrouded, as the trap had been with thick white cobwebs, were the three fat bottles of curacao. Eager as a mother's gaze upon her first-born, Purdy's eye fell on them. Then the match went out and they were plunged in darkness, but Purdy grabbed the bottle-necks with unerring accuracy. A minute later he crawled out backwards into the light, and triumphantly held up the bottles.

Crickem was not so elated. He looked at the labels.

'What does this stuff taste like?' he asked, and he regretfully eyed the tried and trusted sherries and ports that lined the upper vaults. But again he decided to share the taste and dispense with the guilt of the choice.

It was a true summer day. The sun shone out brilliantly, and the fields were bright and busy with the activities of harvest; some yellow with uncut corn, others pale with bleaching stubble. Some dulled with hay still in the sward, others brilliantly green with aftergrass, and spotted all over with cocks of hay. While overhead the sky was a clear deep blue.

The two butlers set out at the pace set by the bay mare; a steady brisk pace. They took the Slane road, that ran through the richest deepest part of Meath, and soon they were going up hill and down, the countryside hidden from them at one moment as they dipped into a small valley between high ditches and revealed at the next moment when there was a rise in the road, or when they rolled up over one of the many railway bridges that rose up like hoops in the flat parts of the land to give a magnificent view across the entire county, with its plains diversified by pasture and grain, and shadowed by the woodlands of its great demesnes. But Purdy and Crickem, when they stood up in the trap, as they did at every other turn of the road, did so not to view this magnificent panorama but to wave their hats and shake their hands at the harvesters inside the hedges, and blow kisses to the girls.

The sight which so delighted the two gallants, was, however, hardly to be compared with the sight that they themselves presented to the people at whom they waved. For the bright scene of summer comes and goes, but the country people who casually raised their heads at the sound of the high-stepping mare, were left staring open-mouthed with astonishment when they saw the two butlers bowling along the road in their outmoded vehicle. Those that were near enough to the road dropped their forks and rakes and lustily waved their straw hats. A few old men ran out towards the road, and taking the pipes from their puckered mouths called out hoarsely:

'Have the old times come back again!'

But it was the women who were most excited. It was the women who felt intuitively that there was something illicit about the two men in black frock-coats jogging along in a horse and trap. And something in themselves responded. Their eyes grew bolder and they threw out their bosoms brazenly.

'There's a sight for sore eyes!' cried Purdy as they passed one field where the workers were all women and young girls. They were tossing hay that had evidently heated in the cocks and had to be remade.

'What we want now,' cried Crickem, 'is two girls of our own.'

But to make a choice; that was going to be the difficulty.

'Look at those for girls!' cried Purdy, pointing to the other side of the road, where there was a knot of young girls sitting on a gate. They had come out to the fields with lunch pails to their menfolk, and now they sat on the gate in their bright cotton frocks and blouses and their flashing white aprons.

'There's a sight for you,' he cried again delightedly, as the women, emboldened by their numbers, looked at them with flashing eyes, and pushed each other forward with false screams and a lot of laughing. And those that pushed others forward, with a rowdy hand or a coarse gesture, offered themselves more urgently with their bright bold eyes.

And the two men on the pony cart drank in the intoxicating sensations given them by the women, as their nostrils and their open mouths drank in the sweet rushing air. But still they did not stop the mare, who cantered gaily onward. Clusters of women were dangerous. Might not the ones that were boldest in offering themselves be the most resentful if their offers were accepted. Might not the triumphant chariot career be turned into a rout, and might they not end, if they stopped, by having to scramble back into the waggon with ignominy, and depart in a hail of derisive taunts, perhaps even of stones. No. They could not risk stopping until they were sure of themselves.

And yet, girls were necessary to make the escapade complete.

'We must get a couple of girls. We won't be right without them,' said Crickem over and over again.

They were frank enough with each other about it.

'No use!' they would say as they passed group after group of women, merely waving at them and raising their hats. 'No use! They're bold enough at a distance.'

'Wait till we're passing through some town,' said Crickem. 'We'd stand a better chance with the town girls.'

'Oh, yes, town girls are the thing,' Purdy agreed.

'Whenever you see a crowd of girls together,' said Crickem, 'you can make up your mind you have a poor chance of picking up with one of them. They wouldn't give in to each other that they like that kind of thing. Wait till we come across a couple of girls by themselves. You'll see we'll come across plenty like that. When you see two girls sitting on the side of the bank you stand a chance with them. And the cooler they are the better your chance, many a time. These ones that roll their eyes and toss their heads know they're safe with the crowd. But two girls sitting on a bank! That's a different thing. What are they doing on the bank? What's in their mind if it's not the same thing that's in your own mind? See!'

And Purdy saw.

All the same when, not long after this profound remark the two gallants passed a high bank on which were sitting two girls with saucy hats, and bright flashing stockings, still they did not stop.

And why? Well, it was probably Purdy's fault. When they first sighted the two girls, Crickem sat up with an eager smirk.

'What did I tell you?' he demanded.

But although he too sat up, Purdy felt a pang of uneasiness. Certain failures of the past came to his mind for the first time in years. Certain miscalculations he had made with Amelia were recalled to him in a rush. And his heart misgave him. Supposing the girls were to turn him down! Suppose they were to snigger when he took off his bowler hat! Supposing, in short, that both of them should want to have Crickem, and want to sit on either side of him, and let him put his arm around them, one in each arm, while he, Purdy, sat alone in the back of the trap, rolling over the countryside, a butt for the jeering of everyone they passed on the road.

They were almost abreast of the girls.

'Good-looking, aren't they?' whispered Crickem.

Purdy pressed his lips together and then opened them with an inspired remark.

'Do you call that good-looking?' he asked. 'I must say I'd like something better on my knee than one of those skinny creatures.'

Crickem turned around. He was astonished; so astonished in fact that he forgot to corroborate his own impression and they passed by the two girls on the bank, who unable to believe their eyes, were sitting up looking after the trap with their mouths wide open. Crickem stared at Purdy. This was the bald little fellow, who was paying alimony to some shrew of a wife, and whom in the matters of women he had always treated with contempt, and yet two of the best turned-out dolls you could ask to see were not pretty enough to satisfy him. Well! Crickem shook his head. He began to lose faith in his own judgment. Perhaps the two on the bank had been a bit flashy. Perhaps there would be better to be had further up along the road. The young man sighed. But then he took heart again. The day was young.

Just then two more girls appeared, walking in the middle of the road ahead of them. At the sound of the horse's trot on the road the girls turned and looked back over their shoulder. Ah! Here was something. One of the girls had red hair and carmine cheeks. Her teeth were flashing, and in her eyes there was just the right amount of impudence and independence. Crickem sat up again and over his face came the familiar smirk. He didn't look at the other girl at all.

But Purdy did. He saw at once that she was the foil that has ever and always appeared beside the heroines of history, literature, and romance. He saw she was fat, plain, pale, and pasty-faced. And he surmised much worse. In all likelihood she would have a tendency to buck-teeth, a squint, or bandy legs. And there was no doubt in his mind that she would fall to him. Instantly he pictured Crickem with the red-head sitting beside him, blowing hot and cold upon him, with her chilly manner and her warm inviting eyes, while he, in all likelihood, would hardly have room on the other seat, with the fat creature's arm laced around him like a vice. Oh, he knew those plain women. He knew those ones that didn't like men. The world wasn't all Amelias! He felt the sweat break out on him. Perhaps after all there were worse faults than Amelia's faults.

The mare raced forward. The girls had moved to the side of the road, the red-head indeed merely moving in a few paces, but already, as Purdy suspected, the foil was going into her tricks. It was she who would be expected to attract their attention; to effect an introduction. With an artificial squeal the fat girl suddenly scrambled up on the ditch and called out to her companion to do the same, thus making an opportunity for the men to get their names.

'Crissie! Crissie! A runaway horse! Get up or you'll be killed!' She screamed again. And then linking the two parties together, she pointed a fat finger at Crissie and called out to the occupants of the on-rolling trap. 'Tell her to get out of the way,' she cried. 'She'll be killed. Oh! Oh!' And she began to scream again without ceasing.

Purdy looked at Crickem.

Crickem's eyes were fastened on Crissie, who, calm and immovable, indifferent to danger, refused to step aside an inch, and glancing collectedly at the trap, called out reprovingly to her friend.

'Don't be silly, Polly. The horse is as quiet as a lamb. And anyway I expect these gentlemen have the animal well under control.' As she spoke, Crissie raised her eyes and they were filled with messages of apology for Polly. But all the messages in those charming eyes were directed at Crickem, and at Crickem alone.

Didn't he know it would be like this! Purdy felt the sweat break out on him again. And the fat creature's name; Polly! That was the last straw.

Once more he would have to take action, and take action quickly.

'Which of them is the worst?' he whispered under his breath to Crickem. 'Which will you have; the fat one or the one with the bandy legs?'

'Bandy legs!' Crickem's smile faded. He almost rose up in the trap. But it was too late. They were on top of the girls and all that could be seen of the saucy red-head was her face. Her legs, bandy or otherwise, were now hidden from them by the mare's girth as they passed them by, without slackening pace. But it must have been the red-head that Purdy had called bandy-legged, for, high on the ditch, plain to be seen, was Polly. And Polly's legs were not bandy. In fact Polly's legs were so fat they would easily have borne the weight of five or six Pollys.

The moment was lost. They had trotted past. And again Crickem did not look back. He turned in amazement to Purdy.

'You don't miss anything, do you?' he said, in awe. 'I didn't see anything wrong with the red-head. When did you get so particular. I thought I was particular, but you beat all I ever came across!' Then he looked back regretfully. 'We'll never get a girl at this rate,' he said, but Polly and Crissie had been left behind in a sweep of the road, and there was no further chance of seeing how far Crissie's legs belied the saucy confidence of her face.

Meanwhile the day rolled on, and the waggon rolled on, and the countryside rolled past them in the opposite direction, and since it was a summer day of unusual warmth and brightness, it need hardly be stated that the galliards met and passed many a pretty girl on the way. But something had happened to Crickem; some chord in his confidence had snapped, and it was he now who was anxious to show Purdy that he too was a bit particular.

They no sooner came in sight of a pair of legs on the road in front of them than Crickem began to criticise the girls.

And then there was the hamper tied to the axle. There was no sense sharing it, it was small enough for two people. It was better to eat it, while they had the chance.

'There will be plenty of time afterwards,' said Purdy, 'for picking buttercups,' and he gave Crickem a dig in the ribs in case the young man might miss the meaning expressed in this fragrant phrase of byegone days.

It was about four o'clock in the afternoon when they pulled in under a shady chestnut tree at the side of the road, tied the mare to the tree, and got out the ham-bone and the bottles of curacao.

'I didn't know I was so hungry,' said Crickem, filling his mouth with cheese.

'Did you see the corkscrew anywhere?' said Purdy, and, rummaging in the hamper with their mouths full, neither of them as much as turned to look at a buxom buttercup that went down the road beside them, leading her cows home from pasture. And when she passed a second time, having no doubt milked the cows in the interval, they were still less aware of her than before, for there had been more meat than you'd imagine on the ham-bone, and the green pickles were heavy. Our friends had overeaten, and asked no more than to lie on their backs, with their hats over their faces, and snore. Buttercups might spring up all around them, and yet cause them no disturbance. The only disturbance they experienced came from within. The curacao made them feel slightly sick.

But as they lay replete under the throbbing sun, through their drowsy minds there wandered visions of all the women and girls they had passed on the roads, and in the fields; all the Crissies and the Pollys; all the buxom women that had stood at cottage doors, and all the blushing slips of girls that had hid their faces and giggled at them. And they were almost as surfeited with visions of hips and thighs, dimpled elbows, and bosoms and bellies, as they were with green pickles.

Purdy, in particular, was worn out.

At last, however, the chill of the early harvest eventide began to steal its way through the grasses under them, and the shade of the tree to which the mare was tied, began to spread its shade upon them. The mare was the first to feel the evening deepening around her, and her sensitive skin quivered as the shades fell blue about her. She began to kick the iron bars of the gate to which she was tied, with an impatient hoof, and to rattle her trappings.

The two butlers sat up.

'How about heading for home?' said Purdy. The day had been long enough for him.

But Crickem, at the first chill touch of the evening air, was restored to his full vigour.

The false feeling of satisfaction fell away from him in an instant, when he stood upon his feet, and the pricks of the chill evening were less insistent than the pricks of his thwarted desires.

Where had the day gone? How had it wasted away like this? He looked at Purdy. It was the old fellow's fault, he thought. If the old fellow hadn't been so particular they might have had a girl apiece now. It would be cold going back in the trap. It wouldn't have been a bad thing to have a hot arm around your middle to keep you warm. Crickem grew warmer at the very thought. They might even have got a couple of girls who would have gone back with them to The Manse. All those empty rooms! All those big beds! What an opportunity lost! A feeling of positive hatred for Purdy shot through him, and he glared at him, but Purdy wasn't looking. Purdy was patting the mare, and rubbing his hand over her haunches that were dappled with dried sweat marks and rough with dandruff and loosened hairs. The day had told on the mare.

'We'll have to give this animal a good rub down when we get back,' he said.

Crickem said nothing. He stood sneering at the crumpled tails of Purdy's coat, and the glossy seat of his pants all stained with grass. He wanted to do something to annoy him. He wanted to make him sting. He wanted to take the complacent look off his glossy fat face. And he knew how to do it.

He walked over to the chestnut tree and untied the mare. He helped Purdy to hitch her without saying a word, but when they sat up on the trap he had the familiar smirk on his face that Purdy knew and dreaded.

'Wouldn't it be a good joke,' he said then, breaking the silence, as if casually, 'wouldn't it be a good joke if the old Manse was burnt to the ground when we got back!'

Crickem had calculated fairly correctly. Purdy was stung; but not as badly as the young man would have wished. His fat cheeks shook all right, but he controlled his start with a little laugh.

'Oh, I don't suppose that's likely to happen,' he said, and endeavoured to forget such an evil suggestion as quickly as he could. Crickem, however, had left something out of his calculations, and that was the effect upon himself of his own remark. No sooner had he uttered it, however, than a superstitious feeling began to form inside him. He wished he had kept his mouth shut, and when Purdy gave a watery smile in his direction and pretended to take the joke in good part, the smile was not more watery than the smile on Crickem's own face. It was Crickem who had to break the silence that he had drawn down on them.

'I wonder could we be blamed if the old place did take fire?' he asked, 'I mean, could we be held responsible?'

He looked at Purdy, whom he had begun to hate less acutely in the last few minutes, and when Purdy looked around to answer him he was struck for the first time at how young his companion looked; a mere youth, thought Purdy in surprise; gawky, inexperienced. He was a bit worried, but not as worried as he had been before they set out. His was the worry of the cautious person that sets in before the deed is done, not the worry of the reckless that waits till the deed is beyond repair.

'There's no use worrying about it now,' he said, in an effort to reassure his companion, who fidgeted nervously on his seat.

And with this, Purdy flicked the whip in the air, and pointed out over the valley below them, for they had entered upon the Slane road again, and indicating the magnificent panorama of Meath, he admonished his companion to enjoy it.

'Look at that view!' he cried. 'Where would you see the like of it!'

And indeed it was beautiful. Although they had passed along this road earlier in the day, its beauty was not so evident, their excitement had clouded their minds and the human activity in the fields had distracted their eyes from the landscape. But now, there were no women in bright red blouses in the foreground. There were no girls in white aprons sitting on the gates. The eye flew over the empty fields to the far rim of the sky where the irregular patches of trees were deepened with blue mist. Trees and bushes, and even the far fields seemed a deep blue under this evening mist. And the blueness everywhere made the vista more immense. Even in the hayfields near at hand the yellow cocks were insignificant beside their own great blue shadows stretching out on the stubble beside them.

'A magnificent view!' cried Purdy again. 'There's no doubt about it, but a horse and trap is the only way to see the countryside. Such a view. You can see the countryside for miles around.' He stood up in the trap and looked all around him, as they rolled up one of the hooped bridges of the railway.

Crickem, who up to this had not paid much heed to Purdy's comments on the view became somewhat more interested. He too stood up in the trap, but he faced forward, and stared ahead over the wide sweep that now lay immediately in front as well as below them for the road swept around a bend at this point.

'We ought to be able to see The Manse from here,' he said, and he tried to distinguish between the various masses of trees upon the sky line.

'Are you still afraid it's on fire!' said Purdy, and he laughed good-humouredly. The day had been so full and satisfying for him. He had forgotten his fidgets and fears.

Crickem bit his lip with vexation.

'It's all very fine for you to laugh,' he said, 'but if I were you I wouldn't be so gay. I don't like to think of the way you were playing with those matches in the wine cellar. Are you sure you stamped on them all? You should always stamp on a burnt match. You never know when it might smoulder and catch light again.' But Purdy laughed more heartily.

131

'The walls of the cellar are lined with brick,' he said.

Crickem said nothing for a minute.

'Think of all the straw from the wine bottles that was on the floor!'

'Oh come! Come!' said Purdy, patronisingly, 'Buck up! I can tell you if the old Manse was on fire we'd have no difficulty in seeing the smoke,' He pointed out again over the vast view with the handle of the yellow whip, and at the same time he opened his mouth and drew in such a deep breath that the buttons on his coat were strained to the limits of their thread and the top button popped open. 'Have you no poetry in you? Have you nothing to say at the sight of that sky! Look at those trees over there in the distance! Look at that mist hanging in the air!'

Crickem made an effort to shake himself up.

'Mist is for heat,' he said, at random. 'It will be another hot day tomorrow.' He stared into the distance morosely. 'It's just like smoke,' he said. 'Isn't it? Blue smoke!'

'Now you're talking,' said Purdy. 'That's just what it's like; blue smoke.' And the better to appreciate this poetic comparison he slackened his hands on the reins and let the mare break her gait. They proceeded at a walking pace, and Purdy gazed ecstatically over the scenery.

'Look at that clump of trees directly in front of us, now,' he said. 'Do you see the clump I mean,' he pointed with the end of the whip and then with a fat finger, and then he began to give more explicit directions. 'Move over nearer to me,' he said to Crickem. 'Run your eye along my finger.' Then he stopped up. 'Wait a minute,' he said, and he pulled the reins short and stopped the mare. 'Do you see that tree in the middle of that field?' he asked.

'Yes,' said Crickem listlessly.

'Well, run your eye along in a straight line from that. Do you see a spire a bit to the left? You do? Very well, now keep your eye on that spire, and raise it a few inches to the far side. Did you do that? You did? Well! What do you see?

'I see the spire,' said Crickem, still more listlessly.

'Good,' said Purdy. 'Well, if you see the spire you must see the clump of trees I mean because they're just beyond the spire.'

'I see them,' said Crickem.

'Well!' said Purdy.

'Well what?' said Crickem.

'Don't you recognise them? They're the trees of The Manse or I'm greatly mistaken.'

'Oh!' said Crickem, and sat up with greater interest.

'Do you think it is?' he asked, for now he had located the clump of trees and was giving all his attention to it although it looked very similar to all the other patches of woodland in the plain below them.

'I'm sure of it,' said Purdy. His chest swelled. 'It must be one of the finest places in the county,' he said. A feeling of pride possessed him. 'Our place must be one of the best wooded places in the county. Look at those trees! Look at the way the mist is thick in them! I bet it's as dark as night in the middle of some of those copses now.'

The mist was certainly deeper. It not only lay in the crevices of the trees and bushes but seemed to rise up over them like a vapour to meet the evening clouds of a still deeper blue that were beginning to gather in the sky.

'I never saw anything so like smoke as that mist,' said Crickem, become touched in spite of himself by the serene expanse below.

133

'That was a good description of yours,' said Purdy. 'A poet couldn't have put it better. Look! Wouldn't you swear it was smoke! And look at those clouds! You'd swear they were clouds of blue smoke hanging in the air.' Then a playful impulse came over him; once more he poked Crickem in the ribs. 'What's this you said,' he asked. 'Wouldn't it be a good joke if it was smoke!' And he threw back his head and laughed. Purdy laughed, and laughed, and as he laughed the reins slipped loose and the mare moved over to the side of the road and began to crop abruptly at the long damp blades of grass that grew up through heaps of stones left on the side of the road by the road-menders.

'Oh, shut up!' said Crickem, and he caught at the reins. 'Are you going to drive, or are you not? Give me the reins if you're not able to drive the animal.' He gave the reins a vicious tug that caused the animal to throw back her head and show her long yellow teeth stained with the green sap of the grass. 'As I said before,' said Crickem, when Purdy wiping the tears of laughter from his eyes took control of the reins again, 'As I said before it wouldn't be such a joke on me as it would on you. It wasn't my idea to go fooling about with matches in a dark cellar.'

Purdy's fat sides shook with laughter. Crickem had a longing to give him a push and topple him out of the trap on to one of the heaps of stones. He bit his lips and glared at the skyline.

'You'd laugh on the other side of your face,' he said, 'if a few sparks came up out of that clump of trees!'

And then, just as he spoke, the young man's mouth fell open, and clutching Purdy by the arm he nearly dragged him off his seat. The reins fell to the floor of the vehicle.

'Purdy!' he cried. 'For God's sake. Look! Did you see sparks that time?' For hardly had he let the words pass from his lips than up from the distant blue trees there flew a covey of red sparks.

For a moment Purdy thought he was being fooled, but unmistakably again a flight of bright sparks flew into the sky.

'Fire!' cried Crickem. 'It's a fire. What did I tell you! It's The Manse! The place is on fire. I knew it! I knew it! I had a feeling about it.' He became suffused with fear. His face was a sickly white. 'You and your mist!' he screamed. 'I said all along it was smoke. "It's like smoke," I said. You can't deny that!'

But Purdy was staring at the distant smoke, that unmistakably now twisted up over the lovely wooded copse, and mingled with the evening clouds.

'It may be just a fire in the woods,' he said dully, but his voice did not carry conviction.

He appeared to be stupefied. Then suddenly he sprang to his feet, and standing up in the cart he caught the ends of the reins and slapped the back of the mare. 'How long will it take us to get back?' he cried, as he fell back into his seat when the mare broke into an unsteady gallop. But Crickem too had scrambled to his feet, and tottering from side to side unsteadily in the galloping trap he held on to the dash-board with one hand and with the other he tried to catch and drag the reins out of Purdy's hands.

'Wait a minute,' he yelled. 'Wait a minute. Think what you're doing. It's the other way we ought to be going! If the place is on fire we had better get out of the county as quick as we can.'

'What do you mean?' cried Purdy. 'Sit down you young fool or you'll fall out of the trap,' and he held tight to the reins.

Crickem tugged harder at the reins. 'Do you realise,' he yelled, 'that we may be held responsible for going out and leaving the place with no one in it.' He gave another violent tug at the reins to try to get them from Purdy and the baffled animal suddenly rose on her hindlegs, not like an animal given to such habits but as one sorely perplexed.

'Let go the reins you fool,' cried Purdy. 'Do you want to upset us into the ditch!'

'I don't care if I do,' said Crickem. 'I'm telling you the best thing we can do is leave the outfit here and make across the fields to the nearest station. We might get a train to Drogheda that would get us to Dublin tonight. In Dublin we'd get the mail boat and get out of the country altogether.'

'Are you mad?' Purdy wrenched the reins back into his own control, and leaned over the trap to pat the haunch of the trembling animal in the shafts. 'If we didn't turn up it might be said that we set the place on fire!'

'And what else did we do?' cried Crickem. 'Curse those matches. Curse you and your bottles of fancy syrup—the damn stuff made me sick into the bargain.'

'We didn't do it on purpose,' said Purdy, 'and if we get back we might be able to help to put out the fire.'

He looked wildly over at the distant trees, where the heavy clouds of night and the clouds of smoke were now mingled together, the underside of them illuminated occasionally with dreadful pink reflections. Night was coming, and with it the nature of the fire was becoming more plain.

'We might be able to do something,' he cried. 'It might be only the stables. It might be only a fire in the woods.' He lashed the mare forward again, and then as

Crickem still stood tottering on his feet, he gave him a push. 'Sit down if you don't want to fall out of the cart,' he said. Then on a second thought he glanced at the young fellow again, with contempt. 'If you don't want to go back, I'll let you out,' he said. 'But I'm going back!'

Crickem skulked in the seat without answering. Then in a mealy voice he muttered something under his breath.

'What did you say?' called Purdy.

'I said it wasn't my idea to go fooling about the cellar, with matches,' said Crickem vindictively, 'And it was you struck the last match!'

For several minutes then they careered along the road in silence, Purdy standing and lashing the mare onward, Crickem sitting crouched up in the trap, his face bleakly fixed in the direction of the glow that grew brighter minute by minute in the darkening plain.

But as Crickem sat hunched up and staring at this glow, the dark masses of tree and shadow to the left of the bright glow was suddenly pricked here and there with white points of light. For a moment the young man stared at these lights without interest and without comprehension. But all at once he threw up his head.

'Purdy!' he shouted. 'Look at the lights!'

'What about them?' said Purdy irritably. 'They're the lights of the town.'

'I know that,' cried Crickem excitedly. 'I know it. But don't you see, they're beyond the fire. Beyond it! Do you hear me!' He screamed the words at Purdy. 'It isn't the old Manse at all. It's some other place. Do you hear me? Some other place!' And half shouting and half crying he staggered to his feet again, and leaned out over the horse's back.

Purdy could not believe the evidence of Crickem's eyes, and, continuing to lash the mare forward, he strained his own eyes over the distance. But as he stared his hands grew looser on the reins and the jaded animal instantly slackened her pace, and after a minute dropped into a walk.

'You're right, Crickem!' said Purdy at last, and flopped back into the seat, wiping the sweat from his face with the flat of his palm. The mare came to a dead stop.

The two butlers sat in the motionless trap. The night air cut into them. The sweat broke freely from them. The mare, too jaded to graze, gave occasional short erratic crops at the dank unseen grass under her feet by the wayside.

'Well!' said Crickem after a few minutes. 'What do you think of that!' He laughed awkwardly. He was feeling ashamed. For a minute he wondered if he could pretend he had been joking all the time, that he had known all along it was not The Manse that was on fire. But he was too fatigued and broken down by the strain to sustain the effort of pretence. He merely sat in the seat, slumped where he had been crouched.

But after sitting a few minutes like this, Crickem looked at Purdy who was sweating profusely and seemed as if he might sit where he was all night.

'Well!' said Crickem. 'That gave us a jolt all right.' He laughed again weakly. Then he nudged Purdy. 'Well! Why are we sitting here? Let's get on our way again.'

But Purdy, who had risen to the occasion when danger had threatened was deflated now; he sat stolid on the seat.

'What would we have done if it was The Manse?' he asked, and he turned heavily to Crickem. 'How would we have faced Malcolm?'

But Crickem was in no mood for these speculations. It was getting downright cold. His fingers were beginning to get numb.

'Look here,' he said, 'if you don't want to get home, I do. Give me the reins. Move up there,' and stepping across the short stiff legs of Purdy he took his place on the driving side. The whip he could not take; it was clamped fast in Purdy's fist as if in the fist of a dead man. Bending the reins, Crickem lashed at the jaded mare who began to move forward again, her legs plaiting under her with fatigue.

Crickem himself was in excellent spirits.

'I always said I was a lucky fellow,' he said. 'I have the luck of the devil. I don't know why I was worried about the fire at any time. Nothing like that ever happens to me. I never yet got into a scrape I couldn't get out of again. I'd get out of hell if I ever got in. But I won't!' He poked the inert Purdy. 'Sit up, Purdy,' he said. 'We're coming to a village.'

There was an unusual stir in the small village.

'We must ask where the fire is,' said Crickem. 'Do you know I believe it's Liscard!' he said.

Liscard was a neighbouring demesne and the two men from The Manse had some acquaintance with the staff there.

'I wonder would we go up and look at it,' said Crickem, as Purdy did not answer, for on their right now, quite near, they could hear the commotion of people shouting and the air was filled with the nauseating odour of charred wood.

'Do you want the horse to drop dead under us?' said Purdy then. He didn't want to see the fire. It made him shudder to think of it. It reminded him too much of what might have been.

'I think it would be a bit of sport to go up,' said Crickem. 'I wonder if his lordship was there when the fire broke out. If he wasn't you can imagine the sweat old Evans was in.'

Evans was the foreman at Liscard.

'Poor Evans!' said Purdy. He knew him a long time.

'Poor Evans my eye!' said Crickem. 'I'd just like to see him now.' He turned around. 'I bet he's hopping like a frog. Come on. Be a sport,' he said. 'Let's go up the road a bit. Think of the game we'd have looking at old Evans. And think of the fat old cook. She'd be a nice bundle to catch in a sheet! And think of the maids! Think of them screeching! Think of them jumping out of the windows into a sheet with their skirts blown out like balloons.' He slapped his thigh and roared laughing. 'Think of their petticoats!' he said, almost choking with laughter. 'Think of their drawers!'

But Purdy was thinking of Bina. Bina was the cook.

'Poor Bina!' he said.

There had been times when he had thought that if it had not been for Amelia! Ah well! There was no use in such vain thoughts.

'Will you come?' said Crickem for the last time. 'I'll tell you what we'll do. We'll tie the old nag to a tree and cut across the fields. Not that there's any need to tie the old bag of bones to anything; it's taking her all her time to put one foot before another.'

Purdy came to life.

'If we tie that animal to anything,' he said, 'we'll tie her to the door of a public house. I'm badly in need of a drink.'

Crickem hesitated another minute.

'All right,' he said. Perhaps when the old fellow was warmed up with a few whiskeys he'd feel differently about going to the fire. 'Get on, you trollop!' he said, lashing the mare again.

The village was only a hundred yards away, but it took them five minutes to beat the mare over the ground.

'We'll have to give her a bucket of beer too!' said Crickem in high fettle. 'We'll never get her home if we don't. We have another six miles to go if we have a yard to go.'

Purdy was scanning the dark village street for the lighted door of the public house.

'It's seven miles from here to the front gate of The Manse,' he said absentmindedly.

Crickem snapped his fingers.

'I'll tell you what we'll do,' he said. 'We'll get a bit of oats from the publican here in this place, and stable the old jade for a while. She'll never make the seven miles without a rest. And we can go across the fields to the fire. She'll be as fresh as a filly when we get back. How is that for a good plan?'

They had reached the small public house and Crickem drew rein, an entirely unnecessary gesture for the animal had come to a natural stop at the barrier of light that flooded out through the doorway of the public house.

The young man sprang to the ground.

'Are you sure it's all right to leave the mare,' said Purdy, looking at the dejected animal whose head drooped down between its forelegs.

Crickem made no answer. He had disappeared into the lighted bar, where bottles and glasses gleamed silver and gold in the light of a hanging oil-lamp. The place had an air of activity most unusual in a small village. The counter was ringed with wet marks as if numberless glasses had been filled and emptied across it in recent minutes and several empty glasses still remained on it.

There had evidently been a big trade done in the last few hours. Those who were quenching the fire had found frequent necessity also to quench their thirst. Behind the counter there was not only the publican but a young girl in a red jumper, an elderly woman, and a small boy, all members of the publican's family who had been drafted at short notice to cope with the unusual situation.

When Purdy and Crickem made their appearance the publican, who had evidently been taking a rest, hurriedly stirred himself again to remove the soiled glasses, in armfuls from the counter. The stout woman snatched up a cloth to wipe them. The young girl in the red jumper sprang to activity, and pushing back her black hair with a sweep of her hand came forward and asked them what they wanted to drink.

'You seem to have had a busy evening,' said Crickem to the young girl, pointing to the soiled floor, but leaning over the counter to stare at her.

'It's the fire at Liscard,' said the girl. 'The whole village is up there. And it's giving them such a thirst. Every other few minutes there's a crowd rushing back here to wet their throttles.'

The stout woman moved over nearer and seeing that Purdy and Crickem were alone, and were not the vanguard of another rush of trade, she ceased from wiping the glasses and joined in the talk.

'I suppose you're going up to see the sight too, people are coming from far and near to see it,' she said. 'I wish we could go up there. I believe it's a sight you'd never forget. One whole side of the house is gutted,' She sighed. 'It's a sight worth seeing. But we can't leave here. We got a glimpse of the flames out of one of the windows upstairs, but every time we got to the window a rush started here below and we had to come down again.' She pointed to the young boy. 'Even the young lad had to stay and help. It's a great pity. It would have been such an education to him. But it's a bad wind that doesn't blow someone good,' she said, as she took the coin that Crickem tossed down on the counter.

Meanwhile the publican had said nothing, but he was staring at Purdy with a peculiar expression. Purdy who had been in the place once or twice hoped that the publican did not recognise him. He had not spoken a word, but had taken up his glass and begun to stare into it. He wished that Crickem would not keep up the chatter.

The women drew out a till under the counter and threw Crickem's coin on to the heap of silver and copper coins that jostled each other like a shoal of live fish.

The publican was still staring at Purdy. Suddenly he edged the woman away from the counter, and took her place, leaning out across the board on his bare arms from which the blue shirtsleeves were rolled back.

'That was a terrible thing that fire,' he said, and he addressed himself to Purdy.

'Was there much damage done?' said Purdy, forced into talk.

'Damage enough,' said the publican moodily. Then he looked up. 'The other place was worse,' he said. 'The other place was burnt to the ground, I hear.'

'The other place! What other place?' said Purdy.

The publican looked curiously at him.

'Didn't you hear?' he said.

'What?' said Purdy.

Crickem was leaning across the counter, with one eye on the publican and the other upon the stout woman as she stood with her back to him washing the glasses. He had succeeded in making a not altogether unwilling captive of the young girl's hand.

'It's the most curious thing that ever happened in my time,' said the publican to Purdy. 'Two big mansions to go on fire in the one day, and within a few miles of each other.'

143

At the other end of the counter Purdy saw Crickem drop the girl's hand. His own body was growing cold.

'Two big fires?' he asked in a faint dim voice.

'Within a few miles of each other,' said the publican. 'Did you ever hear anything like it. Some say the sparks from the other place must have blown across the river and set fire to this place.' He jerked his thumb over his shoulder to indicate the scene of the local fire.

The stout woman joined the conversation again.

'We were all out on the hill at the back of the shop looking at the flames of the other fire, so we can't complain too much about not seeing this one. We saw something anyway, didn't we, Packy?' She tousled the head of the small boy.

'It was a better blaze than this one,' said the child in a shrill bragging voice. He was humiliated at not being out with the other young boys leaping and yelling in the flickers of the fire.

'It was worse than this one, all right,' said the publican. 'They saved the best part of the house up at Liscard. Only the servants' quarters were burned and there was talk of tearing them down anyway. But the other place was burned to the ground I believe. They got the fire under control in time at Liscard, but it seems the other place was empty. There was no one in it at all.'

Purdy saw Crickem moving over nearer to him. He looked up. Crickem's face was as drawn and white and the pimples stood out on it like lumps in porridge.

The two butlers looked at each other.

'Did you hear that?' said Purdy.

'I did,' said Crickem, and as if the publican spoke another tongue and Purdy was an interpreter, he spoke again to Purdy.

'Ask him where the other fire was, can't you?' he prompted.

But Purdy had begun to tremble. His lip shook, and he felt his eye beginning to twitch. His head reeled, and when he looked up at the publican it was Amelia's face that floated for a moment before his eyes. He opened his mouth to speak, but instead he suddenly turned back to Crickem.

'Let's get into the air,' he gasped, and he stumbled out into the darkness, followed at once by the dazed Crickem.

The publican looked after them. The publican's wife and the young girl exchanged glances with each other.

'What ails those fellows?' said the girl, peeved at the gallant Crickem's abrupt departure.

The publican stretched out an arm to embrace the two empty glasses the men had left down so hastily.

'I thought I knew the small fat fellow,' he said. 'I thought he was a butler at The Manse.'

The woman scoffed.

'Didn't you see they were strangers,' she said. 'They knew nothing at all about the fire up there.'

'That's right,' said the young girl. 'They were strangers. They didn't even ask where the other fire was, although you'd imagine even strangers would have asked that!'

She looked at her wrist and put it up to her lips. It was red from the way the young man had gripped her, before he took such a sudden notion to dash away.

A Happy Death

'Are you up there, Mother?' The child's thin voice shrilled up the dark stairs, as she stood at the bottom and looked upward, her small, white face tilted back on her thin neck.

'What do you want?'

The mother came to the bannister rail on the landing overhead, and leaned across it. It was the custom of the household to eliminate footsteps whenever possible by carrying on conversations from room to room, and even, as in this case, from one landing to another, but the lodger in the lower-front room, who was understood to be connected with the stage, had a cold in the head and had not gone out to the theatre that day, and it was in deference to the unusual presence by daytime of a stranger in the house that the woman came out to lean over the bannister.

'What are you shouting for?' she demanded. 'What do you want?'

At the response, however unsatisfactory, from the woman above, the child straightened her neck with relief, but a minute later some urgency in what she had to say to her mother made her strain her face upward again.

'Are you coming down, Mother?' she said, in a whimpering voice that seemed to expect a short answer.

'What do you want me for, might I ask?' the mother demanded, uncompromisingly. 'Hurry up! I can't stand here all day with my two hands idle down by my sides.'

146

The child was reluctant to give the reason for her request. She thought desperately for a minute, trying to find something to say that would bring the woman downstairs. She had apparently no faith in the efficacy of the truth, but as the woman on the upper landing shrugged her shoulders and made a move to go back into the room she had been dusting, the child was forced, against her judgment, to make what use she could of the truth, weak as it was.

'He's bad, Mother,' she said. 'He's coughing and moaning.'

There was no need to mention a name. There was only one man in the family, and the lodgers were all women. A pronoun identified him at any time. He was rarely called Father by any of the children, which was hardly surprising since he had less authority in the house than any of them. As for their mother, it was years since she had called him by his Christian name, and there would appear to be something unseemly now in her doing so. Indeed, it was such a far cry from the time she had called him Robert that it hardly seemed possible to the children that Robert and he could ever be the same person. Not that they had ever heard much about Robert, either, but judging from the few fragments of the past they had pieced together from occasional words their mother had let fall, it seemed to them that Robert must have been the kind of young man with whom they themselves would have been proud to have been seen out walking. He seemed to be the romantic kind of young man who could never grow old. He certainly could never have become the hollow-faced nonentity that stole apologetically in and out of the house, and ate his meals in the darkest corner of the kitchen between the sink and the yard door. Why! Robert was their ideal young man. And to

Alary, the oldest girl, who had a crippled back, due to a spinal injury in her childhood, Robert was the dominant figure in the long romances she wove as she sat sewing all day. Mary was apprenticed to a dressmaker, being unfit for anything more strenuous. To the youngest child, Nonny, who was now calling up the stairs to her mother, it was doubtful if the name Robert meant anything at all, for Ella had long given up even the most casual remarks about the past by the time Nonny was born.

Nonny was now eleven years old. And, this morning, with her small face, startlingly white in the dark hallway, she looked less than eleven as she stared anxiously up the stairs, at a loss to know what to do. At last she stood up uncertainly and went up a few steps.

She could hear her mother in the room above. She could hear the sound of the sweeping brush knocking against the wainscoting and against the legs of the bed.

'Please come down, Ma,' she pleaded. 'He's sick. He's bad. He's sitting in the kitchen moaning.'

The woman came out to the landing again, but her intention was only to pacify the child.

'Did you ever see him any other way?' she asked.

The child, whose eyes had lit with a flicker of hope, said nothing at this, but after staring helplessly up the stairs, her teeth bit slowly into her lower lip, and, sitting down abruptly on the stairs, she broke into silent, helpless tears.

The woman looked down at her impatiently and frowned. She resented this implication of sympathy with the man in the kitchen. She resented any sympathy with him, from any of the children. She always fought her corner with them viciously.

'It's easy for him to sit around and complain. Look at me! My back is broken with trying to keep this ramshackle house in some kind of order. I declare to heaven I seldom or never see the daylight; stuck indoors from one end of the day to the other, with a sweeping brush in one hand and a mop in the other. Did I ever think I'd live to see the day that I'd be sunk to this level? I that was never called on to soil my hands in my mother's house, and had nothing to do when I wanted a new hat or a pair of gloves but walk out to the shop and put my hand in the till!'

It was an old song. The children knew it by heart. They had heard it so often they never doubted the truth of it, and before they were of an age to form a judgment the poison of it had entered their hearts. But they got sick of it sometimes. All the same, they despised their father when he took Ella's part.

'That's what spoiled your mother,' he said. 'She had too much money, and not enough to do with it. She had nothing to do but walk out into the shop and put her hand in the till and take out all the money she wanted.'

Indeed, the girls were never quite clear what the trouble was between their parents. Their mother's complaints, and their father's justification of her, were expressed in such similar words they missed the distinguishing emotion that underlay the words.

On this day, as Nonny sat on the stairs, the tears streaming down her face and her satchel strapped across her thin shoulders, the mother was more than usually irritated. She came out again to the head of the stairs.

'Why aren't you gone to school?' she demanded. 'Do you know the time? Get up out of that and get out of my sight.'

As she spoke, however, a door opened in the lower hall, and the lodger in the front room came out. She did not at once see the child crouched on the steps of the stairs, but she stared down the dark passage to the kitchen from which at that moment there came a low moan. The woman on the upper landing drew back hurriedly to avoid being seen. The child knew without looking up that her mother was standing back out of sight, but that she was listening intently to all that went on below, her features hard and unrelenting, her hands tightened irritably around the sweeping brush, and her bitter expression heightened by the uncompromising way in which her hair was tied up in an old duster. Out between the bannister rails the child could see the other woman, the lower-front lodger. She peered down out at her. And a look of cunning came into her face. Her foxy little eyes took in the painted cheeks and dyed hair and the big breasts heaving inside a tight red silk blouse, as the muscles of a fine mare ripple under the silk skin. She saw the gaudy turquoise jewellery that dangled from the woman's ears and crusted her fingers and throat. And she sensed their purpose unerringly; they were designed to give pleasure. She longed to have this warm, big-breasted woman go in to her father.

She stirred on the stairs, but the woman did not notice her. She moved her foot. The woman looked as if she was about to go back into her room and shut the door. The child coughed, and then, overcome by consciousness of her secret motives she was seized by a fit of timorous shivering and could not raise her head to see if she had been noticed. But the lodger had heard her. Putting up her hand hastily to the palpitating red silk blouse she gave a startled exclamation.

'Nonny! How you startled me, child. Why are you sitting there in the dark? Why aren't you at school?' Then, looking at her more intently with the forced stare of the shortsighted, she spoke more sharply. 'Was it you I heard moaning?'

'No.' Nonny, conscious of the unseen listener, was afraid to say more.

'Who was it so?' the woman asked. Then getting no answer she looked down the dark passage again. 'Was it your father?' she asked.

The child nodded dumbly, hoping the woman overhead could not see her. But the lodger's next question betrayed her.

'What's the matter with him? Is there anyone with him? Is he sick?' Lifting her head she listened for a minute. 'There he is again!' she said. 'Is there no one to do anything for him?' She started as if she would make her way down to the kitchen, and although the child longed to let her go, fear of the woman overhead was uppermost in her, and she knew she must not let the lodger into the kitchen. She thought hard, and then as the woman took another step forward, inspired with a sudden duplicity, the child spoke again shrilly.

'It's all right,' she said, shrill and loud. 'My mother is coming down to him.'

'Oh!' said the lodger, and she looked irritably at the child. 'Why didn't you say that sooner?' She felt the wastage of her sympathy. She felt thwarted in her desire to be of use. But the child did not heed her. She sat on the stairs, hard and tight, waiting to hear her mother descend. She had triumphed over her. She had forced her to come down against her will. Already, she could tell from the sounds above that her mother was gathering her cleaning utensils together to bring them down with her. 'I may as well go back to my room,' the lodger said, ungraciously. She patted her hair absently. 'Let me know if I can do anything.'

The child sat up. She must detain the woman, or her plan would fail.

'He's calling you, Mother,' she called again urgently.

The lodger turned back.

'You've better ears than I have,' she said, and she listened again. But the small delay had fulfilled its purpose.

'I'm coming,' the mother said sourly, and she began to come down the stairs.

The lodger stepped forward eagerly. She'd wanted to get a look into that kitchen. None of the lodgers had ever put foot in it, and a great deal of curiosity about it was shown from time to time in the gossip between the different roomers.

'Can I be of any assistance?' she cried.

Ella's face was expressionless, but she was torn between resentment at the other woman's interference, and a consciousness of the necessity to be civil.

'No, thank you,' she said. 'He's all right.'

'But I heard him moaning,' said the woman.

Ella stepped over the child huddled on the bottom step.

'He thinks he's worse than he is,' she said, and then, as if to dismiss the stranger, she turned back to the child. 'What are you doing there?' she said in a harsh loud voice. 'You'll be late for school!'

She caught the child by the strap of the satchel and lifted her to her feet and pushed her forward. In the narrow hall the woman from the lower-front room felt that she was blocking the child's way. She saw no course but to go back to her own room. The child, however, suddenly realising the inadvisability of being left alone with her mother, held the flapping satchel to her side and darted up the hallway past the lodger. She had got what she wanted. She had brought her mother downstairs. There was a defiance in the way she shut the hall door after her with a loud clap.

152

The lodger turned in to the open doorway of the lower-front room.

'You know where I'm to be found if you want me,' she called back over her shoulder.

'I won't want any one,' said Ella, tartly. 'He's not as bad as he'd have people think!'

Beyond an occasional mention like this, she made a point of never talking about her husband to the lodgers; never telling them her affairs. She walked down the hallway, and as she did, the man in the kitchen was seized by another violent fit of coughing, which, however, he seemed to be trying to suppress as he heard the footsteps in the passage.

Ella, however, after a secretive look about her to see that the child had really gone to school, and that the front-room lodger had closed her door tightly, walked quickly past the closed door of the kitchen and went and stood at the back door. She had her own plans. She knew her own business, she told herself savagely, and she looked around the yard to find something to occupy her. She was determined not to go into the kitchen. She thought with irritation of the work she had been doing when Nonny interrupted her. If Nonny had not been such a busybody she would have had the top of the house cleaned by this time. Could she go up again, she wondered, now that Nonny was gone? She was inclined to turn and go up again when she remembered the woman in the front room. Ella jerked her body irritably. There was another busybody! There was another person poking her nose into what didn't concern her! Why couldn't they leave her alone? If she went back upstairs, and he continued to cough and moan, that woman would be out in the passage again wanting to know what was wrong. Ella turned back to the yard door. She might as well put out of her head all idea of going back upstairs. She looked around her to find some way to use up the nervous energy that was consuming her. Suddenly, as she stood at the back door, she started into activity. She'd clean out the yard. A vision rose up before her of the yard as she had kept it in the first year of her marriage. Robert used to say that he didn't miss a garden she kept the yard so nice. She used to whitewash the walls every spring, and she had butter boxes painted white and filled with red geraniums. But it wasn't long before she got sense. It wasn't long before she came to the end of such foolishness. Still there was no need to have a place like a pigsty. She looked around at the walls on which there was no longer a vestige of lime. They were covered with a powdery green lichen. The same unhealthy green growth covered the sunken flagstones, making them slippery and malodorous. And everywhere the refuse of years was strewn: rusted canisters, empty boxes, old bottles, and articles of broken crockery.

She could get rid of some of the rubbish anyway. That was one thing she could do. She rolled up her sleeves. She could clean out the drain; it was choked up, and lately the water never went down completely so that there was always a stagnant pool lying over the grating like a disk of discoloured glass. She caught up a piece of rusty wire and began to tackle the drain. She began to work with a furious energy and as she did so, it seemed to her that in a little while the yard would be again white and sweet-smelling as it was years ago, and that nothing would be lacking but the white-painted boxes and the red geraniums. And they could be easily got. Robert would get them.

At the thought of him, however, her depression returned, and hearing him cough again at that moment, she frowned. Then she remembered her secret plans, and obstinately shutting her ears, she began to probe the drain with the rusty wire. As long as the lodgers would leave her alone! She dreaded to hear the creature in the front room coming out again to the hall to listen. She dreaded to have her come along again with her interfering offers of help. Why couldn't she see that her help wasn't wanted? Had she ever been asked to help? Had she ever been given any encouragement?

Ella pulled up the wire and with it there came up a clot of green slime that gave out a foul stench.

She never encouraged the lodgers. She never told them her troubles. She never told anyone her troubles, but her pride in her own reticence was spoiled for her by a guilty feeling that if she had concealed her resentment from strangers she had vented it all the more fiercely on the poor wretch himself, and although she defended her conduct on the grounds of loyalty, in the depths of her mind she was uneasy. And it did not make things any better to think that he took all her gibes in silence. As a matter of fact, that was what made her most bitter; his silence.

'I suppose he keeps his complaints for the ears of his friends down at the library,' she said to the children time and again. 'I suppose he makes himself out to be a great martyr when he's talking to them.'

The children said nothing on those occasions. It was true their father must have a great many friends among the subscribers to the library where he worked, because he was always bringing home presents he got from them, sweets and cake, and pots of honey or jam.

'He makes out he's to be pitied, I suppose,' Ella would say, as she took up the things he had brought, having waited until he had gone to bed before she as much as looked at them, in case it might give him any satisfaction to see her do so. And then she would let the children eat as much as they wanted without stopping them, as if she hoped they would sicken themselves and that there would be a scene over them next day. As a matter of fact, whether it was a coincidence or not, it seemed as if he never brought home anything without there being dissension over it.

'I wish people would keep their rubbish to themselves,' she'd say triumphantly, when one of the children would get sick, or when the floor would be messed with crumbs, or when a wasp would come into the kitchen to annoy them, drawn by a sticky jam jar.

On those occasions he used to rouse himself to defend the donors.

'They sent them out of kindness!' he'd say.

'Kindness?' Ella would curl her lip contemptuously. 'Pity would be more like it! I suppose you tell them how badly treated you are.'

He would make no answer to this and so she had to fall back on another familiar gibe.

'I'm glad to see you're ashamed,' she would say.

But in her heart she knew that she was making false accusations against him, and that if he talked about her to strangers it would only be to tell them about the old days, about how pretty she used to be when she was a girl, and about how they had eloped together in spite of her parents, and in spite of their having no money, in spite of how young they were – she was only nineteen that summer, and he was only twenty.

Still the thought of his loyalty to their outworn romance did not soften her, and she told herself that it was easy for him to talk about those days, down at the library, where there was no one to see how the romance had turned out, where there was no one to see the drudge he had made her, and the way she had gone to pieces. She'd like to tell people about the old days too, but she had to hold her tongue, for who'd believe now that she was ever young, or that she ever had soft hands and fine skin. Sometimes she'd like to tell those painted old actresses that rented her rooms that she'd had more beaus than any girl in the town where they'd lived while her hair was still down her back. But they wouldn't believe her.

That made her hold her tongue. They'd only ask themselves why she married a broken-down wreck like the man in the kitchen if she had such a great choice. They wouldn't know how good-looking he was when he was young, any more than she could have known then how much he'd change.

That was what galled her most. It wasn't the fact that she was worn out and had lost her looks, she could have put up with that, but it hurt her sense of pride that he should have lost his own good looks, and grown into such a poor shrivelled wretch of a man. Who'd ever have thought it? And yet, she supposed, there were some girls who would have looked ahead, who would have foreseen how things would turn out. Why! her own mother had been able to see clearly what would happen. That was why her mother had been so dead set against the marriage. Her mother had seen what she was too blind to see, that the very things that attracted her to him were the things that would have made another girl cautious. She loved his white skin that was as fine as a girl's. How did she know it would get sickly and yellow? She loved the way the blue veins showed in his white hands. How was she to know that was a sign of delicacy? And one summer, when he was swimming in the river outside the town, she had come upon the riverbank suddenly and seen his white body, hairless and smooth, flashing through the heavy river water. How was she to know that hair on a man's body was a sign of strength, and that only a foolish, ignorant girl would disgust to it? She knew nothing, it seemed, in those days. And she was so obstinate. She wouldn't look at any other fellow after she met Robert. They all looked so coarse. There was her third cousin, Mat, and her mother thought he would be a good match for her, but she couldn't bear the thought of him after Robert. She hated his thick coarse skin and his black hair that always smelled of stale pomades.

'He's dirty!' she said to her mother. 'He has warts all over his hands.'

'Warts aren't the worst things in the world,' her mother said. 'Warts are a sign of strength. And anyway you could get them off with caustic.'

The thought of treating Mat's warts made her sick in the pit of her stomach. The thought of touching his thick oily skin at all made her shudder. But her mother was right. There were worse things than warts. And as for strength! She met Mat a few years ago, and he was as strong as ever, although he was four years older than she. He was like a bull. Such health! Such a red face! Such good humour! He had grown into a fine man. And wasn't it right for a man to be strong? Wasn't it natural for men to have coarse skin and strong hair. They had to be rough to work the way they did. Anyone but she would have known that Robert wasn't made for hard work. Fine skin and soft hair were only for women. Warts indeed! How particular she had been. Why! the welts on her own hands sometimes now after scrubbing down the whole house, were as bad as warts any day. But there again she didn't mind that. All she minded was for the way he had broken down himself. It was for that she blamed him. She had been so proud of him. She would have worn herself to the bone working for him if he had kept his looks and stayed the way he was back home when she used to steal out of the house and meet him in the Long Meadow back of the churchyard. He always looked so much cleaner than other men. He wore white shirts and white collars, and they were always dazzlingly white. And his clothes were always brushed and pressed, with creases in them as sharp as the blades of a knife. And his shoes were always shining. You could see yourself in his shoes. She'd gladly have worn herself out if he had kept up his appearance. She'd have broken her back polishing his shoes. She'd have worn her fingers to the bone to keep him in white collars and shirts. But you can't keep the colour in shirts forever, and a shirt never looks the same after it's patched. And shoes won't give the same shine when the leather is cracked. As for brushing his clothes! It came to a point where she used to hide the clothes brush.

'They're worn enough,' she'd say to him, 'without you brushing the threads asunder!'

Long ago in the evenings in the Long Meadow, when they were making their plans for running away, they used to count on the fact that they had plenty of clothes anyway.

'They won't wear out for a good while,' Robert used to say. 'We have enough clothes to keep us going for a long time.'

But it was surprising how quickly the clothes wore out. Before they were a year married every suit he had was threadbare. But he wore most of them out sitting about on the benches of the registry offices looking for work. And when he got an odd job now and again, it seemed as if you could see the clothes wearing away with the strain. The elbows would get rubbed, the fabric thin, and the back of the trousers would begin to shine, and in the winter the coat would get dragged out of shape with the way he had to pull up the collar against the cold. Clothes didn't last long when you put them to the test. She could see now how unreasonable she used to be about the rough clothes Mat used to wear.

'I can't wear clothes as fancy as certain gentlemen in this town who sit about reading poetry all day,' Mat said once, giving a dig at Robert.

'Robert isn't reading poetry,' said her mother. 'He's studying.' Her mother was set against Robert, but when she was talking to Mat she never let on to be against him. It was part of her mother's plan to make all Ella's suitors appear to be worth nothing in their own eyes, but worth a great deal in the eyes of each other. But Ella couldn't let that remark pass. She was determined to contradict it, partly because she wouldn't give in to her mother, and partly because she wanted to annoy Mat.

'It is poetry!' she said. 'He reads nothing but poetry!'

She was proud then of the fact that Robert read poetry. That was another thing she could laugh at now. She used to like to see him with a book of poetry in his pocket, or rather she used to like the rest of the people in the town to see him. She didn't like him to read it to her though, and he was always wanting to read it aloud to her. She only wanted to talk, or to tease him. Once in a while she liked to look into the books, and see how strange they were, for the more incomprehensible the poems were to her the prouder she felt of him and the more confidently she could boast of him to others.

'What good is poetry to anyone, I'd like to know?' her mother said, and to this she always made the one reply.

'Don't show your ignorance, Mother,' she used to say.

And then too, although she was often impatient with him for reading when they were out in the meadow, she knew that after he had read a few poems in the book he was always more loving to her, and she felt too that it was because he read poetry that he could say such flattering things about her hair and her eyes and her lips. Other men were so tongue-tied. You'd catch them looking at you. That was the only way you'd know what they thought of you. And even then it was your bosom or your legs they'd look at, but Robert was always praising little out-of-the-way things about her, like her ears or her fingernails. He loved her ears. He'd talk about her ears sometimes for ten minutes. And he said her fingernails were like shells. What other man would ever say a thing like that? Shells! It was the poetry put such things into his head. It was the poetry made him different from other men. She had known that then, but to her cost she had known it better later on. More than his compliments came out of the poetry books; all his nonsense came out of them as well. She wasn't long about telling him so, either. And in the end he admitted she was right. The day she gathered up all the old books and threw them into the fire he said nothing for a minute, and then he said she had done right.

'You're right, Ella,' he said. 'They were my undoing. A man can't expect to walk with his face turned up to the sky without losing his foothold on the ground. You must keep your eyes on the ground.'

'Oh that's more of your talk!' she said, but she was glad she had forced him to give in to her.

He gave in to her in most things, and if he protested at all it was only a feeble protest.

'You used to like to have me read to you, Ella,' he said one day.

'I never liked it!' she said, in a fit of temper. 'I only let on to like it!'

But she regretted saying that when she saw the look on his face. She wasn't long in learning that he could take any stings she gave him about the poverty and degradation into which they had fallen, but he could not bear her to say anything that spoiled the past. She took back her words that day.

'I didn't mean what I said,' she muttered grudgingly, but she was swallowing her words so that she couldn't be sure if he heard her or not. 'I've more to do now than listening to poetry, with those children to get ready for school.'

That was the first quarrel they had. 'What can I do?' he said. 'What do you want me to do? I'm doing my best.' He had got a job as an assistant in a lending library at this time, but the salary was small. 'I give you every penny I earn!'

That was true. But it wasn't enough.

'I don't know why it isn't!' he said. 'There are bigger families than this living on less!'

'And how are they living!' she flashed out at him, and she drew his attention to his clothes. 'I want you to look respectable,' she said, 'like you used to look at home. If you'd only do as I say.'

'What do you want?' he asked again.

'Why do you keep asking that!' she said. 'You know what I want! I want to let the front room, and add a bit of money to the house.'

But it was two years before he gave in to let her take lodgers; not that he could be said to give in, even then, but she took things into her own hands and let the room.

'It's for you I'm doing it,' she said. 'The first money we can spare I'm going to buy you a new suit, the one on your back is falling to pieces. It's no wonder you got a hint about them cutting down the staff at the library! They saw the state of your clothes. They wouldn't want to have a shabby person giving out the books. It wouldn't look well. People are particular about things like that!'

'That's not why they gave me the hint,' he said. 'What's the use of them having signs up all over the place asking for silence, if I keep coughing all the time? I got a bad fit of coughing this morning.'

'Oh, don't start complaining. If you had a decent overcoat, you'd get rid of your cough.' She thought for a minute. 'While we're letting one room we might as well let two. The children could all sleep together, and we could let the middle room as well. Then I could buy you a new overcoat. That would get rid of the cough, you'd find. Never fear! It's not the cough that they don't like; it's your shabby appearance.'

They didn't get the overcoat. The day the rent was paid on the rooms, two of the children got the measles and from that day on through the whole winter there wasn't a single week without some new expense.

'Now what would we do without the rent?' she asked, at the end of every week when she laid the household bills beside his salary, and went over to a tin box on the dresser and triumphantly took out her own money.

Although the money all went to meet the bills, still she didn't forget about the clothes for him. She was bent on getting them. But she never seemed able to scrape up enough money.

'What's the use,' she said one day, 'of having a parlour and a dining room? We never go into the parlour.' Her eyes were deep with calculation. 'The parlour would make a grand bedroom, only some people don't like sleeping downstairs.'

He didn't see what she was aiming at, and he joined in the conversation on its face value.

'Delicate people wouldn't mind,' he said. 'Some people are not allowed to climb a stairs.'

'The very thing!' she said. 'I'll put an advertisement in the paper, saying there's a room suitable for an invalid.' She made it seem as if it was his idea, and he wasn't able to protest. As it turned out they got a better rent for the parlour than for any of the bedrooms.

'Who'd ever have thought it!' she said, as she took down the tin box and counted the money in it. 'I'll get you a new suit,' she said, 'as well as the overcoat. The mistake most people make is not getting enough clothes at the one time. If you have enough clothes you can be easy on them, and wear them turn about.' She had been very excited and animated, but he was hardly listening.

'I don't think the new clothes will make any difference,' he said morosely.

'Oh, you make me sick,' she said impatiently.

Nevertheless, when she brought home the new suit, her heart missed its first beat. He didn't look like he used to look back home before they were married. There was some change. She couldn't say just what it was, but there was a change. What harm! she said to herself – it'll take time to bring him back to what he was. I'll get him some new shirts and new collars. She looked at his feet – I'll get him new shoes. She looked at his hair – I'll get him some brilliantine for his hair. Then her eyes brightened – I'll get him a gold tiepin! she said. The thought of the gold tiepin caused her mind to spin round in furious excitement. She was determined to make him again what he was when they were courting. 'We could let the other room. We could eat in the kitchen. It would save my feet, too. I'm worn out carrying heavy trays backward and forward.'

She bought Robert the new collars and the new shoes. She bought the brilliantine and she bought the gold tiepin, and the morning he was going out in the new clothes she was unusually excited.

'There's a lovely colour in your cheeks, Ellie,' he said.

She ran over to the mirror and laughed happily at her reflection, but when she turned round she noticed how pale he was himself. Her heart misgave her again, but she pushed him toward the door with affected good humour.

'You'll see! There'll be no more hints about cutting down the staff. I'll make you look the way you looked when you were hired. I don't blame them for getting uneasy. You were looking terribly shabby lately.'

She watched him out of sight, and that day she felt that perhaps the bad times they had gone through were over, and that things would take up again, and be like she thought they would be before she was married.

But the minute he walked in the door that evening she knew something was wrong. When you went downhill it wasn't as easy as all that to get up again.

'Well?' she said, and her face darkened, and the light that had shone in her eyes since morning died out.

He stood in the doorway and looked at her in a strange way.

'I knew it wasn't the clothes,' he said.

'What do you mean?' she cried. Why couldn't he speak out plainly!

'It was the coughing,' he said, and then, as if to convince her, he was shaken with a hard dry cough. 'They said they were sorry, but they couldn't have me disturbing people trying to read.'

She stared at him, and he stared back at her helplessly. Then, before she said anything, he recovered himself and put up a hand to his necktie.

'Where did you buy the tiepin?' he asked. 'Would they take it back and refund the money?'

At this some of her old fire came back. 'Leave that pin where it is!' she cried, and she slapped his hand down from his neck just as she'd slap one of the children's hands. He stared at her. All at once he felt like one of the children. He felt that her authority over him was going to grow into something enormous and unnatural that would shame his manhood. He was confused and weary, but yet he felt that he must defend himself against this wrongful authority of a woman over a man. And although he couldn't collect himself for a minute or two he knew that he had a weapon against her. What was it? He tried to concentrate, and then suddenly he remembered.

'You needn't worry about the money,' he said. 'I'll still be bringing in my share.'

He spoke defiantly but she didn't seem to heed his words. It wasn't the money she had minded. She had forgotten about the money. It was the humiliation of their not wanting him anymore at the library. She had been so proud of him when he first got the job there. She used to pass by at night when the windows were lighted, just to see him, sitting at his desk in his white collar giving out the books and stamping the date on the flyleaves. And although she had had to give that up when she had the lodgers on her hands, it was only that morning she had been thinking that she'd try and walk down before closing time and see him in his new suit. She had been thinking of it all day. She'd like to have caught a glimpse of the tiepin. She'd like to see if it attracted any attention.

And now they didn't want him there anymore!

She couldn't believe it. A nervousness overtook her suddenly. Was there anything wrong with the clothes?

Were the sleeves too short? Why were his wrists sticking out like that? – and how thin they were!

There was nothing wrong with the clothes, however, and she was forced to take heed of the way his frame had shrunk. He had changed. Yes, he had changed, and it wasn't the money she was thinking of at all but of this change, when he spoke. Yet she looked up at him.

'If you're not wanted at the library, where will you get the money?' she asked, dully, because she wasn't interested in this aspect of the thing, but as she looked at him she felt frightened, because she saw that he himself was frightened of telling her where he was going to get it. 'Where will you get it?' she asked again, more urgently.

'At the library,' he said.

'I thought you said...?' She stared at him stupidly.

He swallowed hard and moved back from her.

'They said they didn't like letting me go –'

'Well?'

'– they said they didn't like letting me go, but that there were people complaining about my coughing.'

'Well?'

'– so they said that I'd have to leave the reading room.'

'Well?'

He simply couldn't go on. He began to cough again.

'They said they could give me another job – if I had no objections to it,' he said at last, '– a job where I wouldn't disturb people.'

'In the office?' she asked quietly enough.

'No.'

'Well, where?' There was fear in her eyes and before that look of fear his voice failed and he was hardly audible.

'The man that looks after the books in the basement – the stock-man, we call him – is leaving at the end of the week,' he said. 'They thought maybe…in these hard times…temporarily you know…till something better turns up…that some money would be better than none.'

He allowed the words to fall from his lips, nervously, because her silence upset him. Why was she so silent? He had expected abuse.

But she was stunned; stupefied. The man that handled the books! A porter! A kind of janitor, you might say! Suddenly she burst out crying, and through her fit of tears her anger could only break out erratically.

'A porter! How dare they make such an offer! How dare they! How dare they!' She sat down weakly on the edge of a chair. Robert stayed on his feet, looking down at her. He was somewhat confused. It appeared that she was not annoyed with him; that all her anger was directed against the people at the library. But one thing was clear. He was not going to suffer a storm of abuse anyway, and with this thought he felt relieved, and as the phlegm that he had been trying to keep back rose again in his throat he was about to give himself the further physical relief of coughing when he was suddenly seized with a feeling of fear. She wasn't going to let him take the new job. That was her plan. He summoned all his strength once more. He'd have to take it. He'd have to keep his independence. He'd have to pull his weight in the house. And so before he was overcome by another fit of coughing, he managed to summon breath enough for one remark. 'I'm going to take the job,' he said chokingly. And then the coughing started and he had to sit down.

That day had been the beginning of all their misery. That was when the real trouble had started between them. It was not until that day that the irreparable bitterness had come into every word they said to each other.

He persisted in taking the job. The new clothes were laid aside, and the tiepin was stuck on the wallpaper over the mirror. He wore his old clothes frankly after that. Ella gave up trying to darn them or patch them. She no longer even brushed them or made any effort to keep them clean. He wore the new shoes, though, because after a bit his feet came out through the old ones. But the rest of the clothes were put away in a cupboard.

'They would only attract attention,' she said. 'They would only draw people's attention to the fact that you were lowering yourself below your station!'

Her bitterness knew no bounds. Every hour that he was in the house she upbraided him, and where before she had regarded the money from the lodgers as an addition to their joint money, now she regarded herself as the sole support of the family, and sneered at the small sum that he laid on the table every Saturday.

'Is this for your keep?' she used to ask, and throw it contemptuously to one side. And at other times, when they were eating their meals, she would laugh bitterly as she filled his plate.

'You get good value for your money,' she said. Sometimes she called him The Boarder. 'There's more profit on lodgers than boarders,' she'd say.

Things went from bad to worse. He got more and more shabby-looking, and as well as that he seemed to shrink and grow smaller and meaner-looking every day. The more sickly and ill he became, the more bitter she grew toward him.

One day, when he left his few shillings down on the table, she snarled at him.

'Why don't you keep it!' she said, throwing back the money to him. 'Keep it and buy lozenges with it; not that you'll get much for that!'

He seldom protested against this treatment, and when the children appeared occasionally to take his side he always discouraged them. 'Your mother is tired, girls,' he used to say. 'Don't let her think you are going against her. She has a lot to put up with, and she wasn't used to hardship.'

When he said that Ella was not used to hardship, Robert's eyes would sometimes seem to dim with recollection, and sitting there in the squalid kitchen he would stare out the window where a few bits of green fern in a pot on the sagging windowsill had power to draw his heart back into the past. He would sit there, thinking especially of the Long Meadow back of the churchyard in the old town where he and Ella were born. And when he came back up out of the depths of these memories, he was brighter and more cheerful looking, and the girls felt reassured enough to resume their plans for their own enjoyment. They felt they could forget him with impunity, and they crushed against each other, and jostled each other for preference of place in front of the dirty mirror, mottled with splashes, that hung over the sink, as they powdered their faces and combed their hair before going out for the evening.

'None of you have hair like your mother,' he said, sometimes on those occasions, and he would start to describe how Ella's hair had been, how bright, how glossy, and how it curled around her forehead if the weather was damp. But they didn't want to hear.

'There's not one of you like her,' he said sadly, and Dolly, the second youngest tittered.

'It's a good thing we're not,' she whispered under her breath, because they couldn't see back into the past when Ella was young and decked out for love. But Mary shuddered. She was, in fact, somewhat like her mother, and she trembled in her secret soul at the thought that if her mother was once beautiful and yet got like she was, then she, Mary, might someday get like her mother.

'Let's hurry!' she'd say, anxious to be out in the impersonal streets. Being the most sensitive of them all to her father's suffering, she was nevertheless least able to bear the sight of it, just as, most sensitive to the strain between her parents, she was least able to stand it, and rushed out of the house as often as she could.

'Goodbye, Father, goodbye!' They would soon be gone, leaving him in the dark kitchen, knowing that Ella would not stop working and scrubbing until he was out of it too. She would not please him by stopping. She would not give him the satisfaction of seeing her sit down for a few minutes to rest. He began to go to bed earlier and earlier, until soon it was only a question of taking his meal and standing up from it to go to bed. When he was out of the way, he thought, she might sit down and eat, or rest herself by the fire.

One Saturday the strain was too much for Mary. After her mother had made some contemptuous remark about the weekly money that he left obstinately down on the table every Saturday, she burst out before him.

'Why are you always picking at him, Mother? What do you want him to do? Kill himself? He can't earn any more than he does. He shouldn't be working at all! He's not fit for it.'

The mother stared at her.

'Keep out of what doesn't concern you,' she said angrily. But after a minute she softened. 'I'm not making him work. I'm against it. I was always against it from the start. Isn't that the cause of all our misery?' She was speaking to Mary, but out of the corner of her eye she tried to see the effect of her words on the man. 'I want him to stay at home. I want him to give up that humiliating job. What he earns isn't as much as what I get for one room!'

Mary was surprised. She looked at her father.

'Why don't you do what Mother says?' she asked.

But Robert shook his head. 'You don't understand,' he said.

'There you are!' Ella went out of the room impatiently.

But if Mary didn't understand, Ella herself understood less. The only difference between herself and Mary was that Mary honestly tried to understand, but she had shut her mind against him long ago and never tried to see his point of view. She saw her own only, all the time, day after day, and when he got fits of coughing, or an attack of the cramping pains across his chest that he got lately, her own viewpoint narrowed down the more.

'I don't know what notions you have in the back of your head,' she said to him, 'but let me tell you this! You're keeping me back. People won't take rooms everywhere and anywhere, and when they hear my husband is a janitor they think the place isn't class enough for them. And when they see you going in and out, in your dirty old clothes, coughing and spitting, that turns them more against the place; whereas if you were to give up that job and stay at home and wear your good suits and put on clean collars it would make the place look respectable. You could help me out too. There's many a thing you could do. You could order the provisions. It would look well to see you going into the shops. And you could be seen about the place. That counts for a lot. It gives a place a respectable appearance to see a well-dressed man taking his ease in the middle of the day. It would let people see we weren't lost for their last penny. It would let them see we were independent, and that if the price didn't suit them they could go elsewhere. As it is they think because my husband is a janitor I ought to be glad to take whatever they like to offer me!' A frown settled on her face as she thought of past scenes of haggling over the price of the rent, but it lifted suddenly as she let her mind fly forward to a vision of things as they would be if she had her way. 'I'd like to see you with a clean collar on you every day,' she said, 'and your good suit, and your tiepin, sitting on the bench outside the front of the house. That would give a good appearance to the place.'

She paused to picture him sitting on the bench, and then as if the picture was not complete she bit her lip and seemed to be thinking. After a minute she looked up eagerly. 'You could have a carnation in your buttonhole.'

She was so carried away with her idea that from that day forward she never stopped appealing to him. But gradually the appeals grew sour, and took the form of complaints. He, however, remained steadfast in his resistance to her. He resisted her all the time. And the weaker his power to express it, the stronger his resistance seemed to grow, until sometimes it shone at the back of his eyes in a wild light. He was steadfast in his determination to keep his job. She was steadfast in her determination to make him give it up. But although they were equal in obstinacy and will power, she had an advantage over him because of his own decreasing strength. He'd never endure the hardship. His cough was worse week after week. And so, as she went about the kitchen, she used to watch him out of the corner of her eye. He thought he was going to best her, but she knew that she'd win in the end. And when the children worried about his cough, and came to her, and tried to make her get a doctor for him, she smiled in a curious way and gave them evasive answers. For it seemed now that the cough was her friend. It would accomplish what she had failed to do; it would force him to give up.

And when that day came she'd have him where she wanted him. She'd get down his good suits. She'd shake them out and press them, and she'd put a great gloss on his collars, and she'd get him two new pairs of shoes at least, as well as a couple of pairs of socks. She'd get black lisle socks with coloured clocks embroidered on the ankles. As for his cough! That didn't worry her. She'd cure that in a few weeks. When he had nothing to do but sit out in the sun and take his ease the cough would go. There would soon be a great change in him. He would soon get back his looks.

Ella straightened her back. The yard didn't look much better, but she had made some improvement in it.

Just then there was another fit of coughing in the kitchen, and after it she heard a distinct moan. Several times she had fancied she heard moaning, but she'd been able to persuade herself that she was mistaken because she had been making a good deal of noise herself in the yard. But now as she stood idle to rest her aching back she heard it clearly. If only the lodger didn't hear it! If she heard it she would be likely to come out again. They were so curious and interfering. And if that inquisitive creature came out now, it would spoil everything. Doggedly Ella stood and listened to the sounds inside the small window that opened on the yard from the kitchen. She felt that as long as there was no interference with her plans she would soon come to the end of her struggle with him. She was near the end of it now, she felt, and with this thought she permitted herself to move nearer to the kitchen window and listen more intently. But when she listened deliberately there was no sound. Then, when she was moving away, the man in the kitchen was seized with a most violent attack of coughing that was only interrupted by moans and gasps that seemed to be as involuntary as the coughing. The woman leaned forward. He was bad. He was worse than ever he was. A sudden wild elation took possession of her. At this rate he wouldn't be able to go to work today. This was the beginning of the end. What time was it? She strained her head backward to try to see the time by the church clock that could be seen in the distance between the city roofs. Ten o'clock. Could it be that late? Why, he should have been gone long ago! She listened. Her elation grew. Morning after morning he had been getting later and later, but he had never been as late as this! How she had hoped time and again they would discharge him altogether. Seemingly, however, they were prepared to stand anything from him. They pitied him, she supposed, and her resentment burned more bitterly at the thought that he should make himself the object of pity, of charity. Then, as the clock began to strike, she listened intently to the chimes pealing out loudly overhead. He must not be going out at all today. Exultantly she wiped her hands on the sides of her dirty dress. Her day had come. He was defeated at last. Now she had him where she wanted him. She would not be humiliated any longer by having people know that her husband was a janitor. He would be a gentleman again. That was why she had married him; he had been such a gentleman.

Ella sat down on an upturned box in the yard. She felt weak all of a sudden, but it was a gratifying weakness; bearable, and endurable, after a long hard fight in which victory, although certain, had been a long time deferred. After a few minutes the tiredness from the heavy work in the yard began to stream away from her, and with it there seemed to stream away the unhappiness that had lain on her now for so many years. Suddenly she felt that all was going to be well. She looked around at the squalid yard, and up at the loose bricks of the house, that needed to be pointed, and then she looked at the windows of her house, where, in their early years of occupation, neat curtains of white frilled muslin had made all the windows alike, but where now the different occupants of the different rooms had hung their own different curtains. A tenement! That's what it was. But all that would be changed. She would get a better-class lodger. She might try giving board as well as lodgings. There was more money to be made that way, and it was more respectable. Things would be easier now that she would have Robert at home with her. Before he put on his good clothes at the beginning of the day he could do odd jobs for her about the house. They would coin money. And there wouldn't be as many expenses as there were long ago. The girls were all through school except Nonny. Mary's apprenticeship to the dressmaker would be at an end in two months' time and she could ask for a salary any day after that, or set up on her own. She was as good as any dressmaker already. And Dolly was no worry. Dolly's salary at the factory was more than Robert ever earned, even in the good days when he was in the reading room. Then, too, Dolly was as good as married. And Nonny? Ella's worn face brightened even more. She had not done too well for the girls. But there was still time to do something for Nonny. It would be nice to send her to classes and get her made into a typist. Typists didn't get tired and drawn-looking. And she could keep her hair nice, and her hands would be soft and not pricked all over with needles like Mary's, or dyed with chemicals like Dolly's.

Ella looked down at her own hands. If Robert was at home all the time she'd have more heart to keep herself clean. She pulled a hairpin out of her untidy knot of hair, and began to pick the hard black dirt from under her nails. She put up her hand to her hair again. It wouldn't be so coarse if it was washed once in a while. She felt her neck with her fingers. It was dry and rough. But was that any wonder? She only washed her neck when she was going out in the street. You got into dirty habits when you were all alone all day in a dirty, dark house. It would be different if Robert was with her all day. She'd get through her work early, and they might go out for a walk. They used to go out every Sunday when they were first married. She could remember well how proud she was of him. The brightness in her face was a hard defiant brightness. She'd be proud of him again. The suits she'd bought him a few years ago were still as good as new. And they were a better quality than could be got nowadays. As for his appearance, he'd get back his looks in no time after a few days' rest. That was all he needed; rest. He would look older, of course, but he would be distinguished looking, and that was what counted with people.

She began to visualise how he would look, clean and rested, and dressed in his good suits, but the only Robert she could see was the Robert of long ago, the Robert who used to sit on the wall outside his father's house reading poetry and looking down the street to see if she was coming. Once or twice she made a deliberate effort to take his age into consideration, but the Robert she called up before her eyes was a Robert decorated rather than blemished by the marks of age.

She drew a deep breath. Things had been bad, but they were going to come right in the end. Now that the

struggle was over she was prepared to acknowledge that
she had been bitter, but not without cause. An intolerable
burden had lain on her for so many long dark years. And
although behind her was the dark, decaying house, with
its damp and slimy yard, its ramshackle windows through
which there came so often the stench of conflicting smells
that hung about the house all day long from the various
and inferior foods the lodgers cooked in their rooms at
night, nevertheless it seemed to her that these things
were nothing, mere details, or external manifestations of
a nameless, obscure trouble that had lain over her ever
since she was married. A nameless obscure obstacle had
been set in her way and prevented her from fulfilling the
bright dreams that had glanced back and forth in her
pathway so convincingly and alluringly when she was a
girl, contemptuously swinging her foot under the table
while her mother abused Robert and said he was good for
nothing. Perhaps it had been some fear that her mother
was right, and that she was wrong, that had lain on her all
those years. And Robert himself seemed to have taken
her mother's side. He seemed readiest of all to agree that
he was worthless and that she had thrown herself away
on him. Why had he not helped her to keep up a show?
He had given in so early to other people's opinion of
him. He had not put up any fight. He hadn't ever cared
if he put her in the wrong with her own people. But oh,
now wasn't she glad she had not given in to him! She
had held out all the time. She had fought. And now she
had won. In her limited experience and knowledge she
knew little of the abstract differences of the sexes, but
from some dim memory of a national-school primer she
had an idea that women were the upholders of spiritual
values and she felt that in all the weary years she had
been championing a cause. People might have blamed

her for her methods, but they didn't understand: she had had her plans. She had known what she was about. And now her reward had come. Even Robert would have to see that she had been acting for the best. She had been making a way for them both out of the dark forest in which they had been imprisoned, and together now they would flash out into the open glade. That it would be like the green glades of their early youth she did not for a moment doubt.

She stood up. As her tiredness and misery had given way to excitement and exultation, so this exultation had in turn given way to a feeling of infinite peace. She moved toward the back door that led into the house.

But as she entered the mean hallway, her nostrils were assailed by imprisoned odours of the stale past, and she heard his feet scrape on the broken cement floor of the kitchen. And immediately her spirits were dampened. She felt tongue-tied. The habits of years were not to be broken so easily. What would she say to him? For she would now have to deal with the real Robert; the bodily Robert, and whereas it had seemed in her mind, as long ago it had seemed in her heart, that they were one person, indissoluble in intimacy, who could say or do whatever they liked to each other, she had no sooner heard him cough and scrape his foot on the floor than she was aware again that two people never are one, and that they were, as they always were, and always would be, two separate beings, ever at variance in their innermost core, ever liable to react upon each other with unpredictable results. She was uneasy. She had lost her surety before she had crossed the threshold.

And when she heard him call her name in a strange voice, as if trying to penetrate some incredible distance between them, while she was actually within a few yards of him, with her hand on the kitchen door, all her old irritation came back.

'I'm here,' she said. 'There's no need to shout.'

'Didn't you hear me moaning?' he asked feebly and without accusation. Her antagonism gathered.

'Are you ever doing anything else?' she asked. Her flock of hopeful thoughts had taken flight again.

Robert was dressed for work, and the coarse ugly clothes put a barrier between them instantly. But he, who for many, many years had been so sensitive to the strain between them, seemed suddenly unaware of it now. He put out his hand, and it seemed as if he was unconscious of all the other barriers that the years had erected between them. Before she had time to draw it away, he had taken her hand in his.

At the feel of his hard, coarsened hand when it caught hers, Ella drew back roughly and attempted to release her own hand. But Robert only held it tighter and in his eyes there was a strange expression, and he looked at her in a curious way, almost, she thought, as if it were twenty years back and that she was standing in front of him in the Long Meadow. He seemed to ignore or not any longer to see her worn face. And when she tried again to pull her hand away, he seemed not to understand the rough gesture, or to think of it as the capricious withdrawal of bashfulness.

'Don't draw away from me, Ella,' he said. 'I have something to say to you. I was calling you all morning. I wanted you.'

She was disconcerted. The man in front of her had the shrunken appearance of the man she had lived with in misery for the last twenty years, but his voice and his manner were those of the young man who used to read poetry to her long ago. As a few minutes earlier in the yard, once again she got the astonishing sensation that she had made her way out of the depth of a forest in which she had strayed for a long time. Over her head the trees were laced together less tightly. Through chinks between the leaves the light was breaking in ever brighter shafts. But whereas in the yard she had thought she would have to explain all this to Robert, it appeared now that he too had broken his way through to the light. Snatching back her hand, she put it to her head. It was too sudden. It had all come about too unexpectedly. They had flashed out into the glade too fast. She was dazzled. And so she tried to draw back and take refuge in the habits of the past.

'I heard you!' she said. 'And so, I suppose, did that creature in the front room! What did she think, I wonder? It's a wonder any of them stay in the place at all. And as for coming in to you – you know as well as I do that I can't be running in and out every minute for nothing. I have things to do! I wasn't out in the yard for my own pleasure, I assure you!' The flood of words, once released, poured out in a bitter stream. Then as she saw him staring at her, she faltered. 'Anyway,' she said, defensively, 'I didn't know whether you were calling or coughing!'

Still he stared at her, but his eyes were gentler.

'Would it have been such trouble to come to the door and find out?' he asked. And she was put into confusion both by his glance, and by the fact that he had never before in all the years made any protest against her, even a gentle protest like this one.

'Every step counts,' she said doggedly.

She persisted in hanging back in the sheltering darkness of former habits. But when she looked at him she realised that he had already travelled far faster than she. His eyes shone. And in spite of the way the fits of coughing had stooped his shoulders of late, his head was high.

'Every minute counts, too,' he said. And this time when he put out his hand and took hers, she let it remain with him, and further than that, looking at him, and feeling her hand in his, she ventured a fearful step forward with him into the brightness.

'Are you not going to work?'

He looked at her steadily.

'You've always looked forward to the day I'd have to stay at home, haven't you?'

So he *was* going to stay at home! Without further hesitation she rushed into the light.

'You're not going?' she cried. 'You've got sense at last!' She looked back for an instant with a vain regret. 'If only you'd given it up long ago, as I asked you,' she said, but her joy was too headlong to be impeded. Her heart exulted even as she spoke. 'You were killing yourself down there! And for what? As I often told you, I get more for one room than you earn in a week.' She paused. 'At least I would if I had the right kind of people in the house as I could if the rooms had a bit of decent paper on the walls and a few sticks of furniture in them.' She sprang to her feet. 'I'll go up and look at the front room this minute and see the condition of the walls. Even a dab of distemper would work wonders with it. And we could give the woodwork a coat of white paint. Better-class people like white paint. They see the worth of keeping it clean. I'd never have put on that ugly mahogany paint if it wasn't for the poor type of people I had to take. I knew they weren't likely to go to the trouble of keeping white paint clean.' She was silent for a minute, and her mind was busy making calculations. 'New curtains wouldn't cost much,' she said. 'And we could get a few pieces of furniture out of the money in the tin box.' She ran over to the dresser and took it down, but instead of opening it herself, as she always did, she thrust it into his hands. 'How much is in it?' she cried, taking him into partnership. 'Count it.' Her own mind had leapt away and was making other plans. 'If we got thirty shillings for the front room,' she said, 'I'd give notice to quit to the women in the middle room and we'd do it up too.' She looked at him as she spoke, but unseeingly. 'We might be able to do it ourselves, indeed, and then it would only cost us the price of the paint. I often thought that if I had help I'd never need to get a paperhanger; I could do it as good myself, so now, with you at home to help me, I might manage to do it.' She had been talking in a headlong fashion, but suddenly she felt weak from the fever of her excitement. She went over and sat down on a chair at the other side of the table, opposite him, and as she did her eyes rested on him with more attention as he sat with the tin box in his hands.

'You didn't open the box?' she exclaimed suddenly in surprise, but rushing ahead she interpreted his motives for herself without waiting for a reply. 'I know it's hard to think of spending the money, but we can look on it as an investment.' She sighed happily. 'That box won't hold all the money I'll make now that you're going to be a help instead of a hindrance.'

But when Robert made no reply at all, not even to her last remark, which she felt to be very gracious and generous, she looked sharply at him. To her astonishment there were large tears glistening in his eyes, and a heavy tear was making its way slowly down his coarse cheek, running irregularly between the stubbles of his unshaven face.

'What's the matter with you?' she cried, starting up anxiously.

'I don't feel well, Ella,' Robert said weakly.

'Oh, is that all?' She leaned back with relief. 'I wouldn't mind that. A few days at home will set you up again as good as ever.'

But the tears continued to roll down his face.

'I'm afraid I'll be more of a hindrance than ever now!' he said, and then when he conquered a fit of coughing he looked across at her. 'How could I be any help papering the rooms?' he asked passionately. 'How could I help you at anything? I'm fit for nothing now.'

Ella pressed her lips together. So this was the way he was going to act. She stood up and glared across at him, about to give him a cutting answer, but what she saw in his face silenced her. He did look bad. There was no mistake about it. For a moment her resentment against him returned. To think that he might die now just at the moment of her triumph! But a minute later her heart began to ache and she recollected that when this stubborn creature died, there died also the young man with the fair hair who used to sit on the wall reading poetry, and furthermore there died also the fine man in the new suit, with a gold tiepin in his cravat and a carnation in his buttonhole, that she counted on having the lodgers see sitting on a bench outside the house. She ran over to him.

'Don't talk nonsense, Robert. You had yourself worn out, but now things will be different.' As she spoke she patted him on the shoulder and tried to brighten him up too. 'Why don't you change your clothes and sit in the sun? I'll make a cup of hot soup for you.' She darted over to the cupboard to get a saucepan.

Robert did not stir.

'Do as I say,' she said. 'This kitchen is no place to sit.'

For the first time in years she seemed to see its filth and squalor, and leaving down the saucepan she ran about straightening the chairs, gathering up the rags and rubbish that littered them, and finally, snatching up the sweeping brush, she began to sweep an accumulation of dirt and crumbs into the corner under the sink. This furious activity absorbed her entirely for a few minutes. Then she turned around.

'You couldn't find a healthier spot in the world than that bench outside the house. Why don't you go out and sit there? Why don't you go out there now?'

'Ella, please! Let me sit where I am for a while,' said the man wearily.

She laid down the sweeping brush, only half convinced that he was unwilling to comply. Then she gave in to him.

'Well, you can sit out there tomorrow. And it will give me time to have your suit aired and pressed. But you'd better not sit here in the dirty kitchen. I'll help you into your room.' She went to catch him by the arm. But he shrank from being touched.

'I'd like to stay where I am for a while,' he said pathetically, and then got such an attack of coughing there was nothing for her to do but go back to what she had been doing until he got over it. The coughing sounded bad. It distressed her to hear it. He seemed worse all right. And when he stopped coughing he tried to speak but she couldn't hear what he was saying. She went over to him and bent down her ear to him.

'I like to be here where I can watch you, Ella,' he said.

She laughed uneasily.

'Oh go on out of that!' she said roughly, but it was a roughness he knew of old, a roughness of embarrassment, a righteous unwillingness to give in to the pleasurable vanity roused by his words. 'I'll have a drop of soup for you in a few minutes. Wait till you see! You'll be a new man after it.'

It took a long time to make the soup, because in her excitement she tried to do several things at the one time, only thinking to run over and stir the soup when it boiled over and there was a smell of burning. She dragged the ragged net curtains from the window and threw them into a basin of water. She snatched down the mirror that was over the sink and tried to wipe off the flyblows that covered it like a pock. But when the soup was ready at last he could only swallow a few mouthfuls.

'What harm!' she cried. 'It will be all the thicker for leaving it on the fire. You can have it later on.'

Later on, however, he was less inclined for the soup than before, and although she patiently held the spoon to his mouth and coaxed him to take a spoonful, he swallowed only a few drops. The rest ran down on his chin and slobbered his clothes.

At last he protested against the effort of trying to swallow it.

She looked at the clock.

'But you must eat something. You've been sitting there all day without a morsel inside your lips!' A frown of worry came on her forehead. 'What will I do with you?' she asked, but more to herself than to him, for although he kept his eyes fixed on her, watching all her movements, she was beginning to have a curious feeling of being alone. There was certainly no use in expecting any cooperation from him. She wished the girls were home. The day had flown and yet it would be a long time still till they got back from work. Nonny would soon be back from school, but what use was Nonny? She'd be peevish and tired and crying for her dinner.

There was a sound in the passage. That was probably Nonny now and there was nothing ready for her to eat. Even the soup was boiled away. Well, Nonny would have to wait. Ella went out and banged the kitchen door shut.

It was not Nonny, however. It was just a door that had slammed in a draft. The child did not come in until some time later.

The instant Nonny did come home, and stepped into the hall, however, the child was aware at once that some change had come over the house, although she could not tell what it was. The dark hallway was the same, and the same damp smell came out from the walls. There was the same cold, empty sound as she ran down the bare cement passage. Yet something in the atmosphere had lightened and brightened. She pushed open the door of the kitchen, but as she did so her mother shot out a hand and pushed her back into the passageway.

'Go easy!' the mother cried crossly. 'Your father is asleep. What's the meaning of making such a noise? Can't you walk gently? Have you no respect for people's nerves!'

The child stopped in astonishment. This was something new! Her mother had never before greeted her in this manner. Then recalling that her mother had said something about her father, she looked scared.

'Where is he?'

'He's in the kitchen,' the mother said. 'You can go in to him if you go quietly.'

Fearfully and on tiptoe, not knowing what to expect, Nonny went in, but her father was still sitting where he sat that morning, only now his feet were lifted onto a stool and there was a blanket thrown over them. There was also a pillow behind his back.

The child looked timidly at him, but when she saw that he was not going to speak to her she stared at him curiously. Ella had to push her out of her way at last, and after that the child stole about the kitchen getting herself some bread and butter. When she had cut and buttered two or three uncouth and crooked slices of bread, she crept out again on tiptoe to eat them in the yard. She had not been sent out to the yard, but all the time she had been in the kitchen she had felt nervous and uncomfortable and she had knocked into the chairs, and clattered the cups on the dresser, and once she had stumbled. Each time she made a noise she felt her mother turn and glare at her, although she did not dare look up at her. It would have choked her to eat in the kitchen. It was better out in the yard. She sat down on an upturned box and began to chew the bread and ponder on the change that had come over her mother. It used to be her father that was ordered about and glared at, and it used to be herself that was petted. She sat chewing the bread without relish. And she wished her older sisters were home.

The first thing the older girls noticed when they came into the house was the smell of soap and disinfectant, and they saw at once that the passage had been swept. Then, before they went into the kitchen they saw Nonny sitting disconsolately on a box in the yard. They went to the door of the yard to talk to her and tease her, but when they saw the way the yard had been cleaned up and tidied, they forgot Nonny. What was the meaning of this? They exchanged glances, arching their eyebrows. Then they smelled the soup. This was most unusual. And all these unusual things prepared them in some way for a change, so that unlike Nonny, when the older girls went into the kitchen they went quietly, and were hardly surprised at all to see their father wrapped up in a blanket in the corner. As if they were in a strange house, the two girls politely refrained from looking around at the freshly scrubbed dresser and the clean curtains, but they were aware of every change, and under their feet they missed the grit and dirt that was always on the floor, and, when they went to sit down, they were astonished to find the chairs were free of their usual clutter. There was no sign of their supper, however, and their mother, who was always in a fuss at this time of day, belatedly getting something hot for them after their day's work, turned around to them with an anxious face and ignored all mention of food.

'How do you think he is looking?' she asked them earnestly, and although they had not been told their father was any worse than usual, they felt instantly that he must be bad, from their mother's solicitude for him. It shocked them too to hear her speaking of him to his face as if he neither heeded nor heard.

'He didn't go to work today,' Ella said. Then she questioned them anxiously once more. 'How do you think he looks?'

Mary drew back, uneasy at talking about him in his presence.

'Don't mind him! He won't hear you,' Ella said. 'He's sleepy. He's been like that all afternoon.'

Dolly was less sensitive. She stared into the corner where her father sat.

'He looks bad,' she said bluntly.

Ella said, scathingly, 'He's very bad!'

Dolly was tired and hungry and her mother exasperated her.

'He's no worse than he has been for months past,' she said viciously.

For a moment Ella pondered over Dolly's words and her face clouded with worry as she looked distractedly at Robert, then as she became conscious of the mood in which her daughter had spoken, her face darkened still more.

'If that's the case,' she said, 'you might have spoken sooner! You might have drawn my attention to him.'

The rebuke was hurled at Dolly, but the bitter glance that went with it included Mary in its wide reckless orbit. The two girls looked at each other again. Like Nonny they had never before been in disfavour with their mother, but unlike Nonny, they sensed that after twenty years the habits and instincts of acerbity were unlikely to be stifled at will, and that at best they could be but diverted from one person to another. They felt that it was they, now, and not their father, who stood in the path of their mother's wrath.

Ella herself, however, was unconscious of all except the needs of the invalid. After her bout with Dolly she looked at Robert critically, but after a few minutes she was able to disregard her daughter's words again and blind herself to his poor appearance.

'He'll be all right in a day or two,' she said defiantly, and she went over to him and repeated the same words, but in an utterly different tone of voice; half coaxing, half bullying. 'You'll be all right in a couple of days, Robert,' she said, and she tucked the blanket tighter around him and gave the pillow behind him a jerk.

Robert said nothing. His eyes were shut. It gave Ella a shiver to have him sit so patient and quiet. She caught up the blanket and gave it another and unnecessary shake, and she gave the pillow another and more violent jerk.

All of a sudden, looking at his sunken cheeks, she felt that no assurance from the children would be of any use to her. He must assure her himself. For the third time she repeated the words but this time they were in the form of a question.

'You'll be all right in a couple of days, won't you?' she asked, and although she stood over him with her arms on her hips in a truculent attitude that seemed to defy him to give her any answer but the one she wanted, into her voice there had crept a whining tone that was new to her.

Robert opened his lustreless eyes and looked up. And for a moment there was a sign of struggle in his face as he tried to summon up enough duplicity to give a cheerful answer, but he was already too far gone in weakness to do any more than tell the truth. The truth was the easiest. He had no energy for subterfuge.

'I don't know,' he said. 'I feel bad.'

'Oh, nonsense,' Ella said impatiently, but she wasn't convinced by her own exclamation. He did look bad. She could see that now. What would she do? She looked around her helplessly for a moment, but the only words that came to her were the old, ready words that she had used a hundred times. 'You'll be as well as ever you were in a few weeks. And you'll have the best of times. You can lie in bed till the day is well aired, and when you get up you can put on your best clothes, and go out and sit on the bench in front of the house, and be called in to your meals, with plenty of time to eat them slowly and chew your food. Oh you'll be all right. Wait till you see. That bench gets all the sun. I don't know how it is, but the sun shines on it from one end of the day to the other. I often wonder that the lodgers don't make more use of it. But, as a matter of fact' – and here she brightened considerably – 'as a matter of fact, I'm just as well pleased they never got into the habit of sitting on it, because of course you won't want to make free with them when you're sitting out there yourself.' The bright picture she drew of him, sitting proud and aloof on the bench in front of the house made her forget the dismal picture he presented huddled in the chair. 'You'll be all right in a couple of days,' she said. 'After all you have something to look forward to now. It would be a different matter if you were going back to that old library! Yes! You have something to look forward to now, Robert!'

But the truth had stolen into the diminished citadel of Robert's soul and, taking advantage of the weakness of his body, it was in possession now for the rest of his earthly sojourn.

'It's not much to look forward to, Ella,' he said, and he looked up at her. 'I thought I'd come to a better end! I thought we'd make more of our lives than this!' And in spite of the leaden weights that hung on his arms, he struggled to put out a hand from under the covering and make a gesture to include the house.

'What do you mean?' She was frightened.

'It's not much to live for – is it?' Robert said. 'The thought of spending the end of your days sitting in front of a lodging house. Do you remember what we planned? Do you remember how we wanted to be together always, just you and I, without anyone else? Do you remember the way we used to be so mad when your young sister Daisy hung on to us, and wanted to come for a walk with us, and we couldn't get rid of her? And now,' his voice weakened, and he had to stop to draw a long breath, 'look at the way things have turned out!' He made a disparaging gesture. 'Look what happened!'

'What happened?' she asked in a whisper. She truly did not know.

He seemed to be getting weaker every minute. With a great effort he concentrated his forces for an answer, but he could only manage to give utterance to it in fragments.

'Strangers,' he said, and drew a long breath. 'Strangers everywhere.' He began to cough. She wanted to hear what he had to say, but it was so painful to watch him she was ready to forgo her curiosity. But when, rather than see him labouring to talk, she tried to interrupt him, he put up his hand to make her listen to him. 'We wanted to be together, Ella. We wanted to be alone. That's why we left home. And here we are finishing our days in a houseful of strangers. Strangers; strangers; strangers. Strangers in every room. I'm so ashamed! To think we should come to this!'

His voice was stronger toward the end of what he was saying, but suddenly he stopped speaking and sat silent again, and this time it seemed that it was words that had failed him, and not his voice.

In the silence the two girls who, after the first few minutes of curiosity, had begun, like Nonny, to look around and prepare some sort of food for themselves, began now to whisper to each other. Dolly took up her father's words.

'I told you,' she said, turning to Mary. 'I often said it was degrading to keep lodgers. I am always afraid they'll find out at the factory that we keep a lodging house. They'd look down on me so much!'

From the corner her father had caught the sound of her voice, but it seemed he could not see well because he suddenly broke out again in a passionate complaint, and his anger gave a spasm of strength to his voice.

'Listen,' he cried. 'I hear people talking over there at the sink. Who are they? Why must there be strangers everywhere? Why must they be in here?'

The girls were startled.

'He's delirious,' Dolly said under her breath. 'He doesn't know who we are!' And she turned around as if she would go over to him, but Mary suddenly caught her by the sleeve and held her back.

'He knows who we are all right,' she said. 'He just doesn't want us here.' But she herself made no move to go out because to stay where she was seemed less conspicuous, and Dolly, who hardly comprehended her, just stood where she was also, staring at the sick man – a pot of tea in one hand and a cup in the other. But now Nonny who under cover of the older girls had stolen back into the kitchen, and had been listening to the last few words that had passed between her sisters, caught at their skirts in fright, unable to understand what was wrong. She had known all day that something was wrong and had hoped to find out when the other girls came home, but although she had hung on every word that was uttered the meaning of the words was incomprehensible to her.

'Who doesn't want us?' she asked, dragging urgently at Mary's skirt and then at Dolly's. Getting no satisfaction from them she was just beginning to cry when suddenly their mother created a diversion. For Ella had suddenly flung herself on her knees in front of the sick man.

'Why didn't you ever tell me you felt like that?' she cried, in bitter reproach. 'I thought you wanted us to make money. You used to say we'd make our fortune in the city. I only tried to help.' She put her hand to her forehead distractedly. She was bewildered. They had wanted to make money, hadn't they? That was why they had come to the city, wasn't it? She tried to recall the long talks they used to have in the days before they ran away from home. But it was all so long ago. She couldn't remember. Yet surely they had been determined to make money. Wasn't that what all normal people wanted – to make money, and rise in the world?

But Robert was muttering something different.

'The two of us. Just the two of us; that's what we wanted,' he murmured. 'To go away together, and not have your mother all the time nagging at us!' His face brightened as he spoke, and it was almost as if it was of the future he spoke and not of the past that had never fruited. 'The two of us. Just the two of us.' He began to smile. But suddenly his glance grew dark again and he tried to see across the room into the corner where the girls were whispering together. 'And now,' he cried in a loud bitter voice, 'now I'm going to die in a house full of strangers.'

The girls looked at each other. Dolly plucked her mother by the sleeve.

'Tell him it's only us.' But her mother swung around.

'Don't bother me, I'll tell him nothing. What are you doing in here anyway? Get out of the room. Can't you see you're irritating him?'

In their surprise the girls made no protest, but moved to the door, and as they went they heard their mother speaking to their father again, but her words were hardly coherent.

'It's not too late. We can go away now, Robert. We'll get a cottage. We'll go away, and get a little cottage, and be together, Robert! Robert!' She raised her voice as if she would force him to hear her. 'Do you hear me? We'll get out of this place. We'll get a cottage, away out in the country, just the two of us; like you wanted.' She sprang up and rushed across the kitchen. 'There was a cottage advertised in yesterday's paper,' she said, and the girls could hear her searching for the paper. Then they heard her run back to their father. 'I can't find the paper now,' she cried, 'but it's somewhere about the place; I'll look it up. That cottage might be the very thing for us. Three rooms, it said, three rooms, and a garden at the back. Think of it, Robert! You'd like that, wouldn't you?' She was suddenly secure again, a person who could not be bested. For a moment it had looked as if something had gone wrong. But everything would be all right after all.

Outside in the passage Dolly and Mary listened.

'Did you hear that?' Dolly said. 'The two of them! And what about us?' Angry spots of red burned in her cheeks.

But Mary looked pale. 'I think Father is delirious,' she said. 'I think he's forgotten about us.' Her eyes opened wide. 'I think he doesn't remember we were ever born!'

'But what about Mother?' Dolly demanded. 'She knows we were born! She's not delirious. What does she mean, talking about a cottage in the country with three rooms?'

All of a sudden Nonny began to whimper.

'Now see what you've done,' said Mary to Dolly. 'Hush, Nonny. It's nothing to worry about. Mother and Father are only planning a holiday.'

But it was their mother alone who was making plans. She dashed out into the hall just then.

'Where is yesterday's paper?' she cried. She was angry and querulous, as if one of them had deliberately withheld it from her. She went over to the miscellaneous pile of things that she herself had gathered together in armfuls earlier and flung out into the hallway, but she was too distracted to know what she was doing. Mary went over to help her and soon found the paper. When she handed it to her mother Ella snatched it up and eagerly searched out a small paragraph in the advertisement columns. Then she ran back to the kitchen with it.

'Look at that,' she cried, and pressed it into Robert's hands, but she was too impatient to wait for the tired eyes to focus on it and she caught it up again. 'I'll read it for you,' she cried. 'Listen! Three rooms! And a garden! Think of that, Robert. Just what we want. Just suitable for two people. Just what you wanted. Just the two of us.'

In the hallway Dolly put an arm around Nonny. She felt suddenly sad, but it was not sadness for herself, it was for Mary and Nonny. After all, she would be getting married soon. She looked down at Nonny. She might be able to have Nonny to live with her. Then what would become of Mary? But Mary was smiling.

Yes, Mary was smiling, although it was a weak, sad smile. And it faded when they heard their father trying to say something. Their mother evidently could not hear what it was either because she came to the door and called them.

'What is he trying to say?' she asked, and she beckoned them to come back into the room.

The girls listened. Their father spoke again. Dolly couldn't catch what he said at all, but Mary bent close to him.

'It's too late now.' That was what Robert said.

Mary raised her sad eyes. 'He said it's too late now, Mother.'

'Too late? What does he mean?' Ella stared at Mary. She wanted to contradict him, but she had no longer the strength to argue. 'Tell him he'll be all right in a couple of days,' she said to Mary. 'Tell him the country air will cure him. Tell him about this –' and she pointed to the paper in her hand. 'Tell him about the cottage that's advertised here.'

But when Mary bent down again to her father he put out his hand, and with a violence unexpected from one in his weak condition he gave her a push and knocked her back against the table.

'Strangers,' he said bitterly. 'Strangers everywhere.'

Mary turned to her mother.

'I think he's raving, Mother,' she said, but even as she spoke she was struck by the expression in her father's eyes as compared with that in her mother's face. Her mother was the one who looked distracted, whereas her father, in spite of his rambling talk, was looking at her with a fierce and, it seemed, a conscious antagonism. But such a groundless antagonism was in itself unnatural. 'You ought to get the doctor for him, Mother,' she said.

Ella however was not listening.

'It's her mind that's wandering,' Dolly said impatiently. 'Just listen to her!'

For Ella was sitting down with the paper in her hands, staring at the advertisement for the cottage.

'I'm sure there wouldn't be many people would want that cottage,' she said. 'I'm sure they couldn't ask a high rent for it in the heart of the country. I'm sure we could get it.'

'What will we do?' Mary asked despairingly of Dolly.

The man in the corner was muttering louder and louder, and shouting out against the strangers that he seemed now to imagine all around him. He even made efforts to struggle to his feet in order to get at them and put them out of the house.

'We'll have to do something,' said Mary, wringing her hands, and she caught her mother by the arm. 'Mother! Mother! Listen to me! We ought to get the doctor for him.'

Ella shook off Mary's hand.

'Get me a scissors,' she said. 'I'll cut this piece out of the paper so that it won't get lost. Someone might tear up the paper on me.'

But Dolly went over and took the paper out of her mother's hands.

'We can talk about the cottage later on,' she said, 'but we must get the doctor for him now.'

It was Nonny who brought things to a head. She was sorely perplexed; the strain had told on her. Sisters were only sisters, but what she wanted was a father or a mother. And now there was this strange talk about her parents going away. Where were they going?

And what was to become of her? She looked from one of her parents to the other. Which of them would tell her? The distraught condition of her mother and the bright alive look in her father's eyes determined her to turn to him, and running over she buried her golden head in the blanket about his knees. Instantly there was tension in the room. Mary started as if to pull her back, but she was too late. She could only stand by and stare.

It seemed for a minute that Robert knew the child, so concentratedly did he stare at her, but after a moment they saw it was the concentration of unutterable anger. Gathering up unbelievable strength, he put out his thin bony hands and gave Nonny a violent push backward.

'Who is this child?' he cried. 'Take her away. Am I never to have any peace?' And then raising his voice he began to shout. 'Strangers!' he cried. 'Strangers! Strangers!'

There was dead silence after that, and then Nonny began to scream. Opening her mouth to show her small stunted teeth, she screamed and screamed. Ella came to her senses.

'Come here, Nonny,' she cried, and she caught the child to her breast. 'He doesn't know you, darling,' she said appeasingly, and tears began to flow down her own face.

'We'll have to take matters into our own hands,' said Dolly. 'I'll go for the doctor. What doctor will I get?'

But there was no need to take things into their own hands. Nonny's tears had roused Ella. She had begun to capitulate to the force of events. She got to her feet. She was more urgent now than any of them.

'We should have got the doctor hours ago,' she said, and now she was blaming everyone. 'I'll go for the doctor myself,' she said. 'He wouldn't come quick enough if one of you went. But I'll make him come.' And snatching her coat she ran toward the door. 'I won't get the dispensary doctor. I'll get a private doctor.' At the door she halted. 'Which is the best doctor to get?' she cried, and then she ran back into the room and threw herself down on her knees again. 'I'll get the best doctor in the city for you, Robert,' she said, shaking him to make him hear. 'He'll have you as good as new inside an hour!'

Mary was strained to breaking point.

'Get some doctor anyway, quick, Mother, for God's sake,' she said, 'or it will be too late.'

When the doctor came he said that Robert would have to be taken to hospital. The girls dreaded the effect this would have on their mother, yet Ella took it fairly well and began at once to busy herself with preparations for his removal.

'Get the best ambulance you can, Doctor,' she said, and she kept impressing this injunction on him all the way down the hall as he took his leave.

And when the ambulance came it was she who saw to everything, and made the ambulance men promise not to jolt the stretcher, and even went out into the street with them and sent away the crowd of children that had collected to gape at the spectacle. She would have ridden to the hospital in the ambulance with him but the regulations forbid such a thing.

'No one is allowed to ride in the ambulance, ma'am,' the stretcher bearers said as they prepared to take their departure.

She had to give in to them of course, but she ran to the front and spoke to the driver.

'Drive carefully,' she cried to him, and then, just as they moved away she remembered something else and she ran along the path beside the moving vehicle. 'Take care you don't let him be put in a public ward!' she cried. 'I want him put in a private room.'

As the attendants did not appear to hear her she turned frantically to her daughters. 'Hurry, girls!' she cried. 'Go after them. You can go quicker than me. Go down to the hospital, and be sure he's put into a private ward. And tell the nurses he's to get every attention. Tell them that. Let them know we can pay for it all. Let them know he has people that care about him. That counts for a lot with those nurses.' They were standing out in the street, and the girls were ready to go, but she called them back. 'Wait a minute. You'll need money. I want to give the porter at the desk a tip. It will let him see that Robert is a person of some importance. He'll be able to let us in and out, you know, on the sly, outside the regular visiting hours.' She rummaged in the pocket of her skirt and pulled out several notes and some small coins. 'Have you enough, do you think?' she cried, as she pressed the money into their hands. They took the money and turned away, but as they went they heard her calling after them urging them to hurry. Yet they had not reached the end of the street when they heard her running after them. 'Come back a minute,' she cried, and she was panting from lack of breath. 'I forgot to tell you – find out if there's anything he wants, and if there is, get it for him. Insist on seeing him. You'll be allowed up to him if you're persistent enough.'

'Aren't you going to come to the hospital yourself, Mother?' Mary asked.

'I am, of course,' said Ella, 'but I want to go down to the shops and get him a few things. I'll bring them with me. His nightshirt is a show. I want to get him a new one. I wouldn't want him to be ashamed in front of the nurses. And I'll get him some oranges. Oranges are a great thing to have beside your bed when you're sick.'

Robert, however, was a bit far gone for oranges. And as Dolly remarked to Mary it didn't make much difference to him whether he was in a private ward or not, although their mother, when she arrived, was insistent that he be changed. For Robert had been put into a temporary ward, until a bed would be vacated in one of the wards proper, and although it was a long airy passage with only another occupant in a bed at the far end, Ella kept after the authorities all that evening and all the next day to get him moved into a proper ward on the first floor.

The girls were embarrassed at the fuss their mother made.

'They'll move him when they get a chance, Mother,' said Mary, 'and this place is nice and bright.' She was thinking of the damp room at the back of the kitchen where he had slept for the last twenty years.

Dolly protested also, and she tried to kill two birds with the one stone, and make her mother see how bad their father was.

'I don't see what it matters where he is at the moment, Mother,' she said. 'I don't think he knows where he is at all. He doesn't take any notice of anything.'

'It does matter,' Ella insisted. 'We must let the nurses see that we are particular about him.' She looked down at the lifeless figure stretched on the hospital bed. 'He's quiet because he's resting. That's what he needs; rest. Don't disturb him.' She looked around. 'I hope there won't be noise here,' she said, and the girls were embarrassed again because of there being only one other patient in the ward. This patient was a brawny young man, whose leg was tied up in some kind of splint, and whose main object was to get the nurses to sit on the side of his bed and talk to him. He looked good-natured and considerate and they hoped he would not think their mother's remarks were a reflection on him. They whispered together and then Mary drew her mother's attention to him, but Ella when she turned to look at him saw only the table beside his bed, for on it there was a plate with a large bunch of purple grapes. 'Grapes!' said Ella. 'I should have got Robert some grapes. I heard one time that a person can swallow the pulp of a grape when nothing else will stay in the stomach.' She opened her bag and pulled out a half crown. 'There's a shop around the corner. I saw it when I was coming in here – and they had lovely fruit in the window. Run out and see if you can get some grapes.' She looked back at the other bed and her eye fell on a pile of papers and magazines. 'Get him some papers too. He used to like reading the paper.'

Mary hesitated. She did not take the coin.

'I have the money you gave me yesterday,' she said evasively.

But Dolly spoke out.

'What's the use of spending money foolishly?' she said. 'He's too far gone to eat anything. And it's only nonsense to think of him reading, when he doesn't even know where he is!'

'Mind your own business,' her mother said sharply. 'You ought to be ashamed of yourself, talking of saving money at a time like this. Wouldn't I get him anything in the whole world that he wanted?' She raised her voice and bent over the man in the bed. 'Wouldn't I?' she cried. 'Wouldn't I, Robert?'

Robert was moved next day to a ward on the second landing. Ella was more or less satisfied.

'It shows they think something of him,' she said, and she looked around her with satisfaction. 'You can see that this is a good ward by the class of patients in it.'

There were five other beds in the ward. One was unoccupied. In one there was a young man who was still under the influence of an anaesthetic. In another there was a small boy with a bad leg. The third bed was occupied by an old man who was allowed to get up and move about the ward in his dressing gown. And one bed they could not see because there was a screen around it.

Ella looked at the other patients and noted the crowded condition of the small enamel tables beside their beds, and everything she saw with these other patients she wanted to get for Robert.

'I must get him some apples,' she cried, as she saw the old man painstakingly peeling a large red apple while he sat on his bed with his legs dangling. And when she saw some story books on the young boy's table she went home and rooted out two or three mildewed volumes of poetry in old-fashioned bindings with gilt edges that had somehow been saved from destruction, and she brought them up to the hospital. 'When he starts to come round to his senses,' she said, 'he'll be glad to see them.'

Dolly nudged Mary. 'It's a good job there's a screen around the bed at the end so she can't see what's behind it, because if she brings any more stuff in here it will have to be put under the bed.' She laughed.

But Mary could not laugh. She looked down the ward uneasily. 'I wonder what's the matter with that patient? He must be dying.'

The bed at the end of the ward had a screen around it all the time, and nothing could be seen of the patient, although at visiting hours a thin nervous woman in black came up the ward and noiselessly passing behind it took up a position of vigilance at the bedside of the patient. Through the joints of the screen the thin black figure of the woman could be seen sitting silent and tight-lipped, her fingers ceaselessly moving as she passed the beads of a worn rosary through them with the dextrous movements of a card player slickly dealing out cards. The woman never seemed to bring anything to the patient behind the screen.

'He's too ill to appreciate anything, I suppose,' Mary said.

'She has more sense than Mother,' Dolly said. 'I suppose she's his wife.'

The woman was at that moment passing down the ward, unsmiling and walking noiselessly with her eyes to the ground. The two girls looked after her curiously, but they were recalled to their surroundings by Ella.

'Calf's-foot jelly!' she said in a loud voice, speaking out of a deep reverie. 'There's nothing like it for a sick person. I'll get him a jar of calf's-foot jelly.'

'For goodness' sake, Mother, don't bring anything else for a while,' said Mary. 'Wait till he's able to enjoy things.'

Dolly nudged her.

'Don't be giving her false hope,' she said. 'He'll never enjoy anything again.' And she looked at the man in the bed, the counterpane motionless under his inert body, and she looked at the littered table beside the bed. 'Those grapes will get rotten,' she said. 'He'll never eat them!'

As a matter of fact, after a day or two the grapes began to lose their bloom, and the girls themselves ate one or two of the oranges. The magazines began to get crumpled and used-looking and marked with wet rings from the glasses and medicine bottles that the nurses left down on them. As for the poetry books, the nurses put them into the locker under the table because they were only cluttering up the small space of the cubicle.

But still Ella brought in paper bags of fruit and biscuits and sweets. And all the time Robert remained unconscious of her ministrations, or at least as indifferent to them as he had been to her promises of the bench outside the house and the carnation for his lapel. He just lay on his back looking up at the ceiling, and Ella's consolation in the fact that he sometimes nodded his head when she bent down and spoke to him was spoiled somewhat by the fact that he also did it once or twice when no one was speaking to him at all. He divided his time between long periods of complete unconsciousness and shorter periods when he seemed to recover consciousness only to carry on long incoherent conversations with himself in an undertone.

When he was three days in the hospital there was hardly room to sit beside him in the cubicle with all the things Ella had brought with her to try and attract his attention.

'Look, Robert,' she'd cry, bending over the bed and holding out something for him to see. But Robert gave no sign that he saw anything.

Finally the nurses got impatient with Ella, and spoke irritably to the girls.

'I wish that woman would stop bringing in this rubbish,' one of them said one day when she found it difficult to make a place for the thermometer on the top of the crowded table. She turned to Mary. 'Can't you make your mother see that he is too far gone to take any notice of these things? What kind of a woman is she? Why can't she behave like other visitors? Look around! No one in the ward is treated the way she treats this man. No wonder he doesn't come back to his senses. She has him bothered. She shouldn't be let in here at all!'

Mary was embarrassed. She resented the harshness of the nurse. But Dolly could understand the nurse's irritation and she defended her. 'It's true for her,' she said. 'I wonder why Mother's behaving like this? I suppose it's remorse for the way she treated him in the past!'

But Mary looked away and the sad look came into her pale thin face and her eyes shone with tears.

'It's not as simple as that,' she said. 'Mother doesn't feel any remorse. If she did she would be more upset. It would probably break her heart. I don't think she realises how unkind she has always been to him. I don't think she is aware of the way their lives were wasted away in bitterness. I think it just seems like a bad spell they got into, and that it will pass away and they will come out again into happy times like they used to have long ago. She doesn't blame herself at all. She thinks they were both the victims of misfortune.'

Dolly looked at her sister. She didn't fully understand what Mary was saying. She was thinking how different they were. She is more like Father, she thought. I'm more like Mother. And she felt irritated with Mary's subtlety and gentleness.

'I think it's us who were the victims of misfortune,' she said. 'We've heard nothing but quarrelling and fighting since the day we were born.' Suddenly she wanted to hurt Mary. 'Thank goodness I'm going to be married soon and get away from it all.' Then as she looked back at the unconscious man in the bed a disturbing thought came into her mind. 'If he dies now I suppose I'll have to put back my wedding plans for another six months.'

Mary's face quivered and she looked anxiously at her father. 'Mind would he hear you, Dolly!'

'Don't be silly,' said Dolly. 'You're as bad as Mother with her grapes and her nonsense. Can't anyone with an eye in their head see that he's unconscious?' But she looked at him guiltily, regretting her words. Then she went over and bent down. 'Father!' she said, and her voice was firm and authoritative, unlike her mother's cringing appeals to him. 'Father! Can you hear me?' There was no recognition whatever on the white face. Dolly straightened up. 'It's my belief that he won't come back to his senses at all.'

Mary nodded her head in agreement. 'Poor Mother,' she said. 'I wish for her sake that he would come around just long enough to notice all she tried to do for him. If she could have the satisfaction of his seeing all the things she brought him.' She brightened. 'It would be nice for him too. I'd love him to know how she tried to make up to him for the past. He would think it was like the old days.' She caught Dolly's arm eagerly. 'Do you remember he used sometimes to talk about the time when they were young, and how yellow her hair used to be, when she went walking in some meadow with him. I often think of that. I think that if he could only see all she's doing for him now it would be just like as if the sun had burst out again after a long time, and it wouldn't matter how dark it had been, or how long the darkness had lasted. Nothing would matter if that sun shone again, bright, bright, bright, even for a few minutes.' She moved nearer to the bed and gazed down at her father with a passionate look in her eyes. 'If only he'd open his eyes. If only he'd speak. How happy they both would be!'

But Dolly shrugged her shoulders. She was still irritated by the thought that she might have to postpone her own plans.

'I don't think they deserve to be happy!' she said bitterly.

'Don't say that,' Mary said sharply.

'I will!' said Dolly. 'I'm sick of it all.' But as her father murmured and seemed to be in pain, she was filled with remorse. 'Do you think he's suffering?' said Dolly. 'Poor Father! I suppose he deserves it.'

'Deserves what?'

'Oh, what you were saying about the sunshine, and all that. I wish for his sake he could see the way she is trying to make up to him. If he did, I suppose he'd die happy.' But her softness only lasted a moment. 'I can't say our mother deserves much though!' she said. 'It would serve her right if he died without getting back his senses.' She looked angrily at the plate of grapes. Several of the grapes were beginning to rot, and around them a fly buzzed. 'I'm going to throw them out!' she said, and breaking off some of the rotted grapes she caught them up in the palm of her hand with an expression of disgust and looked around for somewhere to throw them. At the far end of the ward there was an open window, and walking across to it she threw them out into the street. 'I don't care!' she said, in answer to the unspoken criticism of her sister's face. 'I was sick of the sight of them.'

When Ella arrived the first thing her eye fell on was the plate of grapes from which the large bunch had been cut. Her face, that was furrowed by fatigue, straightened out, and a light came into her eyes.

'He ate the grapes?' she cried, in delight.

The girls said nothing although Mary's lips moved and if Dolly hadn't been listening she might have told a lie, and said he had eaten them. But she felt her sister's eyes upon her, defying her to give in to such weakness.

Ella read their faces. Her eyes grew dull again. She took out a soiled handkerchief and began to wipe her neck. There was sweat on it from the strain of climbing the stairs in a hurry.

'Don't cry now, Mother,' Dolly said crossly, and Ella looked meekly at her and put away the handkerchief. Her old obstinacy was breaking down. She was getting uncertain about everything. She would have liked to talk about her disappointment over the grapes, but she was afraid of Dolly. But just then the Sister-in-Charge came into the ward. She was a small red-faced nun, with a kind face, secure and complacent in her own beliefs. Ella turned to her eagerly.

'I thought he ate the grapes,' she said, and she sat down despondently on the bed, another paper bag of fruit unopened in her hands.

But the Sister had heard the complaints of the nurses. She disregarded Ella and spoke in an undertone to the girls.

'I think it would be better if she could be made to understand that he's too far gone for these things. It's only waste of money.' She looked at their poor clothes, and Mary blushed. She knew what the nun was thinking.

'We don't mind the money!' she said defensively.

Ella raised her head. She overheard the last sentence.

'That's right,' she said, looking at Mary. 'Spare no expense!' She even appealed to the Sister. 'Is there nothing I can get for him?' She turned and threw herself across the coverlet of the bed. 'My poor darling,' she cried. 'Robert! Robert! Is there nothing I can do for you? Why don't you know me? It's Ellie. It's your own Ellie! Ellie – who'd do anything in the world for you!' But the impassive face had no reply, and she turned back to the others. 'If only there was something I could get for him; something to ease him!'

The girls said nothing. They looked at the nun. The nun looked back at them as if she would like to have conferred with them alone, but since this was impracticable just then, she nodded her head to signify that she could not neglect the opportunity afforded by Ella's own words. She put her arm around Ella.

'You want to do something for your husband, do you, you poor woman? Well, there is only one thing you can do for him. You can pray that God will give him the grace of a happy death.'

Ella drew back from the nun's embrace.

'He's not going to die!' she said fiercely.

But the nun had entered into a familiar domain. She ignored the nervous murmuring of the girls, and even a slight stir in the man in the bed.

'We must all die, sooner or later,' she said. 'It doesn't much matter when we go. But what does matter is the manner in which we die! Will we get the grace to die a happy death, or will we not? And if we are unable, like this poor man, to pray for that grace ourselves, what more can those do who love us than pray that God will give us the grace we are unable to ask for with our own dying lips?' The words fell easily from the untroubled lips of the nun, like a lesson long learned, and it echoed in the ears of those around with the familiar notes they had heard a hundred times in sermons and mission lectures. Then the nun's voice grew warmer, and more personal. She took Ella's hand and pressed it.

'Pray for him, my child. Pray that God will give him that inestimable thing that surpasses all else in the world – the grace to die a happy death. You can give him no greater thing.'

Ella pulled away her hands but this time it was to wipe her face. Her tears had begun again. The nun looked around her quickly, and taking up a bunch of the decaying grapes she held it in front of Ella.

'Think of all the Masses that could have been said for the benefit of his soul with money that was spent on this perishable matter!'

There was a pause. Had the nun succeeded? The girls held their breath. In the next bed the old man who had been putting on his socks sat listening, with one sock on and one sock off. The nun herself could be seen silently moving her lips in prayer while under the fold of her habit her fingers ran over the wooden beads of her rosary.

Suddenly Ella stood up.

'How long is it since he was at the Sacraments?' she asked the girls.

They all exchanged glances. She had not only comprehended the nun's words, but with her impetuous nature she had already outstripped her in thought.

'Do you think is there any danger he would die without recovering consciousness?' she asked, but she didn't wait for an answer. 'We should have sent for the priest for him,' she said. 'We should have done it long ago. Why didn't someone mention the matter to me?' But when the girls made a stir as if they would do something about it, she pushed them aside. 'I'll attend to this. Some priests are more sympathetic than others. I don't want him to be upset. Some priests have very poor manners! I'll get a Franciscan; that's what I'll do. The Franciscans are all lovely men.' Her enthusiasm swelled into a great flood.

Like the bench in front of the house, like the cottage with the three rooms, like the grapes, the oranges, the books of poetry with the gold edges, now it was eternal salvation she wanted for him. She was ready to dart away at once to get it. But she stopped, frightened, and caught at the nun by the arm.

'What will I do if he doesn't recover consciousness? He won't be able to make his confession! He won't be able to talk!' She was startled. She was terror-stricken.

'The priest has already paid him a routine visit,' the Sister said more gently. 'And of course we'll let him know the minute there is a change. He has been anointed and been given conditional absolution.'

But this wasn't good enough for Ella. For days it had been impossible to convince her that he was dying, but in her determination to procure him all the rites of the Church she was instantly reconciled. These rites might be the last thing that she could procure for him.

'Conditional absolution isn't enough,' she cried. 'He'll have to come around to his senses.' Suddenly she threw herself down on the bed again. 'Robert! Robert!' Then she looked around her wildly. 'He'll have to come around. Couldn't the doctor give him something to bring him around, just for a few minutes; just for long enough to make an act of contrition?' Then she remembered something else. She straightened up. 'There should be a blessed crucifix placed in front of him so that his eyes would fall on it if he opened them. Just to look at the crucifix could save your soul, even if you weren't able to speak. Did you know that? I always heard that said. Where will we get one?' She began to fumble in her pocket for money to send the girls out to buy one. The nun put out a hand to calm her, and detaching the long brass crucifix that dangled from her belt she proffered it. But Ella pushed it aside. 'It should be made of wood,' she said authoritatively, and drawing still further upon some obscure fund of theological superstition she cried out again. 'A habit!' she cried. 'He should have a habit ready. If he only got one arm out in the sleeve of it he'd be saved. The left arm; nearest the heart.' Hastily drawing out a greasy purse she gave it to Mary. 'Get a habit,' she ordered, 'and a crucifix. I'll stay here and try and bring him around.' A fever of energy had made her cheeks glow, and from the depths of some repository of knowledge and superstition, long undisturbed, she brought up a score of suggestions. 'If we held a lighted candle in front of his eyes, he might open them!' she cried. 'If we wet his lips he might speak! Do you think it would be any use to wipe over his face with a cloth wrung out in cold water?' She was determined to bring him around, if only, as she said, over and over again, if only for one moment.

From that hour there was continual excitement. Ella was in and out of the hospital as often as she could gain admittance, and in the intervals she did not rest but sped all over the city, going from church to church lighting blessed candles and arranging to have Masses said for her special intention. The special intention was always the same. The prayers were all offered for Robert's return to consciousness. And when she was in the ward there was such confusion that they put a screen around Robert's bed, while the mother of the small boy in the opposite bed made so many complaints about the noise they had to move the boy to another ward.

'What will we do with her at all?' said the nun who had first put the idea of a happy death into her head. For Ella was inconsolable. 'After all,' the nun said at last, 'you haven't such great cause to worry. Your husband led a good life. He was a good man. And he has already been given conditional absolution. God is merciful, you know. But what would you do if you were that poor creature?' She nodded down toward the end of the ward where, behind the screen, the woman in black was just discernible sitting alert and vigilant beside her husband's bed. 'That poor woman down there has cause to worry. Her husband is unconscious too like yours, but how different his life has been!'

Ella was barely listening, but the girls looked curiously at the screen.

'An atheist!' the nun said in an undertone, and she made the sign of the cross over her breast as inconspicuously as possible, because the woman in black had raised her head and seemed to be looking in their direction. 'She can't hear us,' the nun said reassuringly as Mary's face reddened. 'And even if she did, she wouldn't mind. She's a saint if ever there was one. She doesn't mind who knows her story. She is aware that it could be a lesson to others. That's what she said to me. And so it will. There he is now, after his life of sin and blasphemy, stretched speechless without the power to utter one syllable in supplication for God's pardon!' The nun shook her head sadly. 'That poor woman's life has been a trial to her from the day she married him, but she never lost her faith in God's goodness. She offered up all her sufferings to the Almighty. And she never ceased praying for her husband's return to the Faith. Even now, she has not lost hope, and every hour that she spends by his bedside is occupied in silent prayer for him.'

The girls felt uncomfortable at this point, fancying that there was an implied criticism of their mother in the nun's words.

'Is he unconscious too?' asked Dolly.

The nun shook her head sorrowfully. 'Alas, not all the time. How much better if he were!'

Dolly did not understand.

'Whenever he comes to his senses,' the nun said, 'it is only to utter curses and blasphemies. Fortunately the periods of consciousness are getting fewer. When he was first brought in here it was terrifying to listen to him. The night nurse would not stay on duty alone. She said it was as if there was an Evil Presence in the ward!' The nun shuddered. Then she looked at Ella. 'It should console your mother, to hear about that man. What would she do if she was the wife of that man?'

But Ella was not to be so consoled by anything. She had set her heart on one thing, and she was determined that Robert would come to his senses.

'If we brought Nonny up to him!' she exclaimed when the girls were trying to make her listen to what the nun had told them about the other man. 'He might hear Nonny. He might heed her where he wouldn't heed anyone else. A child's voice is very penetrating.'

But when they brought Nonny she was so timid she could hardly be persuaded to open her mouth. And when they urged her forward to the bedside, she hung back and clutched at Mary's skirt.

'Call him, Nonny!' Ella ordered. 'Call him. He'll know your voice. He'll hear you! He'll come back to his senses when you call him. Go on. Call him.' Nonny opened her mouth, but she could hardly be heard by those standing beside her. The mother gave her a jerk. 'Who could hear that?' she exclaimed irritably. 'Where is your voice? Call him again. What are you afraid of anyway? Raise your voice. Go on! Call him. Call him again.' But the child was nervous and overconscious, and would only utter a few weak cries. Finally Ella sent her home in disgust. 'No matter! When the priest comes he'll bring him back,' she said. 'The priests have wonderful power in their tongues. Wait till the priest comes.'

The Franciscan Father, when he came, however, occupied himself more with Ella than with Robert.

'You must not give way to despair,' he said. 'You must trust in God. God's ways are strange. God's ways are not our ways.' Then he became more practical. 'There doesn't seem to be any immediate danger, or I would anoint him, but I'll look in later in the night to see how he is getting along. At the least sign of danger I can assure you I will exercise my powers.' He patted Ella's shoulder reassuringly.

'You're not going, Father!' cried Ella. She was afraid to let him away. 'He might take worse suddenly.'

But the priest had other duties, as he explained rapidly to the girls in a low voice.

'I have other sick calls to make,' he said. 'I must try to be where I am needed. I do not think I am needed here – not just yet.'

Afterward they all recalled his last words.

'God's ways are wonderful indeed,' the nun said.

For just as the priest was leaving Robert's bedside, there was a sudden sound of a chair being pushed back and a woman's voice rose in a sharp exclamation. A minute later the screen by Robert's bed was pushed aside and the woman in black rushed into the cubicle.

For a moment the others hardly recognised her. The face that had for so long outstared the enemy wore a defeated look that was at odds with the words she uttered.

'My prayers have been heard,' she said. She looked as if she might at any minute start to laugh foolishly. Ella and the girls could not immediately comprehend what had happened. But the nun understood at once.

'God be praised,' she said, and forgetting Robert, forgetting Ella, forgetting even the Franciscan Father, she pushed aside the screen, and followed by the excited nurse, she hastened to the end of the ward. The Franciscan then, although he had no previous history of the case, seemed to divine what had occurred. 'Thank God I was here,' he said. 'His ways are indeed wonderful!' And like the others, forgetting Robert, forgetting even to push aside a chair over which he nearly fell, he too hurried down the ward to the bedside of the penitent, from whom there had come a despairing cry.

'A priest! For God's sake, get me a priest!' the man cried. 'Don't let me die in my sins.'

It was a miracle. Word of it flew all over the hospital. Nurses and Sisters whom Ella and her daughters had never seen came running to proclaim it. There was untold activity. Screens were hurriedly pushed back to permit the passage of those carrying candles, holy water – a crucifix.

As for the man himself, who had lain prone so long, he had started up from the pillow, and in spite of the hands that tried to hold him down he was almost standing in the bed, his eyes burning as in fever, and the sweat beading his face.

'Mercy!' he cried in a voice for all to hear, and terrifyingly lucid. 'Oh God, have mercy on me, miserable sinner that I am,' he cried. But when way was made at the bedside for the Franciscan he did not recognise his garb and tried to push him away. 'Mercy! Mercy! Mercy!' he screamed. It was as if he already gazed upon the Face of the Godhead, but being perhaps blinded by the lightning flash of his conversion, he could not distinguish upon that Dazzling Countenance the attributes of mercy from the attributes of wrath. 'I am lost!' he cried. 'Lost!' And even when he was at last made to understand that the priest was there, it was some time before he could be convinced that it was not too late for him to seek salvation. Babbling bits of half-forgotten prayers, he clutched convulsively at the priest's hands and covered them with kisses.

In the other beds in the ward the patients were all sitting up in excitement, except for Robert, who lay silent and still behind his screen, which was slightly awry after the abrupt departure of the Sister and the nurse. And then, suddenly, the Sister, who had gone hurriedly out of the ward a few moments previously, came back carrying in her hand two tall black candlesticks in which burned long wax candles, the flames of which, as she moved, flowed backward so swiftly that the eye could hardly see the tenuous thread that connected wick with flame. When the Sister was halfway down the floor of the ward she stopped, and beckoning one of the nurses she nodded her head in the direction of Robert's bed.

'Take that screen,' she said. 'We can get another one later for that patient.'

Before Ella could protest, the screen had been whisked away and a moment later, although Ella still stared in the direction of the penitent's bed, she could see nothing but the shadows of those behind the screen, chief amongst which was the shadow of the priest with a raised crucifix in his hands. Then the Sister appeared again around the corner of the screen. She came toward Ella who was standing alone by Robert's bedside. 'My daughters had to go,' Ella said. 'The little one was frightened and they had to take her home. It's too bad. I thought Nonny's voice might reach him. She has a very penetrating voice.' But the nun wasn't listening to Ella. Her thoughts were still occupied with the man at the other end of the ward.

'A miracle!' she exclaimed. 'That's what it is; a miracle. God works in a mysterious way. How I hope that I may be shown the same mercy when my turn comes. Think of it! A man who lived a life of sin; an enemy of the Church; a blasphemer. Ah yes; it is true indeed; God loves the sinner.' The nun folded her arms in the form of a cross. Then suddenly she uncrossed them again and looked around her. The light in the ward was fading rapidly now. She became aware of the irregularity of Ella's presence.

'I'm afraid it's time for you to go,' she said, but she spoke kindly, and as Ella looked back in anguish at Robert she nodded her head in understanding.

'Don't lose hope,' she said. 'God's ways are wonderful. I'm sure your husband will regain consciousness. You'll see. God will not fail to give him a happy death.' She nodded back over her shoulder at the patient at the far end of the ward. 'You ought to be greatly encouraged,' she said, 'by this marvellous example.'

As Ella went toward the door, she caught a last glimpse of the other patient. The excitement had abated, and except for the Franciscan, who stood at the end of the bed, his hands joined in prayer, and the candles that fluttered and strained upward, the scene was almost the same. The woman in black still sat with stiffly folded hands at the bedside, and the man, exhausted now, lay on his back staring up at the ceiling.

'And no wonder he was exhausted!' Ella said later that night, when she was telling the girls. 'I never heard such shrieks. They were hardly human.' She sighed. 'When that shrieking didn't rouse your father, nothing will rouse him. Oh, what will I do? What will I do?' And frantically she looked at the clock to see if there was yet time to arrange for another Mass for him. 'If he'd only come to himself for five minutes. Five minutes would be enough.'

'Even if he doesn't, Mother,' said Mary, 'you have no need to worry. Poor Father. He'll go straight to heaven. What did he ever do that was wrong? He never hurt anyone in all his life.'

Under her breath, Dolly was muttering.

'The only one he ever hurt was himself. He put his purgatory over him here in this world.'

Ella wasn't satisfied.

'How do we know what sins he might have on his soul?' she cried, and she threw up her hands and began to wail. 'I'll never rest an hour if he dies without recognising the priest. What does anything matter as long as a person gets a happy death? Isn't it the only thing that counts in this world?'

And it seemed to her that morning would never come when she would renew her vigil at his bedside, where by now instead of bags of oranges and apples there was an accumulation of crucifixes and blessed candles, holy water and medals, all of which by turns she pressed against his lips and his forehead and his hands in the hope that they would bring him back from the bottomless silence into which he had sunk.

The next day when it came at last, and they went back to the hospital, passed in much the same manner as the day before it. Robert's condition was unchanged. But there was no sign of the man who had occupied the bed at the end of the ward. The nurse said he had died shortly after Ella had left the hospital the previous night.

'It was an edifying sight,' the nurse said. 'To see a man who wouldn't let the Name of God be mentioned in his presence, die clutching the priest's hand and crying like a child. An exemplary death! Is there any end to God's mercy? To think that a man like that should be given the grace to die such a death!' Then the nurse remembered Robert's state and she reddened. 'Please God your husband will get the same grace,' she said. Ella and she glanced at the bed on which they were all accustomed now to see Robert's motionless face. When she glanced at him now, the nurse gave a startled cry and bent closer. Then she caught Ella's arm. 'His eyes are open!' she cried, and she rushed over to the bed, but Ella, who reached the bedside almost as quickly, pushed her aside with a violent arm.

'The crucifix! Let him see the crucifix!' she cried, and snatching it up she held it in front of him, almost pushing it into his face. 'Robert! Robert! Look at the cross. Can you see it?' She stared into the open eyes, but there did not seem to be any answering response in them. 'Can you see me at all?' she cried. And then, more anxiously still she shook his arm. 'Can you hear me?' she asked. 'Can you hear me? I want you to repeat an act of contrition. Can you hear? Keep your eyes on the crucifix.' And while she held it in front of him, she looked around at the girls. 'The priest!' she gasped. 'What are you thinking about? Get the priest at once!' Then, turning back to the man on the bed, she entreated him to try and hear her. 'Repeat after me, Robert,' she said, and she began to enunciate the act of contrition. '"O my God,"' she said, and waited for him to repeat the words. 'Robert! Can you hear me? "O my God." Say that after me. "O my God, I am heartily sorry for ever having offended Thee." Robert! Robert! Repeat it after me. Can you hear me?' And the last words were almost a wail because, although the light of recognition had flickered for a moment in his eyes, it had gone out again. She leaned closer. 'Robert! Don't you know me? It's Ellie; your own Ellie!' But in spite of her appeal it seemed as if there would be no change in the face on the pillow. Then suddenly a faint light flashed in the dark eyes of the dying man, and the lips moved as if they would say something. Ella put her face down to the pillow. Yes, he was saying something. But what it was she could not hear. She bent so close she could feel his breath on her face, and then, faint as the breath itself, she caught the word that with great difficulty was formed on the parched lips.

'Ellie!'

That was the word.

Ella straightened her aching back with a sob of relief, and as the nurse came hurrying into the ward, followed by the Sister, she turned around to them, her worn face bathed in happiness.

'He has come to his senses. He spoke to me,' she cried. Tireless, she bent down over the bed once more.

'Robert darling, you know me? You can hear me? It's your own Ellie. And she wants you to do something for her. She wants you to make an act of contrition. Repeat the words after me – "O my God –"'

The girls, who had arrived, crept closer, and the nurse, without saying anything, sat down on the chair beside the bed and took the thin wrist in her hand to feel its pulse. Then she looked at Robert's face.

'He's trying to say something,' she said, for although no sound came from the lips, it seemed that the man was making some effort to speak by the way the muscles of his worn face had begun to work. They listened.

Then, scarcely audible, a few words struggled from his lips.

'Ellie, my own Ellie!' he said.

Ellie's face showed some relief, but there was still a certain anxiety in her eyes.

'Yes, yes, your own Ellie,' she said impatiently. 'But now, Robert, I want you to repeat something after me.'

'Just a minute,' the nurse said. Taking a spoon and a bottle she went over to the patient and forced something between his lips. 'Now!' she said, nodding encouragingly to Ella.

Ella bent down again.

'"O my God!"' she said. 'Repeat that after me, Robert. "O my God, I am heartily sorry for ever having offended Thee." Repeat that. "O my God…"'

But it seemed as if Robert had slipped back into his world of darkness. His eyes closed, and an imperturbable look had settled once more on his ashen face.

'Robert! Robert!' Ella's voice implored him to hear her. 'Don't slip back on me, Robert,' she cried. 'You know me, don't you? It's Ellie, Ellie!' she cried.

The dying man opened his eyes again and again he spoke.

Although showing signs of exhaustion, Ella wasted no time.

'Repeat this after me, Robert,' she cried. '"O my God, I detest all my sins,"' she said, and then, confused, she began to forget the wording of the prayer. '"I am heartily sorry,"' she said. '"Never more to offend Thee."' But now she was not looking at the silent lips, she was turning in despair to the Sister and the nurses. 'What is keeping the priest?' she cried. 'Why doesn't he come? This may be our only chance. He may slip back altogether after this!' She was distracted. She was on the point of collapse.

But just then the priest appeared at the door. Under a white cloth he had the Sacrament for the dying.

'God is good,' he said, by way of salutation to those around the bed, who all fell to their knees before the Presence he brought with him. The priest moved over to the bed, but first he stopped to whisper to the Sister. 'If he wants to make his confession,' he said, 'I'd like you all to draw back from the bedside. Just a few paces is all that will be necessary.'

Those around the bed immediately withdrew.

'The goodness of God! Two such miracles in the one day.' The nun took Ella's hand in hers. 'God has heard your prayers!' she said. 'You have a lot to be thankful for. I must admit there were times when I thought your husband would never regain consciousness.'

Then the priest, who had bent over the man in the bed, straightened up and looked back over his shoulder. He appeared to be in some difficulty. The nun stood up and went over to him.

'Do you want something, Father,' she asked, and she prepared to hand him first the crucifix and then the holy water.

But the priest wanted Ella.

'I think he wants to say something to you,' he said. 'He keeps calling your name. It might be better if you remained within his range of vision.'

'Ellie!' said the man in the bed, and he stared up into her eyes, and now to her joy his eyes seemed once again to be clear and lucid and to shine with all the brightness of consciousness. 'Ellie. My own darling girl.' Like the man who had died at the other end of the ward, he struggled to raise himself on the pillows.

'He's near the end,' the nurse said to Mary, and she hastened to support him, but Robert pushed her aside. The nurse motioned to Ella then, and Ella put her arms around him and held him up. He turned his head and looked at her, and it seemed that he saw nothing else.

'Just the two of us!' he said, and he put up his hand and stroked her hair with a perfectly normal gesture. The onlookers exchanged glances of satisfaction, but a minute afterward they were in doubt again, because although now he spoke clearly, the words he uttered were inexplicable to them. 'Your lovely golden hair,' he said. Taken aback, they all looked at Ella's grey hair on which his hand rested.

Ella continued to support him, but she turned frantically to the priest.

'What will I do?' she said. 'Will I repeat the prayers?' The priest nodded his head. '"O my God,"' said Ella. 'Can you hear that, Robert? "I am heartily sorry." Can you hear that?' And this time Robert seemed to hear.

'Sorry?' he repeated, questioningly. Then he closed his eyes for a moment again, but when he opened them they were filled with a rapturous light, astonishing to behold in a face etched with the lines of an almost lifelong sadness and weariness.

'Yes, yes,' said Ella eagerly, repeating the line that seemed to have caught his attention, while the priest nodded his acquiescence. '"I am heartily sorry,"' she said, speaking slowly and distinctly.

Robert put out his hands and eagerly caught at her hands.

'Sorry?' he said again weakly, then his voice grew suddenly strong and vibrant. 'There's nothing to be sorry about, my darling,' he said. 'We were unfortunate, that was all. It wasn't your fault. I wasn't much good. That was the trouble. I should never have taken you away from your comfortable home. I'm the one who should be sorry, not you.' He had raised himself higher in the bed, and some of the lines of hardship had gone from his face, and an assuredness that was like the assuredness of youth came back into his voice. 'But I'm not sorry,' he said. 'You were all I wanted in the whole world. When I had you I had everything. Even when you spoke harshly to me, I knew it was because you were tired. I knew that I had failed you, and I always forgave you.' He pressed her hand tighter. 'Don't talk about being sorry,' he said again, urgently searching her face for the effect of his words. 'There's nothing to be sorry about. You always made me happy, just by being near me. Just to look at you made my heart brighter. Always. Always. It was always like that.' He sighed then with a long peaceful sigh, and seeing that he had relaxed, the nurse motioned Ella to lower him again onto the pillow. Back on the pillow he closed his eyes, then, but he closed them deliberately and not from fatigue, for a smile played over his face, and showed that he was yielding to some happy thought. 'The meadow,' he said then, in a soft voice little more than a sighing breath. 'Do you remember the meadow? How happy we were walking along the headland holding each other's hands. You could never understand why we had to keep to the headland. You used to want to walk in the high grass. "I'd love to wade through it like water." You said that one day. Do you remember? You wanted to wade through and pick the clover that sweetened the air with its warm scent, and when I told you it would spoil the harvest, you wanted to trample it all down. You were so wilful! So wilful, my darling. That was what I loved best in you; your wilfulness.' Suddenly his voice grew stronger and there was a harsh note in it. 'Your mother knew you were wilful. That was why she was afraid to speak out against me. That was why she did no more than throw out hints about my health. My health was all right then. It would have been all right if she had let us alone, and let us stay where we were happy. We could have got a little cottage outside the town, with a small piece of land. That was what I always wanted.'

Suddenly he struggled to sit up in bed again. 'I don't like that woman,' he said.

Ella, who had been listening with suppressed sobs of remorse and joy, suddenly stopped sobbing. Her mother had been dead for years.

'I don't like her,' said the man at the top of his voice. 'I won't be humiliated by her. I'll take you away. I will!' His voice was fierce. 'Will you come with me, Ellie?' he cried. 'I'll make you happy. Trust me! Trust me, Ellie.' The fierceness that flared up so suddenly as suddenly died out. 'Trust me, Ellie,' he said then in a soft sweet voice, the voice of a young lover. 'I'll make you happy. I promise. I know I can do it. We'll go away from here where we'll be alone; just the two of us. Just the two of us. You and I.'

Since the first mention of her mother, Ella had been sitting with a dazed look on her face, unable to comprehend what had happened. She turned around now with a vacant look at the priest. The priest moved over to the bedside.

'Perhaps after all it might be well for you to stand aside where he wouldn't see you,' he said, 'and then I might be able to regain his attention.' But when the priest came within his range of vision Robert's face changed, and his eyes took on again the wild unnatural glitter.

'There's someone coming!' he shouted, warningly. 'I think it's your sister Daisy. She'll want to come with us! And we don't want her, do we? It's so much nicer alone, just the two of us. Let's hide, Ellie. Let's hide, sweetheart. Let's get behind that tree over there!' Dragging his hand free from Ella he began to point wildly.

The priest shook his head, and moved back to the footrail of the bed where he began to confer earnestly with the nurse and the Sister. Ella sat still, stunned into silence. Dolly coughed nervously. She felt embarrassed at the incongruous intimacy of her father's outburst, even in delirium. She turned to Mary in her discomfort. But Mary was smiling strangely, and staring at her father with a secretive smile that was like a smile of complicity. Dolly was aware again, as she had been a few days earlier, of a great difference between herself and her sister. Mary was like their father. She herself was more like her mother. She looked at her sister's face, and then at the face of her father, but as she looked at him Robert began to move his lips again.

'Just the two of us!' he said, the look of rapturous happiness returning to his face.

And something about that rapturous look caused the nurse to start suddenly to her feet and make a sign to the priest. After one startled glance at Robert, without waiting to stir from where he stood, he raised his hand in the blessing of conditional absolution. At the same time the nurse put her arm quickly around Ella's shoulders to lead her away.

Ella pushed the nurse's arm away, and, not comprehending what was happening, she looked in bewilderment at Robert. But the serene smile that had taken the place of the rapture of a moment before deceived her, and she did not recognise in it the serenity of death, until her daughters, both together, put their arms about her and began to reassure her.

'Never mind, Mother. Never mind! He led a good life. He never did anyone any harm.'

Then Ella understood. Throwing up her arms she began to scream.

Still screaming and sobbing, she was led out of the ward, and it was utterly incomprehensible to her that God had not heard her prayers, and had not vouchsafed to her husband the grace of a happy death.

Magenta

The house was closed, and the furniture in the reception rooms was covered with great white sheets. The shutters were up on the lower windows, bolted fast, and only opened on warm, sunny days to let air through the house. The lands were let for grazing, and although the gardens were kept weeded, there was no attempt made to set new plants or renew the soil. There was a man in the garden, and he kept up the general appearance of the place as far as it was possible for one man to do. In time, however, the ivy crept closer and closer over the window-panes till they crossed the glass here and there like a lattice. And although the paths were all easily discernible from the lush grass of the overgrown lawns they were no longer gravel paths but green lanes of moss and weed.

It would be hard to say whether it was more silent and lonely there in summer or in winter, for although the evenings were brighter in the summer time, the rich growth of weed and shrub and underwood stifled the place with greenery, and all day long a humidity from all this foliage pervaded the air and lowered the vitality. In winter, indeed, it was often less lonely, for although the nights fell fast and dark there was a certain spaciousness between the bare branches of the trees, and the grasses were flattened by the wind.

There were two maids employed in the house permanently. They were supposed to keep the rooms from becoming damp, and to answer the door, if a stray person should call not knowing that the place was uninhabited. They had not much else to do, but it was thought well by the trustees of the estate to have some life about the place. The maids were instructed to report any repairs that were glaringly in need of being attended to, and these repairs were noted, and if it were thought necessary they got attention. Twice a year the place was inspected by the solicitor who looked after the interests of the estate. He came down from the city by car and went back almost at once.

The two maids were seldom seen except upon Sundays when they rode with the gardener to the church on a sidecar which was retained for this purpose. The man sat on one side and the two maids rode on the other side, with their hands folded over their putty-coloured rug, and their prayer books clasped in their hands as stiff and new as the day they came out of the shops with their bevelled edges glinting.

The maids were originally daughters of the locality, but long association with the demesne, and the absence of the legitimate owners had combined to give them a false importance in the eyes of the neighbouring farmers; an importance which grew with every year that passed. And the years as they passed had indeed made changes in the two women. Their faces began to gain in dignity what they lost in youth. The face of the older one had grown so thin the angular shape of the bone compelled attention, and gave her a look of great authority when she frowned, which she often did. Her discoloured black hair was scraped back severely and was in keeping with this stern appearance. She was tall.

The younger one was slight. She was softer and not so thin, and her faded fair hair was harder to control. It still curled at the front of the temples, over her insipidly pretty blue eyes.

Both of the women were pale. The damp and the darkness of the passageways had blenched their skins till they had at last the same waxen pallor as the faces that peered out from the dark canvasses in the upper galleries of the house.

When they were out for a walk in the grounds, they often scared the life out of trespassers and poachers who assumed that they were the owners of the estate, and muttered lies and excuses to them as they took themselves off in a hurry. They would hardly have felt the necessity for departure at all, much less for such deferential departure, if they knew they were dealing with two maid-servants.

'They think we are the owners,' said the younger one, giggling, one afternoon as two poachers fled into the bushes at sight of them, leaving a fine fat widgeon in a sack on the side of the avenue. Then she had one of her frequent accesses of timidity. 'I hope it isn't deceitful of us to create a wrong impression?' she said.

'Nonsense,' said the tall Miss Perks, who suffered neither from flushings nor fears. 'We did nothing to give a false impression. If people take false impressions of their own that is another thing. Besides, it's just as well for trespassers to think there are people in residence. It is a protection against undesirable callers.'

This was a point which timid Miss Budd could readily appreciate. She was distinctly nervous of undesirable callers. If she was alone in the house she would keep the door locked, even in the day-time, and she declared that she would die if there was a knock. Fortunately she was never alone. If there was occasion to go to the town, they went together. But such occasions rarely arose. Small messages and purchases could always be done by the gardener or by one of the herd's children.

It was so long since anyone had rung a bell in the house or given an order in an imperious tone, there was nothing servile in their manner, and no one would presume to call them by their Christian names. The young people in the locality could hardly have told you what their Christian names were. When they went to work in the house long ago they had of course been Bessie and Annie, but now no one would venture to make use of such familiar names.

Miss Perks and Miss Budd were as proud as any ladies.

And Magenta, the herd's daughter, was proud to be asked to scrub the floors for them, and polish the outsides of the windows.

Magenta was lucky in so far as that Nature had given her a rich red on her cheeks, and a luxuriant growth of black hair that more or less justified the chance that her mother had taken in departing from the orthodox Calendar of the Saints when she was choosing a name for her.

'You had better take off your coat, Magenta,' said Miss Perks when she handed Magenta the bucket of hot water and the scrubbing brush, and showed her the passages that she was to scrub. 'You can put on this apron. It may be a bit long in the sleeves but we can roll them up.'

Miss Perks held out a white apron with blue stripes, like the ones worn by herself and Miss Budd. The apron had a gloss upon it like the gloss on a man's collar, and it was so stiff with starch that it could almost have stood up on the floor by itself while Magenta stepped into it. But Magenta cried out in horror at the thought of soiling such an immaculate garment.

'Oh Lord save us, Miss Perks. It would be a crying shame for me to put on a lovely clean apron like that, swishing dirty water to left and right, and rising splatters every other minute! My old coat is so dirty it wouldn't matter if I fell into the bucket with it!' She looked down deprecatingly at her dun-coloured brown coat, that was buttonless and rent at the seams, with the cuffs shrunk back from the wrists, and stains and tears fighting with each other for supremacy of number all over the front and the back. 'This old coat is never off my back. You needn't fear for this old coat! I wear it cleaning out the pig sties!' Magenta caught up the bucket.

Miss Perks replaced the apron, reluctantly, on a pile of similar aprons on top of the bright scoured press in the wash-room. She watched Magenta disappear down the passage with the bucket in which the water swayed up to the rim, first on one side and then on the other, as Magenta changed the handle from one fist to another, or shifted the weight from her left hip to her right. Occasionally the water spilled over the rim and left a beading of wet drops on the passage floor in her wake.

'I wish she had worn the apron,' said Miss Perks to Miss Budd.

'It hardly matters one way or another,' said Miss Budd. 'I don't see that her coat could be much dirtier than it is!'

'That's the point!' said Miss Perks. 'I wasn't thinking of the coat. I was thinking of the walls and the wainscoting! If she brushes up against the wall with that dirty coat she'll leave a track of grease after her, as sure as if you dragged a piece of fat along it with your hand. I declare she'll do more damage than she's worth. I don't believe it pays to hire her!'

'Poor Magenta!' said Miss Budd. 'She's very biddable. I wouldn't like to deprive her of the few pence.'

'I suppose we should give her a cup of tea?' said Miss Perks.

'It would be a charity, I suppose,' said Miss Budd. 'The child is underfed.'

'Will I set a cup and saucer on the table in the kitchen?' said Miss Perks.

Miss Budd bit her lips and pondered the point.

'You wouldn't consider setting a place for her at our own table in the Hall?' she asked.

'And have her eat with us?' Miss Perks almost screamed.

'It's only for once in a way,' said Miss Budd.

'That's true,' said Miss Perks.

Magenta was deeply impressed at having her tea in the servants' hall with them. She still wore her coat, wet and splattered though it was by this time, but she kept tugging at the skimpy cuffs and drawing them down as far as she could over her wrists. Conversation, too, was skimpy.

'Scrubbing is hard on the hands, isn't it?' said Magenta. 'The dirt gets into the splits in your skin.'

She looked at Miss Budd's hands, but when she saw that they were very smooth and white, her cheeks became a richer peony red than before, and by contrast it seemed as if her teeth became whiter, her hair became blacker, and her eyes became much more brilliantly blue. To get over her embarrassment she looked around the room.

The walls of the servants' hall were decorated with postcards and pages cut from glossy magazines. There was a bright fire blazing on the hearth and because of the heat from it the large window with single panes was open to its full height, and the curtains blew in and out with a slow indolent movement. On the table there was a white cloth and an assortment of cutlery which indicated that those who sat down to the table would have more to partake of than bread and butter. In the centre of the table there was a vase of brilliant flowers for which Magenta knew no name.

'The flowers are lovely!' she said, wishing to say something to please the two ladies. And all during the meal she made remarks of a similar nature. 'Isn't the butter lovely,' she said, as she spread it on her bread. 'I love ham,' she said, as they pressed her to take another piece.

And lastly when she was leaving in the evening, as Miss Perks and Miss Budd went out to the door of the courtyard with her, and she saw the lamp burning up in their room on the second storey of the servants' wing, she was filled to capacity with admiration, and she sighed as she said goodbye.

'It's well for you,' she said, sincerity and envy penetrating through a remark that the ladies might otherwise have thought to be a shade too familiar. 'It's well for you sleeping up a stairs. The cats are always coming in on top of us if we leave the windows open.' She thought of the crowded, hot and noisy bedroom to which she was going home herself, where Sonsy the baby was always getting sick in the middle of the night, or crawling up on her sisters to sleep on top of them like a cat on the bulge of a barrel. 'I don't suppose cockroaches go upstairs!' she said, as another aspect of the differences between her lot and the lot of Miss Perks and Miss Budd came to her mind. But at this point Miss Perks felt matters had gone far enough.

'Cockroaches are a sign of dirt,' she said. 'There's no need for them upstairs or down!'

And sadly Magenta realised that this was probably true.

'I wish I was out at service,' she said, in a burst of confidence, as she reached the path that led across the fields to the herd's hut.

'We'd be glad to give you a reference,' said Miss Perks, and she took Miss Budd by the arm, and prepared to turn back to the house. She felt that by the last remark she put the right complexion on a conversation that had begun to get unnecessarily familiar. 'That's the worst of making free with people,' she said, as she and Miss Budd walked back towards the yard where the light of the lamp in the upper room shone like a moon in the dark. Miss Budd covered her head as a bat flew down almost into her face.

'We'll miss her if she gets a job,' she said. 'She's as gay as a little bird.'

'She won't get a job,' said Miss Perks. 'Who would take her; an untrained, dirty little slut? She has a good heart, but who'd take her into their house? You wouldn't be sure of the pillows. You wouldn't be sure of the cushions. You'd never know what pests she'd bring into the soft furnishings. I don't know that we are wise ourselves in having her into the house here, even to scrub.'

'But she only does the stone passages! She couldn't do much harm to the stone passages,' said Miss Budd, in whom Magenta's youth awoke far faint echoes of her own.

'I suppose not,' said Miss Perks doubtfully, 'But I wish she was cleaner.' And then she laughed. 'Well, you are simple,' she said, 'to think that anyone would take a chit like Magenta into their service!'

'I don't know. After all it's a great thing to be willing; it isn't every girl that's as willing as Magenta,' said Miss Budd, whose own timidity made her put a high value on tractability in others.

'What has that got to do with it?' said Miss Perks, whose authority was inflexible in all circumstances. It even functioned better when there was some opposition.

Miss Perks had such authority indeed, that Miss Budd did not dare to say that she had warned her when Magenta came flying through the yard a few weeks later, with her cheeks flaming and her hair flying, and her voice hysterical with excitement.

'I've got a job!' cried Magenta. 'I've got a job of my own! I'm going to work for a lady in the city. She wrote and told my mother to send me up on Tuesday.' Magenta was speechless. She was out of breath with having run across the fields, and when she got back her breath she was still incoherent from excitement. 'I wanted to tell you!' she cried, as an excuse for having come unbidden, and then she had another access of emotion. 'My mother said I don't need to do any more work until I go away. She said I'll have enough of it before long. I don't have to milk. Molly is to milk. I don't have to clean out the pigs' house. Pete is to do that. And I don't have to mind that little brat Sonsy. Ma's going to do that herself!' Magenta sighed with the ecstasy of her leisure, and then she breathed faster with joy at the thought of how she planned to use it. 'So I came up to let you know about my job,' she said, 'and to see if you might like to get some more scrubbing done before I go. I ought to get a lot done by Tuesday.' She looked around her, and as a pang of loneliness came into her heart she allayed it quickly. 'The lady says I can get home as often as I want,' she said. 'I'll be able to come over now and again when I get home for a day and give you a hand.' She looked enviously up the long stone passage that she had scoured and whitened some days before, and which still shone white and almost spotless. 'The passages stay clean for ages, don't they?' she said. 'I suppose it's because there's no one to walk on them; you should see the state of the floors at home. There's no use scrubbing them. My mother gave that up long ago.'

Miss Perks pursed her lips. Miss Budd shuddered. It took a lot of the good out of hiring Magenta to think that she came from such a poor class of home.

All the same it was bad to think of her going away. She was useful. They'd miss her. Only the other day they had been planning to get the attics swept; that was a dirty job. And now Magenta would not be available. The attics would have to wait, which was a pity because sometimes Miss Budd fancied there was a bad odour up there. The place was probably infested with mice.

They would certainly miss Magenta.

'Would she get the attics done in a day, I wonder?' asked Miss Perks, because Magenta had offered to do anything they wanted before she departed.

'I'm afraid not,' said Miss Budd, and she smiled sadly. 'The poor child. She's too excited to do anything. I can't help pitying her. She thinks it's wonderful to be going away to work. If she only knew what's before her! I often think it's scandalous the way those poor wretched little servant girls are treated in the city.'

Miss Perks and Miss Budd had long ago disassociated their minds from the nature of their own employment. Indeed they had strong views on the servant problem, and many discussions about it.

'I don't know how people can have it on their conscience to treat girls the way they do,' continued Miss Budd. 'They think nothing of putting them to sleep in the basement with the cockroaches and the damp; and no job is too hard for them. As for the food they get!' She threw up her hands in horror. 'The poor girls!'

'Oh well. There's no use crying over them,' said Miss Perks, who resented a certain trace of alliance with the wrong side in Miss Budd's remarks. 'After all, there is something to be said on the other side too. The mistresses don't always get the best of it. They have a lot to put up with, in my opinion. It's only one girl in a hundred that can be relied upon, if there is even that many at all. If it isn't stealing, it's vermin. If it isn't that it's breaking things, and hiding them, or sticking them together to let on they're not broken so they'll fall to pieces when the next person touches them. And if that were all! Oh if that were all! I've heard things about girls! Oh yes! and only I wouldn't want to demean myself by repeating them, they'd make your hair stand on end!'

Miss Budd lowered her eyes, and a virginal blush stole over her cheeks.

'But Magenta isn't like that!' she murmured defensively. 'Magenta isn't that kind.'

Miss Perks was thinking of the inconvenience that Magenta's departure was going to cause them. It annoyed her.

'I don't know!' she said ominously.

Magenta would not easily be replaced. In the first instance, Magenta had never been hired. She had got into the habit of coming up to the house and doing odd jobs for a few sweets. Later it had been for a few pence. Even up to this very day she was not paid. She got surprises and presents from the ladies in the big house. And the surprises and presents were different every week. There was nothing like a steady salary. It would be awkward getting a new girl. It would be all so definite; so different from just sending down for Magenta who loved coming up to them. Sending for Magenta could be regarded as doing an act of charity. Miss Perks was filled with resentment. Miss Budd's remarks had come at a bad time. 'I don't know,' said Miss Perks again. 'The best of these girls isn't far removed from the worst of them. You never know when you can trust one of them. Servant girls are a breed in themselves. As I often say, would they be servants if they were good for anything better?'

Miss Budd sighed. Her mind was filled with thoughts of Magenta. She wondered if she should have asked her if there was anything she needed in the way of underwear. Warm underwear was so important, and Magenta was likely to skimp the money she spent on it and be extravagant with ribbons and bows.

'I hope she'll be happy,' she said.

Miss Perks meanwhile had unaccountably cheered up.

'Happy?' she said. 'Do you realise the treatment she'll get? Do you realise the way she'll be ordered about? Happy!' Miss Perks scoffed.

Miss Budd listened confusedly. Miss Perks seemed to be saying the same thing that she had said a few minutes before and for which she had been cut short. Where was the difference?

Difference however was there.

'She'll have to run here, and run there,' said Miss Perks. 'She'll never get a minute's peace. She'll have no regular hours, and she'll be at the beck and call of everyone in the house. She'll get contradictory orders, and be expected to do twenty different things at the one time. She'll be run off her feet. And a delicate girl like her will never stand it. She'll be back in a few weeks. You'll see! She'll break down!' Miss Perks pursed her lips triumphantly. 'You'll see!' she said. 'Magenta will be back inside six weeks. Mark my words. You'll see! Magenta won't be long away!'

Miss Budd opened her mind to this pleasant thought, but as it penetrated into her mind it cast a dark shadow.

'Wouldn't it be terrible if her health gave away,' she cried. She vividly pictured the rosy-faced Magenta pale, broken down, dying. She put her hands to her heart.

'Oh, I don't think Magenta will let things go that far,' said Miss Perks, with a certain return of asperity. She suddenly remembered the attic that she had intended Magenta to clean. Ah well! it would have to wait. Miss Budd was still thinking nervously of the risk Magenta was going to take with her health.

'Do you think we ought to have said a few words of warning to her?' she said.

Miss Perks was witheringly contemptuous.

'And have her mother say that we were trying to put her off her plans for our own sake! As a matter of fact, I didn't like to say it before, but I think you're making altogether too much fuss and talk about the girl. I know it's only to me, but all the same I'd be afraid it would get to her mother's ears; they'd say we were lost without her. I wouldn't let them see we set such importance on her. It would give them a wrong notion of her value.'

Miss Budd looked guilty of indiscretion. She made an effort to justify herself.

'But I never mentioned her name to anyone else but you!' she said.

Miss Perks drew up.

'Even to me!' she said, 'you shouldn't make so much of her. It takes from your dignity.'

Miss Budd was abashed. From that day she did her best to remember her dignity. Indeed, Magenta's name was only mentioned when some unpleasant job turned up for which she would have been useful.

'This sink is getting into a bad condition,' Miss Perks would say. 'Magenta would have given it a good scouring.'

On those occasions Miss Budd ventured a few remarks about her.

'I wonder how she's getting along,' she said. And then one day, about six weeks after Magenta's departure, she went a bit further. 'Annie!' she said. 'I hope you won't say I'm making too much of her, but I was thinking that it might be a nice thing for us to walk over across the fields and call to the door to ask Magenta's mother how she is getting on in her employment.'

Miss Budd shrank back timidly after this courageous outburst. Miss Perks was standing over the sink at the time. It did badly need a scouring. Her thoughts were not fully centred on what Miss Budd was saying. Then as she was about to answer, her eye caught sight of the pipes that ran across the ceiling under the ventilator. And the ventilator too! Such cobwebs! Where had they come from? How had they gathered? Miss Perks sighed. It was at times like this that one missed Magenta. Miss Perks never minded work, but by that she meant routine work. No one could possibly have made the kitchen table whiter than Miss Perks, or kept the china more orderly, or the flagstones swept cleaner, but it was jobs like sweeping the ceilings, clearing the ventilator-holes, dusting the piping or cleaning out the drains; they were the drudgery.

'What did you say?' she asked Miss Budd shortly.

But when Miss Budd repeated herself, even more timidly, Miss Perks was surprisingly attentive, and seemed to think Miss Budd's suggestion worth considering.

'We might do that,' she said. 'As a matter of fact we might walk over this afternoon. It's lovely weather.' She only made one stipulation. 'Let me do the talking,' she said. 'I want to find out how the girl is getting along and if there's any likelihood of her coming home; but I don't want to give the impression we miss her.'

It was mid-summer.

In the afternoon Miss Perks and Miss Budd put on their best hats and prepared to set out. Miss Perks took her walking stick. Miss Perks was always trying to persuade Miss Budd to avail herself of the comfort of a cane, but in spite of the timidity which gave way in almost every other particular to Miss Perks, Miss Budd's timidity at the thought of carrying a walking stick was even greater. She hadn't so completely forgotten her origin as to be indifferent to what people might say of Bessie Budd going to such lengths. She only went as far as an umbrella, getting an extremely long one with a steel handle, which she maintained was just as good as a walking-stick. There were, however, limits to the occasions when she could avail herself of an umbrella, even furled and tightly rolled. And this afternoon was certainly one of those days.

The sun shone down. Never did the estate look more lovely. The two ladies stepped out across the green wicket in the gate of the courtyard and made their way under the trees through a pathway almost overgrown with laurels, till they came to a creaking kissing gate leading into the big field that was called the Park.

Here in former times deer wandered, and here now a more profitable herd of bullocks cropped the grass. The Park comprised about twenty unfenced and unbroken acres, and dotted everywhere over the vast irregular green expanse there were large park trees. No matter how much grass they soured by their green shade, there was plenty and to spare in this wide parkland.

As they entered the Park, Miss Perks and Miss Budd looked around them at the wide acres of sunlight and the trees in their spreading pools of shadow, and although it would never occur to them to call attention to its loveliness, their appreciation of it was present by implication in Miss Budd's exclamation.

'Poor Magenta!' she said, 'down in some dark, damp basement in the city! I hope we'll hear that the poor child is soon coming home.'

'I sincerely hope we do!' said Miss Perks, for her eye was taking in the fine twigs that were lying under the trees in the field. They would make such good kindling. A few of them would start the fires in the morning as quick as you'd wink your eye; but it would not look well for either of the ladies to be seen collecting them. Magenta, who used to gather them for her mother, could bring in an armload every time she came across the fields.

They walked along. There was a kind of a track through the park, and although it wound about intricately and followed seemingly unnecessary curves, it was better than going straight across the field, for the grass was as high and as rich as meadow, and their feet would soon ache from high-stepping.

When the path had wound its way across the greater part of the field, passing close under some of the smaller trees, and widely circling others, it ran for a distance through a flat open stretch of sunny pasture. Then it made straight for a small copse in the centre of the park and wound around it before it cut straight through another wide-open stretch to the far boundary of the demesne.

The ladies felt quite rightly that they had covered the greater part of the ground when they reached the copse. It was a small copse of silver pines and larch, intersown with high laurels and rhododendrons, the whole plantation being protected from the cattle by a huge encirclement of ditch and embankment. It rose up in the sunny, open spaces like a military fortification. The outer sides of the embankment were so steep the grass had never taken foothold on the yellow clay, which was powdery and dry under the hot sun. Long strands of dusty briar trailed down the sides like barbed wire, and all up and down the sides a colony of rabbits had tunnelled what were for all the world like gun-emplacements.

Miss Budd pulled Miss Perks by the sleeve.

'There must be a lot of rabbits,' she said. 'Wouldn't a nice rabbit pie be tasty?'

Miss Perks ran her tongue over her lip; then she frowned.

'Rabbits are such trouble to skin and clean,' she said.

And then, both of the ladies together, could not refrain from giving a simultaneous sigh. 'If only Magenta had not gone away,' they sighed. 'If only she were back again.' They began to walk faster.

They were nearly across the park. When they rounded this copse they would be in sight of the road, and over the high wall of the demesne, and the thick shrubbery that had grown up inside it, they would be able to see the red clay chimney of Magenta's cottage. Even as they hurried along, Miss Budd thought they might glimpse it through the occasional thinning in the copse.

But when they came around the copse at last, although across the park beyond the distant demesne wall the tip of the red clay chimney stood out clearly among the green trees, brightened by its little flag of blue smoke, the ladies did not look at it at all.

Something else had caught their attention and put Magenta and her mother's cottage completely out of their minds.

Coming along the same narrow path through the pasture on which they themselves were walking in single file was another figure; a woman. Miss Budd, who was walking ahead, slowed down in her surprise. There was seldom anyone to be seen in the park except the herd, or Magenta's poor mother with a bundle of sticks on her back, or a few of the village children furtively crouching under the chestnut trees looking for conkers. A stranger was a rare sight. Miss Budd came to a stop on the narrow green path, and Miss Perks had to give her a dig in the small of the back with the knob of her walking stick.

'What are you stopping for?' said Miss Perks.

'There's someone coming,' said Miss Budd. 'Perhaps we ought to turn back!'

This was the kind of remark that exasperated Miss Perks, the incurable kind of remark that Miss Budd was always liable to make. In a crisis she always lost her head.

'And why should we turn back, might I ask?' said Miss Perks irritably, giving her another and more violent poke in the back, this time more from irritation than any other reason, for Miss Budd had begun to move forward again reluctantly. 'It's not we who are trespassing; keep right on.'

The person coming across the fields was a stranger, and not only a stranger but someone altogether unlike what anyone would expect to meet in the middle of a peaceful Meath pasture. Even at this distance, and the young woman had hardly started out upon her path and was a long way from them yet, it could be seen that her clothes were of a most unusual cut, the kind of clothes that country people always call fashionable, and as for their colour, it was hard to tell which colour predominated, so many frills and bows and feathers of different hues glinted in the sunlight.

'Who on earth is it, I wonder?' said Miss Budd, and she was just about to exclaim at how fashionable the person was when Miss Perks exclaimed the opposite.

'Whoever she is she's a vulgar baggage in my opinion,' she said, 'judging by the showy clothes. Such clothes! It's probably somebody visiting one of the cottagers, and they sent her up here to look at the grounds just to get her out of their way!'

A long distance still divided the ladies from the advancing figure with the nodding feathers. Her attire was clearer now in its brilliant and wafting detail.

The young woman wore a light green silk dress, that frothed into pink silk ruffles at the point where it met the high grasses on either side of the path. Around her waist there was a sash of the same pink silk, and her sleeves, that came to a stop at the elbow, were banded with pink silk ruffles. But her hat, which was large and floppy, was a bright canary yellow, and from it a large ostrich feather dangled down across her back. The feather was blue. In one hand she carried a yellow silk bag that she gaily swung from side to side like a censer as she walked, and in the other she carried a pink parasol, which although it was furled and tied at the top, was bulky and wide with the rows and rows of frills that decorated it all over. But above all, the ladies were astonished to see at this time of year, that the advancing figure wore a large yellow fox fur draped across her shoulders and dangling down to either side of her. Her feet they could not see; these were hidden in the long grass, but it seemed from her mincing gait that her footwear must be either extremely high in the heel or else a bad fit.

In spite of the difficulty with her footwear, however, the advancing figure was getting rapidly nearer. Miss

Budd looked nervously over her shoulder at Miss Perks for information as to how she should behave.

'Will we have to speak to her?' she asked.

'Why should we speak?' snapped Miss Perks. 'If this person knows her place she'll step aside when she sees us.'

'Don't you think she sees us now?' asked Miss Budd.

But just then the question was settled definitely. To the astonishment of the ladies, the figure in the waving flounces at that moment put up a hand and began to wave it in their direction. The ladies looked at each other with startled glances. Then they looked over their shoulders. Who was this person waving at? There was no one else in sight.

'She's waving at us!' said Miss Budd in positive terror.

'Don't be absurd!' said Miss Perks.

But indeed there was hardly any doubt about it that the person was waving at them. Then, as if waving were not enough, clutching her top-heavy hat with the hand already encumbered with the parasol, and catching up her flounces and furbelows with the hand that held the swinging silk bag, the young woman, whoever she was, suddenly quit the path and began to make straight for them, across the thick rich grass; her speed and her hurry, her eagerness and the fullness of her skirts all giving her a most headlong appearance.

And then all at once Miss Budd put up her hands to her bosom. Her heart began to palpitate. And to Miss Perks' astonishment she gave a short cry and raising her own hand she began to wave back at the young woman running towards them. But seeing that Miss Perks was staring at her in astonishment she calmed herself enough to gasp out one word.

'Magenta!' she said. 'It's Magenta!'

And then, without waiting to hear what Miss Perks had to say, Miss Budd threw up her hand and began to wave as frantically as ever the distant figure had waved. It was likely that she too would have darted forward into the long grass, if Miss Perks had not caught her by the sleeve and held her back. Miss Budd, thus detained, turned around with a glowing face.

'Can you imagine it,' she breathed. 'Magenta! And I thought it was some stranger. Magenta! Our own Magenta!' Miss Budd was beside herself with excitement.

Miss Perks however was not only calm; she was stone cold. And she looked at Miss Budd with tight lips, as if she disapproved of something. But if this were so, there was no time now to express it, for Magenta was within earshot, or so at least she deemed herself to be, because she was calling out gaily.

'Hello there!' called Magenta. 'Hello there! I was just going over to see you.'

And stumbling still oftener, clutching her hat more wildly, Magenta ran forward more precipitantly, until she was within a few breathless yards of them.

'Oh Magenta, my dear!' cried Miss Budd, and while the pressure of Miss Perks hand upon her sleeve prevented her from yielding to her impulse of putting out her arms, her eyes were filled with tears of emotional welcome, and her lips were parted with affectionate envy and admiration for the splendour of the herd's daughter.

On nearer view, Magenta's finery, however, seemed to have something wrong with it. There was something slightly wrong with the waistline of the flouncy dress. There was something a shade wrong about the flopping hat. There was even something wrong about the blue feather, and, more subtle still, about the high buttoned boots. And then the ladies saw what it was. They were all, all; dress, hat, feather, and shoes, all a shade, ever such a slight shade, the wrong fit for Magenta. They were all a trifle, just a trifle, too big for her dainty figure. That was why she had had to keep one hand up to the floppy hat. That was why she had stumbled and tripped over the dress. And that was why the white kid buttoned boots that were now to be seen, were wrinkled about her ankles. And as for the fur! At one minute the two ends that hung down in front were in danger of tripping her underfoot, at the next she slung the skin back over her shoulders until the brown sateen lining was more in evidence that the yellow fur.

But of these small blemishes in her splendour Magenta was unaware or unheedful. She rushed up to the ladies and thrusting out her hands, on both of which several bangles of different-coloured glass beads tinkled lightly and gaily, she uttered little cries.

'Well, fancy meeting you like this!' she cried. 'I was just going over to see you. I only came home an hour ago. I said to my mother, "Don't bother about tea for me. I promised the two ladies up at the demesne that I'd call on them the first day I came home. I'll step across the fields. I won't break my word. I'll step across and see how they're getting on." "Won't you wait and have a cup of tea after your journey," said my mother. "I won't," said I, "I'll take a cup with them over at the demesne. They'll be glad of a bit of company, I'm sure".'

All this Magenta twittered in an accent as new as her clothes, and like the clothes, a trifle badly fitting.

'Well, that was very nice of you, Magenta,' said Miss Budd affected, and she turned to Miss Perks. 'Wasn't it nice of her?' she cried. Then she turned back to Magenta. 'You'd never guess where we were going?' she said, and turning to Miss Perks she cried, 'Tell her!' because it was getting awkward that Miss Perks had up to this said nothing.

Miss Perks, appealed to thus, looked at Magenta.

'How are you, Magenta?' she said in her most dignified voice; the voice she kept for the solicitor and the trustees. Then to Miss Budd's astonishment Miss Perks went on. 'There's no secret about where we were going,' she said. 'We were walking over to the post office to post a letter.' And then she turned and gave a most peculiar glance at Miss Budd, a glance which threw her into such confusion that she felt her cheeks get red.

But Magenta was delighted with Miss Perks.

'Oh, if you were only going to the post office,' she cried, 'we don't need to bother! Let's go back to the house. I can take your letters with me tonight when I'm going back to the city, and they'll be delivered first thing in the morning. Goodness knows when they'd be delivered if you posted them in the village. That's the worst of these backward places.'

And, then linking Miss Budd by one arm and Miss Perks by the other, so that they had to walk in the high grass while she had the path, Magenta swivelled the ladies around and began to urge them back in the way they had just come. Miss Budd, who had caught a delightful scent from the swinging tails of the yellow fur, was insensible to anything odd, and was ready to be led by Magenta in any direction whatever. And Miss Perks, although she drew herself up with a start when Magenta linked her, was almost compelled to be as acquiescent as Miss Budd, because as a sail speeds a boat before the wind, Magenta's flounces and furbelows seemed to be wafting them all forward.

'I'm longing to tell you all about everything,' cried Magenta, as she bore them along. 'Wait till you hear! I have some good things to tell you. I'll have you splitting your sides laughing. I was telling my mother and the girls, and they didn't want to let me out of their sight. They came to the door after me, and they hated to see me go. "Hurry back," said my mother. "I don't know why you want to go over there at all," said Sadie. Even my father was interested. "What's your hurry," said he. "Tell us some more." But I knew you'd never forgive me if I didn't come. "They'd never forgive me if I didn't go over," I said. "It's all very well for you," I said to them at home, "you're living on the side of the road, where you have people dropping in and out at all hours, but think of those poor things over in that god-forsaken place, with nothing but trees all around them, and not a soul to talk to from one end of the day to the other." ' Magenta turned and smiled to either side of her. 'So I put on my hat,' she said, and here she turned particularly to Miss Budd, 'How do you like it?' she asked. 'My hat, I mean.'

But Miss Perks could endure no more.

'It's too big for you!' she said. 'Your hat, I mean.'

For a minute Magenta paused as if she was flurried. It was clear she was in two minds about something. Then she lowered her voice, and looked around uneasily at the vast stretching park.

'As a matter of fact,' she said, 'I'll tell you something! Oh, I have such a lot of things to tell you—as a matter of fact it's not mine at all; the hat, I mean!' She hesitated another minute, and in that minute she measured Miss Perks' eye, and made another quick decision. 'The dress isn't mine either,' she said, then capitulating altogether she giggled, 'nor the shoes, nor the gloves, nor the fur.' She stopped giggling. 'Isn't the fur gorgeous?' she said, and unlinking them she stopped in her tracks and stroked it down with her hands. Then proffering a tail to each of the ladies she gave them a cordial invitation. 'Feel it!' she said. 'It's a treat to feel it. Did you ever feel anything like it?'

Miss Budd gratefully put out her hand and felt the fur.

'Oh, it's lovely,' she cried, and then, seeing that Miss Perks had not felt it she joined her importunities to those of Magenta. 'Feel it!' she cried. 'Feel it!'

But Miss Perks drew back.

'I don't like the feel of fur,' she said coldly. Miss Budd felt hurt and perplexed. Then she remembered what Magenta had said about the fur not being her own. Perhaps Miss Perks was uneasy. She herself grew a bit uneasy.

'If they're not yours, my dear,' she said, 'whose are they? And why are you wearing them?'

Miss Budd's face reddened with the indelicacy of her own remark, but Magenta saw no need for delicacy. She threw back her head and laughed.

'Did you think I stole them?' she asked, and she burst out laughing again. 'Did you think I got them in a pawn shop?' She roared laughing. Then stopping the laughing as quickly as she started, she looked around her again and lowered her voice to the same confidential pitch as before. 'As a matter of fact I'm awfully lucky,' she said. 'Some girls have the most wretched time. But my mistress is an exception. Mistress! We're just like friends really. She says it as much for the company as for the work that she keeps me with her. She said she'd do her share of the work if only she had more time. But she's very busy. She's connected with the theatre.' Magenta paused. She seemed to have forgotten what she had set out to say. 'I have so much to tell you!' she exclaimed, by way of stop-gap.

'You were telling us where you got those clothes,' said Miss Perks critically.

'Oh yes!' Magenta rolled her head and rolled her eyes. 'My clothes! Well! Since I went away to this job I never have to buy a stitch!'

'Does your mistress give them to you?' said Miss Budd enviously, and she put out her hand again, timidly, and felt the fur.

Magenta was disconcerted. It was as if an idea had fluttered within her reach, without her having seen it in time to catch it.

'Well yes, as a matter of fact she does,' she said. 'She's given me lots of things, but she didn't give me those. She lent them to me, which is much better.' She turned to explain. 'They're not cast-offs, you see. They're brand new. She lends me anything I want. And she has such a stack of clothes. You should see her cupboards. You can hardly get the door to shut. She has to have a lot of clothes on account of being connected with the theatre. But she doesn't care about clothes. That's where I am so lucky. "Never be in want of something pretty to wear, Magenta," she said to me one day. "If you're going out on your day off never hesitate to borrow anything you like out of my wardrobe."' Magenta looked at Miss Budd. 'What do you think of that?' she exclaimed.

She looked at Miss Perks. But she said nothing when she looked at Miss Perks. To tell the truth Miss Perks looked as if she didn't believe her. Magenta thought for a minute to find some way of convincing Miss Perks.

'Of course,' she said, airily looking up at the ceiling, 'she borrows some of my things.' Then in answer to a silent criticism that still lurked in Miss Perks' eye, she went on hastily. 'I haven't much to lend her, but I am getting a few things together now, my salary is so good.'

If anything, Miss Perks looked less convinced. Magenta thought harder.

'Do you remember that little necklace I used to wear; the one my grandfather gave me, the one with the glass beads and the pearls?'

The ladies remembered it well. Miss Perks looked more convinced. As a matter of fact that necklace had been the cause of words between herself and Miss Budd. She had often been on the point of telling Magenta not to wear jewellery at her work.

'You remember it?' cried Magenta eagerly. 'Well, imagine! The first day she laid eyes on that she took such a fancy to it I had to let her wear it that evening.' Magenta looked at Miss Perks out of the corner of her eye. 'She's wearing it tonight,' she said. 'She absolutely had to have it. She wouldn't take no for an answer. And of course I had to lend it to her. How could I do anything else when she insisted on my taking her fur.' Magenta held up the tail of the fur again and rubbed it against her cheek. Then she leaned out generously and rubbed it against Miss Budd's cheek. '"Why don't you take my fur, Magenta," she said. "Your mother will want to see you looking well." And then she made me take the dress and hat as well. "No need to thank me, my dear," she said. "Put them on, and hurry up, or you'll be late for your train."'

They had reached the edge of the trees again by this time.

'Talking about trains,' said Magenta, as she slipped through the kissing gate and stood watching the two angular ladies come stiffly through it after her, 'Talking about trains,' she said, 'I mustn't stay long. I mustn't be late for my train.'

'Oh, are you going back tonight, Magenta?' said Miss Budd in disappointment.

'Oh I don't have to go. There's no compulsion,' said Magenta. 'But I know she'd miss me. If I didn't go she'd be disappointed. I wouldn't want to disappoint her.' They were in the inner park now, making their way between the laurel and rhododendrons. 'Oh hasn't this place got darker and damper than ever,' said Magenta, interrupting herself. 'I wonder you have your health living under those trees.' Then she went on. 'But as I was saying,' she said, 'if she's out late I sit up for her. And if I'm out late she waits up for me. Sometimes we have a cup of tea together. I don't care much for tea at that hour myself, but I know she enjoys it, so I sip a cup with her. She doesn't sleep well at any time. Those theatrical people never do, I believe. She sits up in bed half the night playing patience. She taught me how to play too. And she taught me how to read the cards as well.' Impulsively, generously, Magenta put out her hands and caught the two ladies each by an arm. 'That's what I'll do,' she said. 'I'll tell your fortunes with the cards. Only don't let on to them at home or they'd be wild with me for not doing it for them. But as I said, I don't pity them!' They were at the green wicket now. Magenta skipped lightly into the courtyard and turned to urge the ladies on. 'Hurry!' she cried. 'I'm dying to begin. I suppose there's an old pack of cards in the house somewhere?'

There was no pack of cards to be found however in the servants' hall. Magenta threw open all the cupboards, and pulled out all the drawers, but without success.

'I can't believe there isn't a pack to be found somewhere,' she cried. 'I never heard of a house without one.' She turned to Miss Budd. 'While you're making the tea,' she cried, 'I'll take a run over the house. I might find a pack somewhere.' And with that she was gone. And the ladies could hear her running along the passages, and banging doors after her.

When she came back after a few minutes she was very dejected.

'No luck!' she said despondently, sinking into Miss Perks' armchair. But all at once she sprang up again as she caught sight of her silk bag on the table. 'There might be a pack of cards in my bag!' she exclaimed.

Miss Perks looked curiously at her.

'Wouldn't you know what was in your own bag?' she asked sternly.

But Magenta disarmed her with a smile.

'The bag isn't mine either,' she said. 'The bag is hers too!' And exclaiming with delight, she pulled out a miniature pack of cards, such as ladies carry travelling, and from which there arose and spread all over the room a strong oriental perfume.

Taking them eagerly, Magenta sat down at the table and pushed aside the tea things that Miss Budd had just arranged. Then, more nonchalantly, she began to shuffle the small cards that assailed the nostrils of the ladies with stronger and stronger waves of the oriental perfume.

'Sit down, girls,' said Magenta. 'Sit down. I'll open your eyes for you now with the things I'll read in your cards.' She threw a glance at the small clock that stood on the mantelpiece, and raised her eyebrows. 'Time flies, doesn't it?' she said, 'even up here.' She turned to Miss Budd. 'You can pour out the tea, if it's made,' she said. 'I can be sipping it while I'm shuffling and dealing.' She nodded down at the cards that were skipping expertly between her fingers, and Miss Budd, who had been staring dreamily at the flounces on Magenta's dress, roused herself with a start and began to busy herself with the teapot. When Magenta had shuffled the cards to her satisfaction, she turned from one lady to another. 'Who is to be first?' she asked. 'Whose cards will I read first?' Miss Budd, whose face had worn a vague eagerness up to now, looked suddenly nervous. At no time had it been made clear that Miss Perks would condone the reading of the cards. But when she looked at Miss Perks, she was surprised at the peculiar expression on Miss Perks' face. The oriental perfume had unsteadied Miss Perks. There was a slight flush on her thin cheeks. And Magenta had not missed it, and so she turned to her, not so much in deference to her seniority but rather to an intuitive feeling that whatever chance Miss Perks had of listening to her own fortune being read from the cards, she would assuredly never bear with the trial of listening while Miss Budd's was being read.

'I'll do yours first,' she said to Miss Perks, and leaning across the table she flung the cards down in front of the older lady, who as a matter of fact had not decided at all whether or not she could lend herself to this indignity. But as Magenta splashed the cards across the table one card was accidentally turned upside down. It was the five of hearts. And on this card Miss Perks' eye fastened. Hitherto cards had been to Miss Perks something the same as the marbles with which children idle away their time. But as she stared at the glossy card, splotched with red hearts and smelling so strongly of the strange eastern perfume, it seemed to her suddenly that the card was a cypher, and that within that thin wafer there was concealed extraordinary information and knowledge. At it she stared tantalised, as at some strange hieroglyphics, and not just the hieroglyphics of some remote historical curiosity, but hieroglyphics that concealed something of immediate concern to herself, Annie Perks. In that card there was a message for her, and for her alone. Perhaps some good fortune was to befall her in the near future! Miss Perks smiled in spite of herself. Then her face changed. Perhaps that card held a warning for her, a message of danger? She looked at it with awe. And to think that she could not read it. Miss Perks looked up at Magenta with a new look in her eye; a new respect. To think that Magenta could tell her what that card meant. Just then Magenta, who had only just noticed the upturned card, put out her hand to snatch it up and include it with the other cards. Miss Perks darted out her own hand.

'What does that card say?' she cried in dismay at seeing it swept up without explanation.

But Magenta only laughed.

'You haven't cut the cards yet,' she said, and she had to positively tug the card to get it out of Miss Perks' tenacious grip. Miss Perks had to let it go and sadly watch it vanish among the other cards.

'Cut them?' She looked humbly at Magenta. 'What does that mean?'

Magenta gave the cards a final flip through her fingers and threw them down again in front of Miss Perks.

'Cut them!' she ordered again, and seeing Miss Perks still uncertain she leaned over and showed her what to do.

Miss Perks, with a strange and delightful feeling, nervously did as Magenta showed her. 'Is that right?' she asked timidly, and, as Magenta snatched up the cards again she tried hard to glimpse the card on the underside of the pack. 'The six of spades!' she cried. 'What does the six of spades stand for, Magenta?'

Magenta slapped the cards down on the table without answering.

'Cut again!' she ordered. It appeared that there was more to this fortune-telling than Miss Perks had imagined.

'The three of diamonds,' said Miss Perks this time, eagerly looking up at Magenta's face.

Magenta's face was inscrutable. The three of diamonds likewise was snatched up unexplained into the mysterious pack. Magenta gave the cards another violent shuffling and threw them down with a flourish for the fourth and last time.

'Pick out seven cards,' she said to Miss Perks.

With trembling hands Miss Perks did as she was bid.

'Turn them face upwards,' commanded Magenta. 'Now pick out seven more,' she said. 'That's right. Lay them on the others.' She put out an impatient hand. 'No, not that way! Face upwards like the others! Now seven more!'

Miss Perks was a bit unstrung by so many orders, all issued so close together. She looked at Magenta with the cards held weakly in her hand. Then she ventured to execute the orders.

'Yes,' said Magenta encouragingly. 'That's right. Face upwards!'

Miss Perks laid down the last card gingerly and looked up again at Magenta. Magenta sat back and surveyed the cards. Miss Perks herself was almost afraid to look at them, but she felt vaguely disturbed because she had caught sufficient glimpses of them to see that there were more black cards than red, but before she had time to reflect much upon the matter Magenta swept all the cards up into her hands again. For a moment Miss Perks trembled with fear that Magenta was going to sweep them all back again into the general wisdom of the pack; their particular significance for her still unrevealed. But to her relief, Magenta kept the twenty-one cards, and spreading them out in a wide fan she held them up in her right hand and began to study them with a serious face.

Miss Perks could now see only the backs of the cards with their insipid recurring design of interlocking circles. But she found something to scrutinise in the face of Magenta, who while she stared at the cards was certainly making strange faces. At one minute she bit her lip; then she relaxed and almost smiled. Then her face clouded over once more. Miss Perks sat waiting. A feeling of intolerable suspense had taken possession of her.

'Well?' she breathed.

Magenta looked at her over the rim of the fan of cards.

'I don't like so many black cards,' she said, morosely, but seeing Miss Perks' face fall she put out her hand and patted her reassuringly on the arm. 'You're going to get your wish anyway!' she said. 'That's one good thing anyway!'

Miss Perks looked startled. She had not made any wish. She wondered if she should tell Magenta. But she was afraid that if she did, Magenta might sweep the whole pack up, and begin over again. Miss Perks could not have endured going through all that suspense again. And not only that, but the cards would be different the next time, and Miss Perks stared fixedly at the twenty-one cards fanned out on the table before her eyes—it was in those twenty-one cards, she felt absolutely certain, that her destiny was written. She said nothing, but bent closer to Magenta.

When Miss Perks bent closer to Magenta, Magenta responded instantly and bent closer to Miss Perks. They were alone in the world.

But just then both of them were recalled to the presence of a third person, Miss Budd, who, all this time, unnoticed by both of them, had been staring and listening stupefied by the way Miss Perks had come under the spell of the cards. Miss Budd herself from the very moment they had been mentioned had been in a fever of excitement, but she had not dared to show her excitement. She expected every minute that Miss Perks would jump on Magenta, just as she had jumped on her when she had admired Magenta's clothes. But now it seemed as if she need no longer keep in her excitement. She leaned across the table and breathed a sigh.

'What did you wish?' she asked, looking ecstatically at the cards and rudely recalling Miss Perks to her surroundings.

'Keep back, Bessie,' said Miss Perks irritably. 'You're breathing down my neck.' And then, as Miss Budd hastily moved aside to comply with her, Miss Perks looked at her with even greater irritation. 'Now you're in Magenta's light!' she said. 'She can hardly see the cards.'

Miss Budd blushed furiously, but her excitement still smouldered. Miss Perks relented somewhat.

'Your turn will be next, Bessie,' she said.

Miss Budd clasped her hands.

'You can be making your wish!' said Magenta, throwing out the small scrap of comfort as she concentrated again on the fan of cards.

'Oh dear, what shall I wish?' said Miss Budd, ecstatic at being given the chance of making a wish, but appalled at the same time by the difficulty of doing so. But Miss Perks was impatient. She silenced Miss Budd with a glance.

'How can Magenta get on with the cards if you keep chattering, Bessie?'

She turned back to Magenta. Magenta's face assumed a serious expression.

'Now there's no need for you to believe everything I say,' she said. 'It's up to yourself whether you want to do that or not.'

Miss Perks grew white.

'Do you see something bad in them?' she asked.

'Oh not at all,' said Magenta reassuringly. 'I'm only just warning you. Sometimes people are terribly affected by having their cards read.' She paused. 'They let it prey on their minds.'

Miss Perks gave a half-hearted laugh.

'Some people take them seriously, I suppose,' she said. She laughed again at the expense of these vague, foolish people. And then, where a few minutes before she had wanted to disassociate herself from her friend Bessie Budd, she turned now to link them together. 'It's different with us,' she said confidently. 'With us it's only a bit of fun!'

Magenta appeared not to like the turn things had taken.

'Speaking for myself,' she said, 'I must say I never had my cards read yet that things didn't turn out just exactly the way the cards foretold.' She looked down abruptly at the cards in her hand and turning sidewise to exclude Miss Budd she concentrated on Miss Perks. 'There's a dark lady here,' she said. 'I wonder would that be you?' She looked critically at Miss Perks. 'I suppose you were dark one time,' she said, offhandedly. 'We'll say it's you anyway.' She looked down again swiftly. 'Well,' she said. 'Well! this dark woman—whoever she is—is after turning her back on a serious illness.'

Although it was Miss Perks' fortune, at this point Miss Budd could not help interrupting.

'What does that mean?' she said, leaning across the table again.

'Bessie! Please!' said Miss Perks. 'You're breathing down my neck again.' Her nerves had become a bit frayed in the last few minutes, but as a matter of fact, although she turned on Miss Budd so irritably, she herself looked enquiringly at Magenta for an interpretation of this sinister-sounding phrase.

'Yes, what does that mean, Magenta?'

For a moment Magenta was confused. She had never heard anyone call for an explanation of the cryptic utterance of clairvoyance.

'That's what the cards say,' she said defensively, and in order to gain time, then she ventured an explanation of her own. 'I suppose it means that you were getting something but it passed over you.' She looked around the room suddenly. 'It's a wonder to me you didn't get it, whatever it was,' she said. 'It must be very unhealthy in this house, with so many trees about.' Magenta laid down the cards. 'That's one great thing about the city,' she said, 'There are no old trees about the place, dripping water all the time.' Magenta shuddered, and still shuddering she picked up the cards again. 'Oh-ho,' she said then, in a low drawl. 'This dark lady may be turning her back on a bad sickness, but there's another person here, a fair woman, and this fair woman is facing into a sickness of some kind.' She looked up at Miss Budd, who had been bending forward again, but who drew back hastily as Magenta's eye darted in her direction. 'I suppose you could be the fair woman?' Magenta said. 'You were fair one time, weren't you?' She looked at the single strand of gold hair that Miss Budd was careful every morning to set out across her forehead in prominence over the rest of her pale, faded hair. 'Anyway,' said Magenta, 'This could be a grey woman just as easily as a fair one. The cards don't say whether it's fair or grey. They just say light or dark. It must be you.' She looked compassionately at Miss Budd. 'You're facing into an illness,' she said. But as

Miss Budd paled, Magenta put out her hand. 'Don't worry, dearie,' she said. 'It may only be a slight illness. It may be only a cold in your head.' She left down the cards. 'I don't know how it is you don't get more colds, both of you. These big old houses are all draughts, and you can't go outside the door without stepping into a puddle of water.' Her cheeks glowed suddenly. 'Give me the city every time,' she said. 'The houses are up-to-date and there's always a nice dry pavement under your feet when you go outdoors.' Once again Magenta took up and put down the cards on the table. 'I'm always out,' she said. 'It's a great thing to have good hours. Of course it doesn't matter to you two.' She looked from Miss Perks to Miss Budd. 'Even if you were free, where would you go? What would you do? That's the worst of a backward place like this, I always think. Of course you have each other,' she said, and she considered this point for a minute and then rejected it, 'but I suppose you get sick of each other sometimes?'

To their dismay the ladies saw that this was a question. Miss Budd looked startled and was about to hazard an answer, but Miss Perks, who had begun to resent the way her cards were being shared with Miss Budd, reasserted herself enough to bring Magenta back to the job in hand.

'What else do you see?' she asked.

Magenta hurriedly looked back at the cards.

'I see a letter,' she said. 'There's a letter coming to you. Are you expecting a letter?'

Miss Perks looked blank for a minute; then her face lit up.

'Why, now that I come to think of it, I am expecting a letter!' she said. 'I am.' She looked at Miss Budd. 'Isn't that remarkable?' she said. 'I had forgotten it, but I'm expecting one all right.'

Magenta nodded her head with satisfaction.

'Well, it's coming,' she said. 'It's on its way. What did I tell you! The cards bring out the truth.' Suddenly she peered closer at the card which she had last fingered. 'Is this letter coming from overseas, by any chance?' she asked.

Miss Perks' face fell.

'No,' she said reluctantly. 'It's not, I'm afraid.' She felt apologetic towards Magenta. She felt she was letting her down. Magenta however was all magnanimity.

'Oh, that's all right,' she said. 'This could be another letter; a different letter.' Then suddenly she giggled. 'Maybe it's the same letter,' she said. 'The postman has to peddle his bike through so many puddles you might almost say that all the letters come across water!' and she continued to giggle until suddenly her eye that was abstractedly gazing at the cards opened wide, and assumed a look of astonishment. 'Oh-ho,' she said again. 'What do I see here! A man! A man in uniform! Now what is he doing here?' She looked up roguishly at Miss Perks, as she had seen her mistress look at a visitor when she made use of this particular expression, but something in Miss Perks' beaked white face caused the smile to fade. 'I suppose it's only the postman,' she said flatly. 'Although you hardly call it a uniform, what they wear around here; it's only an ordinary old coat with brass buttons sewn on it and a bit of braid around the sleeves. You should see the postmen in the city. There's one fellow I know. You should see his uniform! He doesn't deliver in our street. He's in the next street, but I meet him when I'm taking out the dog for his walk. You get to know people easily in the city. He said he's going to try and get the fellow on our street to exchange rounds with him. I wonder why he wants to do that?' Magenta opened her eyes innocently as she asked this question, but at the same time she patted her hair self-consciously and brushed some imaginary flecks of dust from the front of the pale silk dress. Then she sighed. 'I told our postman what the other postman said,' she continued, 'and he was fit to be tied! He said he'd like to see anyone trying to change streets with him! Queer, wasn't it? You wouldn't think they'd care what streets they delivered in, would you?'

Magenta was likely to continue on in this vein for some time, and although Miss Perks would like to have put a stop to her, she did not like at the same time to appear to possess too great a curiosity in her own destiny. But Miss Budd, who had long ago resumed her old position behind Miss Perks' chair and who had also resumed her breathing down Miss Perks' back, came now to the rescue. Her thoughts, that had wandered in a different direction from that taken by Magenta's tongue, was still following the figure in uniform that Magenta had called forth from the third card on the left.

'It might be a soldier!' she said suddenly, and then she corrected herself hastily. 'An officer, I mean,' she said, apologising to Miss Perks with her eyes.

Upon Magenta, whose mind was far away, Miss Budd's remark fell as inconsequentially as a flake of lime from the ceiling. But she rapidly recollected her thoughts.

'That's right,' she said. 'It could be a soldier. But what would a soldier be doing around here? No one ever comes up here, do they?' She spoke under the impetuous impulse of the truth, but a minute afterwards she felt she must not let down the cards. 'Take care would it be a policeman!' she said suddenly! 'You'd better see that you have a light on your bicycle!' But here Magenta was so overcome by a gigantic wave of conversation that she dropped the cards for all the world as if they had been washed out of her hands. 'Have you still got the old bicycles?' she asked, for Miss Perks and Miss Budd, although they had the use of the sidecar for going to church, and for going to the town for the week's provisions, were occasionally seen, in the fine days of early summer, taking a decorous ride around the roads in the vicinity of the demesne on two brightly-shining bicycles, with gleaming handlebars, that would have been taken for brand-new every summer were it not that they were somewhat high in the saddle, and straight in the frame; in short were it not that they were somewhat old-fashioned. 'I often think of those old bicycles,' said Magenta. 'Since I went to the city I often think of them, and I have to laugh all by myself in the street.' She made an explanatory gesture with her hands. 'You'd never see a bicycle in the city. People would split their sides laughing if they saw you on a bicycle in the city.' And, as if in her mind she was picturing the ladies making their way through a crowded city thoroughfare on their high old-fashioned bicycles, there and then, sitting at the table in the servants' hall, Magenta laughed so much the tears ran down her face and made streaks in the powder on her cheeks, and she felt so weak from all this exertion that she put her arms down on the table, and her head down on her arms, and the green silk dress heaved up and down and all the pink silk ruffles fluttered.

'The room is getting very hot,' said Miss Perks suddenly, and she drew back her chair abruptly. She had been getting closer and closer to Magenta. 'I think you could open the window, Bessie,' she said to Miss Budd.

The air was certainly heavy. The strong odour of Magenta's oriental perfume was mixed now with a heavy odour of perspiration, and as Miss Perks looked at her she saw that on Magenta's back and shoulders the green silk dress was moist from the heat of Magenta's shaking body, and it clung to her; her warm pink skin showing up in patches and blobs through the thin silk. While, under the armpits, Miss Perks saw that a wide arc of moisture was spreading over the green fabric, discolouring it, and leaving an ugly brown rim where it ceased. Miss Perks moved back her chair still further.

At the sound of the chair grating on the floor, Magenta raised her head, and still shaking with amusement, she picked up the cards which she could hardly see through the tears of laughter in her eyes.

But Miss Perks was coming to herself again with every minute that passed, and now seeing in Magenta's hand only a few plain, spotted cards, without as much as a knave or queen among them, much less a king or an ace, she suddenly leaned out her hand and took up the cup of tea which Miss Budd had poured out for her some time previously. She sipped the tea. The tea was cold.

'Spill this out, Bessie,' she said. 'It's cold.' She turned back to Magenta. 'Drink your tea, Magenta,' she said, 'or it will get cold. Don't bother about the rest of the cards. You can go back to them afterwards.'

She adjusted the stiff collar at her neck. The air was really stifling. She looked with distaste again at the green stain under Magenta's armpit. It was spreading wider and wider. She put up her handkerchief to her thin nostrils. The odour of that perfume! Miss Perks drew her chair still further from Magenta and took up the cup of hot tea that Miss Budd had poured out for her. She stirred it vigorously. Then she took a slice of bread.

'Take your tea,' she said to the other two. 'Don't let it get cold.' And then, suddenly putting out her hand she gathered up the cards that lay among the plates and saucers, and sweeping them into the pack she tossed it across to a sidetable, and began to straighten the crockery.

'Oh, your fortune!' cried Magenta and Miss Budd both together in dismay.

But Miss Perks gave one of her old familiar sniffs of contempt. 'I heard enough of it,' she said, and she looked at Miss Budd. 'It's only nonsense.'

'Oh, but it's such fun!' cried Miss Budd protestingly.

'Well, you can wait until after we've had our tea before you have your fun,' said Miss Perks.

Miss Budd blushed. She might have guessed that Miss Perks would have spoiled the fun sooner or later. Still she was going to have her own cards read. Nothing could spoil that. The heat of the room, the overpowering effect of the mixed perfume and perspiration that had brought Miss Perks to her senses had only caused Miss Budd to lose hers completely. Every moment that had brought disillusionment to Miss Perks, had filled Miss Budd with an ecstatic feeling, and all the vague hopes and ambitions that Miss Perks had long ago stifled stirred into feeble life again within her at sight of the mysterious and prophetic cards; the red, the black, but above all, the gorgeous enigmatic court cards.

'Oh, of course we'll have our tea, first,' she cried, in order to placate Miss Perks, and she took a sip of her own tea. 'My tea isn't so cold at all!' she said. 'I won't bother spilling it out. How about yours, Magenta? Is yours all right? Give me your cup if you like and I'll give you hot tea.'

But although she held out her hand for Magenta's cup it could be seen from her weak face that she hoped the meal would not be unnecessarily prolonged by everyone wanting hot tea. Magenta was not looking at Miss Budd, however.

271

'I think I'll have a hot cup,' she said, without even sipping the tea that was in the cup in front of her. 'I hate cold tea.' She handed up her cup to Miss Budd. 'Don't worry,' she said then as she caught sight of Miss Budd's face, and read it as easily as the cards, 'there will be plenty of time for your fortune after our tea.' She leaned across for the pot of honey from which Miss Perks had just taken the cover. 'Don't bother about a spoon,' she said to Miss Perks, and licking the butter from her knife she helped herself to the honey.

Miss Budd spilled out the tea that was in Magenta's cup and poured hot tea into it.

'Here now, Magenta,' she said, and she passed it to her. 'Will you have some bread? Oh, you have some. Some honey? Oh, you have some,' and one after another she absent-mindedly attended to needs that Magenta had attended to herself already. Her mind was not on the meal. Her mind was on the treat in store for her after it was over.

'I never had my fortune told,' she breathed, as she spread a small piece of bread with butter.

'Well, you won't have long to wait now,' said Magenta. 'You won't be able to say that after tonight!' and she took two pieces of bread at the same time to avoid stretching across the table and getting her sleeve into the butter.

They ate in silence for a few minutes. Miss Budd however could not keep her mind from the exciting topic of the card-reading.

'It won't be delaying you too long, Magenta?' she said solicitously. 'Your people won't be expecting you back?'

'Oh, not at all,' said Magenta graciously. 'It's a pleasure. As long as I get back in time to go to the train it will suit me.' She licked her knife again preparatory to taking some more honey on it. 'There's plenty of time!' She looked at Miss Budd archly. 'There's plenty of time to discover all your little secrets!' she said, and she wagged her finger roguishly at Bessie Budd, who blushed all over. 'Plenty of time!' said Magenta. 'Plenty of time!'

'Oh as long as they won't expect you to spend some time with them at home, it's all right,' said Miss Budd. 'As you say, you'll have plenty of time! Plenty of time!' And then in her eager restlessness Miss Budd felt that she must do something. 'I'll just take a look at the clock,' she said, 'to put your mind at rest, Magenta.'

'Oh, I'm sure there's no need in the world,' said Magenta. 'It's early yet.'

But as Miss Budd lifted the small clock, Magenta glanced at it, and even before Miss Budd had looked at it, Magenta had seen the time. With a scream she sprang up from her chair, letting her knife clatter down among the crockery.

'That's not the right time, is it?' she screamed, and she threw up her hands before her face and darted across the room. 'Let me see?' she cried, and brushing past the table so close to Miss Perks that Miss Perks' stiff collar got twisted sideways, she grabbed the clock out of Miss Budd's hands and began to shake it violently as if she might shake the small hands into some position in which they would give less cause for excitement and confusion. 'It can't be right,' she cried. 'It can't be right,' and she shook it again and again, but whether in order to alter its judgment or to chastise it was not quite clear.

'Bessie, what are you thinking about?' cried Miss Perks, and she sprang up and took the clock from Magenta. 'Did you want her to let it fall and break?' she snapped, looking angrily at Miss Budd. 'Stop making such a noise, Magenta,' she said, then turning to Magenta. 'If

273

it's later than you thought you won't improve matters by standing there screaming.' Miss Perks caught up the silk bag and stuffed the cards into them. She caught up the befrilled parasol, and she caught up the perfumed yellow fur, and pushed them all into Magenta's hands. 'You can go straight to the train,' she said. 'We'll go down and explain to your mother, or,' she said, correcting herself quickly, 'We'll send a message down.'

Magenta's hands closed on the bag and the parasol, but their grasp seemed too enervated to hold the yellow fur, and it slid to the floor.

'The train is gone!' she wailed. 'It's gone this twenty minutes!' and down her cheeks in noiseless trickles, more disturbing than all her screaming, came thick hot tears.

'Oh Magenta, what will you do? Oh dear it was our fault! Oh dear, what shall we do?' Miss Budd looked as if she too would begin at any minute to cry helplessly.

Miss Perks pursed her lips.

'It's too bad,' she said. 'I'm surprised at you, Magenta, to be so careless about the time. But,' she drew herself up to her full height, 'but just the same there's no need to take on in this way. If you're late, you're late, and that's all about it. You will have to stay at home tonight and go on the first train tomorrow morning.'

But at the explicit statement of her situation, Magenta gave another scream.

'She'll kill me!' she said. 'She'll kill me.'

'Who will?' said Miss Perks and Miss Budd together, and then they remembered the owner of the silk ruffled dress. 'Oh, your mistress, you mean,' said Miss Perks. 'But if she is all you say she is, she will understand that it was an accident!'

'Oh, you don't know her,' cried Magenta. 'She wouldn't understand. She wouldn't understand.' And here she broke down so completely that Miss Budd had to put her arms around her to steady her shaking shoulders.

'I must say then that she must be a most unreasonable person,' said Miss Perks. 'I know it was careless of you, Magenta, but even the best of us can make mistakes. It's a queer person that doesn't make some allowances for accidents.' Miss Perks stared at Magenta's finery as she spoke, and she could not keep a supercilious smile from gathering at the corners of her thin lips. 'I should think that it would be better to have a normal woman as your mistress than this unreasonable person with her nonsense about friendship and company.'

In the midst of her tears, Magenta made an effort to sustain the character of her employer as painted by herself earlier in the evening.

'But you see,' she cried, 'she didn't know I was coming down here today. I didn't tell her. She was going out and she said she wouldn't be back till late tonight and I thought it would be a great chance to take the day off myself and come down here!'

Miss Budd trembled at the magnitude of Magenta's temerity. But Miss Perks was staring curiously at the green silk dress.

'I thought you said that she knew you were coming? I thought you said that she told you to take that dress and that hat so you'd look nice before your mother!' Miss Perks raised her voice accusingly as her eye fell on the fur. 'I thought she told you to take the fur!'

Alas! Magenta had made an error. She looked at Miss Perks and then she looked down at the yellow fur on the floor. As well as the absent mistress, she was faced now with two more accusers, for Miss Perks with her stern eye, and Miss Budd with small nervous utterances were both accusing her where she stood. All at once she felt a return of the awe in which she used to hold the two ladies, but just the same, she was less afraid of them than she was of the shrew with the dyed hair and the sharp tongue whose drudge she was, and whose Sunday finery at that moment was pasted tight to her back with sweat. With another wail, she threw herself on the mercy of the ladies.

'Oh, what will I do?' she cried, sheltering close to Miss Budd, but appealing with her eyes to Miss Perks who, in the last few minutes, had been rapidly restored to the feelings of superiority that she had jeopardised for a short time during the reading of the cards.

'Stop cringing and wailing, Magenta,' she said, patronisingly, 'and we'll think of something.'

But it was Miss Budd who thought of something.

'I wonder if it would be deceitful,' she said, appealing first to Miss Perks, 'I wonder would it be very deceitful if Magenta went back on an early train in the morning and stole into the house, and pretended that she was in bed when her mistress got back tonight.' Miss Budd trembled with the audacity of her suggestion.

But it was of no use to Magenta.

'Do you think she'd let me go to bed until she came in at night?' she said. 'You don't know her! No matter what hour of the morning she takes it into her head to come home, I have to sit up and wait for her. I often sat up till two in the morning, on a hard kitchen chair, and when she would come in at last as often as not she'd want tea. Oh there'd be no use trying to pretend I was in bed. She'd soon come rapping on my door to find out what I was doing. I never go into my room, day or night, that she isn't rapping at the door and giving orders.' She turned appealingly to Miss Perks. 'There'd be no use pretending I was in all the time,' she said, 'because even if I did do that she'd surely have missed the clothes. She'd have missed the hat for a certainty because I left the lid off the hat box in my hurry going out. And she'd miss the fur. She opens the cupboard every night just to look at it and stroke it!'

'The dress? The hat? The fur? What are you talking about, Magenta?' demanded Miss Perks. 'She told you to wear them, didn't she? Although, as a matter of fact,' she added, glancing at the silk dress, 'she's likely to be annoyed at the way you've got the dress all stained with perspiration under the arms.'

'Oh, where?' Magenta contorted her figure to try to see this damage Miss Perks related, but she desisted in despair as the number and enormity of her tragedies made this new one seem insignificant, and instead she began to cry again, this time with loud noisy tears and gulps.

'Oh come now, Magenta,' said Miss Budd, 'things aren't so bad. If the worst comes to the worst you don't need to go back at all; you can send the lady's things to her by post, with a note thanking her for lending them to you, and saying that your mother needs you at home, and that you regret you cannot go back to her.' Miss Budd smiled with satisfaction at her neat wording of the situation. Then she threw a glance over Magenta's head at Miss Perks, and nodded to convey some private meaning. 'You know you can always get something to do here at the house, Magenta,' she said. 'We'll always be glad to give you any small jobs that we cannot manage to do ourselves.'

But Miss Perks seemed unimpressed with the meaning conveyed in Miss Budd's private nod at her. She looked coldly at Magenta; and then she looked coldly at poor Miss Budd.

'I don't think it's going to be as simple as that for Magenta,' she said.

'Why?' said Miss Budd.

Magenta only stared.

'It's my belief,' said Miss Perks, slowly and deliberately, staring fixedly at Magenta with her sharp eyes, 'it's my belief that Magenta…'

But Magenta threw up her hand and stuck her fingers in her ears.

'Don't say it!' she cried. 'Don't say it!' and then, as if it were better to say it herself than hear it from anyone else she flung herself down on the chair and buried her head in her hands on the table sobbing out the bitter story. 'It's true!' she cried. 'I stole the clothes. I thought I'd be back before she got home and that she'd never know. I stole the clothes. And the bag,' her voice broke into a wail, 'and the fur. I stole the fur!'

A shocked silence descended on the servants' hall.

'I must say I thought as much, Magenta,' said Miss Perks at last. She turned to Miss Budd. 'That's why she said nothing to your suggestion about pretending she was in the house all the time.'

Miss Budd looked apologetically at her friend. 'I suppose it wasn't right to have suggested that,' she said. 'It would have been deceitful.'

'Oh, that's not the point,' said Miss Perks impatiently. 'That's not what I meant.' She turned to Magenta. 'I knew that the woman would miss the clothes,' she said, 'even if she didn't miss Magenta.' She looked piercingly at the culprit. 'I don't suppose she has all the stacks of clothes you said she had?' she asked, contemptuously.

'She hasn't a decent stitch but these,' said Magenta, looking down ruefully at the borrowed garments. 'She wears a white coat all day at the theatre.'

'What's this you said was her connection with the theatre?' said Miss Perks.

'I didn't say,' said Miss Magenta humbly. 'I said she was connected with it.'

'In what way?' said Miss Perks relentlessly.

'She's one of the attendants in the ladies' cloakroom at the Tivoli Theatre,' said Magenta, lowering her eyes. But the sight of the white kid boots of the cloakroom attendant, buttoned tightly to her own thin ankles made her give another wail.

'We must do something for her,' said Miss Budd to Miss Perks.

'I don't see what we can do,' said Miss Perks. 'I might have had some hope of helping her before I heard the type of person for whom she was working! It would be a different matter if she were dealing with a lady. But a person like that is only too ready to make trouble. She's probably glad of a chance of getting her name in the papers.'

'Her name in the papers!' Poor Magenta looked up.

'That kind of woman,' said Miss Perks, 'won't wait for an explanation to turn up. She'll start a hue and cry at once just to attract attention to herself!'

'A hue and cry!' Miss Budd put her hands to her heart.

'A hue and cry!' Magenta's eyes opened wide. 'Do you mean she'll tell the police?'

'I shouldn't be surprised,' said Miss Perks. 'I shouldn't be surprised if she has done so already!'

'The police! Already!' Miss Budd could endure no more. Sitting down beside Magenta she began to cry weakly and quietly, wiping her lashes frequently to make up for the dearth of tears in her weak blue eyes.

But Magenta was not crying. She had stooped down and picked up the silk bag from the floor, where it had fallen a while before to join the yellow fur, and with an awed look on her face she was opening it. Inside the silk bag was the pack of cards that Miss Perks had stuffed away at the first mention of the train.

'Do you remember the man in uniform?' said Magenta, her eyes almost starting from her head. 'Do you remember the cards said there was a man in uniform coming to the house.' She looked up. 'It must have been a policeman!' She paused and drew one long gulping and frightened breath. 'That must be the policeman,' she cried, 'coming after me!' And with that she began to scream again, and scream so loud and so frantically that Miss Perks had to put her fingers in her ears.

But Miss Budd stared at Magenta, and in spite of the condition of her sweat-sodden dress, her stale perfume, and her blotched face, Miss Budd's eyes were still filled with admiration.

'Isn't that remarkable,' she said. 'The cards distinctly said a man in uniform! Isn't it more than remarkable! No matter what anyone says, isn't there truth in the cards?'

Miss Perks threw a glance of contempt at her.

'Oh, stop your nonsense,' she said, 'and help me to bring this girl back to her senses.' And indeed it was time to do something about Magenta; her screams were becoming wilder and wilder, and the pink lace ruffles on the green silk dress were getting more and more bedraggled as she flung her arms about her in despair.